THE
TEST

THE SECRET OF
SPELLSHADOW MANOR
5

BELLA FORREST

NIGHTLIGHT PRESS

First Edition

THE
TEST

THE SECRET OF
SPELLSHADOW MANOR
5

CHAPTER I

ALEX REACHED UP CAUTIOUSLY TO TOUCH THE SOFT feathers on the side of the Thunderbird's face. She cooed, pressing her head into his hand.

"How am I supposed to ride you?" he asked her, picturing his ancestor Leander on the back of his warbird, Tempest. Thunderbirds could definitely be ridden, he knew that much, but there was no saddle, no manual, no obvious way of hopping aboard and hanging on. The last thing he wanted was to go plummeting to his death from a lofty height; he already had enough dangers ahead of and behind him. Caius hadn't seemed to be in a good state when Alex had made his escape, but the warden was crafty, and it was possible that the old man, or the specters that had surrounded him, would be following close behind.

The Thunderbird chirruped, as if in response, distracting him from dark thoughts of ghoulish beings.

"Sorry, girl, I don't speak bird," he muttered, scratching the spot between her eyes. It seemed to please her, as her sleek feathers bristled.

A vivid thought flashed into the forefront of his mind, like a picture playing on a screen. It didn't seem to belong to his own train of thought. Alex turned, feeling as if he were being watched. In the shadow of a nearby overhang, he saw a glint of something. The shape wasn't easy to make out, with the wind whipping around him, stinging his eyes, but it was enough to make him suspicious.

More thoughts followed, bombarding his mind like artillery fire. Each flash, each pop, forced another vision that didn't feel like his own into his head. They were suggestions, almost, of how he might go about climbing onboard the Thunderbird. Some seemed simple, no more difficult than getting on a horse, but when he tried to just hop on, he slipped backwards, almost toppling off the edge of the mountainside. The throb of his injured ankle had dimmed to a slight ache, making his attempts less painful than he'd expected, but her regal feathers were extremely slippery, and he wasn't sure how or where he was supposed to sit. She didn't seem to know either, though she helped him as best she could, nudging him this way and that.

A more complex idea flooded his mind, involving an elaborate feat of gymnastics; he had to wrap his arms around her neck and let her tip him backwards onto her back, the wrong way around. It felt like a joke, but he didn't have many other options.

Alex interlocked his arms around her neck, and she tipped him over with her head. Instead of a graceful landing, he ended up sliding straight off, hitting the ground face-first.

From the shadows of the overhang, he thought he heard someone cackling, but it might've just been the wind.

Dusting himself off and checking for any broken bones or further injuries, Alex decided that complex approaches weren't going to work. He lay his palm flat again, and the Thunderbird eyed him curiously. There was something in the cooperative gesture that intrigued him, and he wondered if that could be the key to getting on her back. She seemed to brighten when he let her press her beak to the center of his hand. It was like permission, almost, as she rested lower on her haunches, her back sloping to make it easier for him to get on.

"I guess I should have asked if it was okay first," he apologized, maintaining contact with the feathers of her

3

neck as he walked around the side of her. It was a clumsy mount, his legs getting stuck between the folds of her wings, the bird chirping her irritation as he grasped and grappled to try to stay on.

He could feel himself sliding backwards again, but didn't want to hold on too tightly to her feathers in case he hurt her. However, he wasn't sure how successful simply clinging to her neck for dear life would be—it didn't seem particularly efficient, or particularly heroic.

He tried and tried again, slipping backwards each time. He tried to grip tighter with his legs, but to no avail. He tried to hold her neck, but he couldn't see anything with his face buried in her feathers—if he did that, he'd be flying blind. It was no good, and with each failed attempt, he could feel his frustrations growing. The bird beneath him seemed agitated too. Finally, just as he was about to slide backwards for the hundredth time, Alex grasped at two bunches of feathers, gripping them tightly in a vain attempt to stop himself falling to the ground.

She shrieked, bucking wildly, throwing him off.

He felt a wave of dread as he lost his grip on her feathers, his body soaring backwards through the air. He hit the rocky ledge, his hands scrabbling for something to hold onto, but the ice made it too slippery and suddenly there was no more rock to grab for, only open, endless air as he plummeted down the sheer drop of the mountainside. The air rushed around him, and he flailed violently, trying to get enough of his faculties together to conjure his way out of this mess and use his travel techniques—but the panic made it nearly impossible for him to focus his mind. The sharp rocks rising up to meet him flooded his thoughts with nothing but terror. He was falling too fast.

Squeezing his eyes shut, he braced himself for the impact.

A second later, he crashed into something solid. Although winded, he wasn't in nearly as much pain as he had expected. There was a softness to the thing beneath him, and the steady beat of movement. He tentatively opened his eyes, feeling the ripple of muscle below as the Thunderbird's vast wings flapped powerfully; they were even more glorious opened out, carrying beast and passenger through the air with ease.

Clutching the Thunderbird's neck with a vise-like grip, Alex felt the cold rush of a glacial wind on his skin as she rose upward again, almost parallel to the sheer rock face. Her speed was as terrifying as it was exhilarating, and Alex could barely catch his breath as she raced toward the sky, though she stopped just short of the first band of clouds that trailed around the summit, her streamlined body circling in the air as she made to return him to the icy ledge of the mountain.

As they flew back toward solid ground, Alex noticed two patches of feathers that were a different color than the rest—a deep, vivid scarlet, hidden in the spots where her neck met her wings. Reaching for the strange patches, Alex felt two bony knobs sticking up from beneath the feathers, which were coarser than her silky feathers, and realized he could grip these protrusions without hurting her. They were like handles almost, with which he could keep himself steady, and he found that she would turn slightly if he put pressure on one in a certain direction, though most of the navigating was definitely up to the Thunderbird herself.

With a loud squawk, she returned him to the rocky outcrop of the mountain, glancing at him sharply with her bright eyes as he hopped off.

"I won't try that way again," he joked, and though he felt a little foolish, and more than a little relieved not to be human mush, he knew he had made progress. Alex stroked the smooth feathers at the side of the Thunderbird's face. "Thank you for saving me," he said softly.

She chirruped, and the sound made him smile.

His near annihilation made him wonder about how his ancestors had learned to fly on the backs of these magnificent beasts. *Were there flight schools or something?* he mused, contemplating how many other Spellbreakers might have almost plummeted to their deaths in the pursuit of learning to fly.

After taking a moment to bring his pulse back down and forcing away the flashbacks of jagged rocks, Alex turned toward the Thunderbird, eager to try again before he lost his nerve entirely.

This time, he managed to climb up onto her back without incident, tucking his legs neatly behind the folds of her wings, feeling like a jockey waiting at the starting line of a derby. It was an awkward position to sit in, and he knew his legs were going to ache afterwards, but he didn't mind if it meant he could fly on the back of the beautiful Thunderbird.

"I suppose I should give you a name," he said, leaning closer to her.

She trilled, turning to look at him, her neck twisting like an owl's. There was an intellect behind her eyes that had Alex convinced she could understand every word of what he said.

"You think so too?"

She trilled again, louder this time.

Alex smiled. "Okay, what shall we call you?" he pondered. "How about Sugarplum?"

She gave him a deeply unimpressed look, her head tilted to one side.

"Okay, not Sugarplum. How about Dasher?" he said, gaining another apathetic expression from the giant warbird.

"Hm." Alex's mind turned toward the stories of her

ancestors. Glancing at her gleaming silver feathers and hearing the crack of lightning overhead, a thought came to him, fitting of both her heritage and her appearance. "How do you like Silver Storm?" he asked.

She chirped, cocking her head.

"I'll call you Storm for short," Alex added.

Storm rested the tip of her beak on Alex's forehead for the briefest moment. He grinned, taking it as a sign of her approval.

"Okay then, Storm, let's see what you can do."

Turning back around, she stepped toward the edge of the mountainside once more, perching precariously on the lip of it. Alex could see the drop below, and his heart began to pound, though he forced his eyes to look dead ahead. As he took a deep breath, the Thunderbird's whole body lurched forward beneath him. For a moment, it felt as if he was falling again, but her wings caught a ferocious air current that sent them surging upward. The wind was ice cold and stung his cheeks, but he hardly noticed it as Storm settled into flight, soaring toward the thunderstorm above.

Once he was sure they weren't about to dive to their deaths, he began to relax and enjoy the ride. Storm shot up through swollen, black clouds that left his clothes drenched and his face soaked, her agile form wheeling around thunderbolts, ducking and diving around the lashes of electricity that whipped toward them. Though time was of the essence, Alex couldn't help but feel a thrill of excitement as he chased storm clouds and danced with the rain.

Through a parting in the dense cloud cover, he could make out the top of the mountain, and was surprised to see what looked like a shrine, glimmering at the very pinnacle. It was shaped like a Thunderbird, and forged from what appeared to be solid gold. Alex wondered if it was supposed to be a likeness of Tempest, the mountain's namesake, reminding him of the broken town that lay in its shadow.

Was this Leander's birthplace? he wondered, looking toward the ruins that seemed so small from above.

Storm seemed offended by Alex's distracted attention, her eyes glinting as she dove suddenly, racing down the side of the mountain, showing him the full force of her agility as she tucked into a loop-the-loop. Alex clung on for dear life as the bird continued her gleeful display, twisting through barrel-rolls and corkscrews, until Alex felt sick with adrenaline.

Through one ill-timed loop-the-loop, Alex lost his grip on her bony handles and fell for a brief moment, only to be caught again with smooth precision. Storm chirped delightedly, even though the move had left Alex feeling decidedly nauseous.

"Please… no more tricks," he pleaded.

Storm trilled, her eyes glittering intelligently as she

looked back at him. He felt as if she were mocking him, and it made him grin. Surely, they were about to embark on a great companionship. The thought made him pine suddenly for his friends. While he was busy learning how to fly and having fun, he still had no idea whether they were safe or not. There was a reason he had learned to fly in the first place—to join Lintz, Ellabell, and Aamir at Falleaf House.

Alex maneuvered Storm back toward the mountain, trying out his amateur navigational skills. She followed the instruction easily, responding to the light squeeze of one leg, or the gentle pull of her shoulder-holds. It was simpler than he had expected, and he felt a rush of pride as she followed his lead, flying steadily back toward the ledge.

Landing, however, was a different matter entirely. He urged her downward, toward the rocky outcrop. She flapped wildly, trying to control her own movements while Alex squeezed her shoulders to steer her elsewhere. A loud squawk stilled his hands—he allowed her to do her own thing, and she dropped down onto the ice and snow. Alex awkwardly dismounted, sliding down onto the rock.

"Sorry, I'm still learning," he said, stroking Storm's feathers.

She ruffled them in disgruntlement, but her eyes told him that he was forgiven. His mind turned back toward his friends, and how he was going to find them. He pulled the beetle beacon from his pocket. A faint ripple of magic still coursed through it, but Alex didn't know what good it would do him.

A vision pulsed into his mind, showing him how to feed his anti-magic into the mechanisms and smother the faint swell of golden magic within, in order to track its owner. Alex shivered. The train of thought was too precise and too coincidental to be from anyone but Elias.

The realization made him suddenly anxious again, about what had actually happened when he had tried to read Elias's mind. He had thought Elias had vanished for good, but apparently the shadow-man wasn't quite done pestering him just yet. The pain of the act had all but gone, but Alex could still feel a strange warmth in the depths of his chest, and he knew it had something to do with his shadowy acquaintance.

"I know you're there!" Alex called, directing his words toward the rocky overhang. "Elias! You can come out now. I know it's you!"

But Elias didn't come.

It didn't placate Alex, however. If it truly was Elias out there, the shadow-man would appear when he was good and ready, and not a minute before. The present moment clearly didn't suit Elias, as much as Alex wished to get their reunion over and done with. He didn't know how he felt about the idea of Elias still being around, especially after everything he had done, to his father, to Ellabell—all the deceit. It was impossible for Alex to shake the anger that still coursed through him, but he could sense Elias was near, and knew, with a sinking feeling, that he may not have a choice when it came to Elias's continued presence in his life.

Now, he was convinced that something deeply unwanted had happened between himself and Elias back at Kingstone, and he could only guess at the repercussions. Wherever that creature went, Alex's misery followed, and any help the shadow-man gave would surely come at a price.

CHAPTER 2

A S MUCH AS HE HATED THE SOURCE OF THE information, Alex decided to follow the vision he'd seen in his mind.

Holding the beetle tightly in his hand, he ran his anti-magic through the mechanisms, feeding the black and silver strands through the cogs and over the magic already within, coating the gold with the contrasting gleam of his powers. The two streams of energy merged, brightening for a moment before fading to a dull glisten.

Nothing happened.

Alex frowned, knowing he had followed the vision

exactly as he had seen it. Frustrated, he shook the beacon, as if it might miraculously make the thing work, but still nothing happened within the metal carapace.

"I thought you were supposed to be helpful!" he shouted toward the shady overhang.

He waited a few moments more, and even fed a few more strands of anti-magic into the mechanism, willing the device to flash or beep or do something at least, but still nothing happened. With a growl, Alex threw the small oval of metal away, watching it arc through the air before it tumbled away into a snowdrift.

Annoyed at being back to square one, Alex sat down on the edge of the rocky outcrop and gazed out toward the horizon, willing it to grant him some form of inspiration. He wondered if he could simply get on Storm's back and fly aimlessly, hoping to end up in the direction of Falleaf, but he had no idea where the fourth haven was, or if it could even be reached from this realm. It seemed hopeless, and with the potential threat of specters following in his wake, he wasn't comfortable staying put. There had to be something he could do—a way to reach the others without the beacon.

Storm pecked at the back of his head. He pushed her beak away, but she was insistent, ruffling his hair and tapping lightly on his skull.

"Stop it!" he said, trying to duck away from her latest

attack, but she would not stop. She nudged the side of his face like an overexcited puppy. Alex shot her an annoyed look.

With a high-pitched chirrup, she clamped her beak onto the back of his shirt and dragged him away from the edge of the mountain with surprising strength, yanking him toward the snowdrift. He cried out in surprise, trying to get her off him, but she simply would not let go.

As he neared a pile of snow, he realized why. A dim light flashed against the ice shelf just in front of the snowdrift, blinking a steady rhythm. He dove toward the freezing snow and scrabbled to dig the beetle out. As he clutched it in his hands, the beetle gave a low whine, the snow having dulled its shriek. Alex didn't care about the sound—it was the light he sought, the northernmost bulb showing the way to Lintz and the others.

Excitement pulsed through his veins as he turned back toward Storm, who was eyeing the beetle curiously, perhaps wondering if it was a tasty treat. She tried to peck it from his hand, but he quickly moved it away.

"You wouldn't like the taste," Alex teased. He held his palm flat, waiting for her to touch her beak to the center. "We need to go north," he told her, still not certain how much she could understand.

It seemed she had a vague idea, however, as he

clambered onto her back and held on tight. Before he had even managed to get settled, she was charging toward the lip of the mountain, taking to the air in one smooth movement, her wings spreading wide. He didn't know how long it would take to get to Falleaf House, or if it was even possible, but the Thunderbird's apparent understanding put him at ease.

As they flew, Alex took in the landscape around him. There were endless forests, peppered with the shattered remains of ancient towns, and sparkling rivers that wound through the deep green canopies, off to some unknown ocean. To the east, strange shapes emerged on the horizon. Alex thought they might be a distant mountain range, but as the scene grew clearer, he could see structures that looked distinctly manmade shining from within the dull gray rock. Golden spires as tall as any skyscraper rose from vast, palatial buildings that shone against the glare of the sun, the elegant dwellings poking up from gaps in between the peaks of the mountain range.

Alex wondered if it was somehow the real world, glimpsed through the fabric of the magical realm, or if it was something else, something private and reserved for the crème de la crème of mage society. It certainly looked regal enough. There was nothing ordinary about the buildings; they were almost otherworldly, with a gauzy haze covering them, like a mirage in the desert. It looked to be a barrier of some sort, protecting whoever lived inside. Part of him wanted to take a closer look, but he knew that his current schedule would not permit such a luxury—they had to get to Falleaf House as quickly as possible; there was no time for detours, however tempting.

"How are we going to get to Falleaf House?" Alex asked Storm, feeling slightly silly for speaking to an animal who couldn't talk back. The Thunderbird, however, continued to surprise him.

After a moment or two, she began to speed up, beating her wings faster and faster until she was rocketing through the sky at an alarming rate. It didn't seem possible that a bird could fly so fast, and where once Alex had felt exhilaration, he now began to feel the adrenaline-pulse of fear. It was too fast. He was barely holding on.

With a loud snap like the crack of a whip, Storm broke the sound barrier. She flew faster still, not showing any signs of slowing down. Alex clung to her neck and gripped her sides with his legs, unable to keep his eyes open against the rush of air blasting in his face.

The scene around him stretched and blurred, and he could feel his whole body being pulled in different directions. The wind whipped against his face, but nothing looked normal; there were no clear images, nothing he could recognize as real. It had all become warped and weird, everything bent out of shape and alien to the eye.

Then, with a satisfying whoosh, everything shrank back to normal again, snapping into place.

They had emerged in a different realm.

Alex realized that his Thunderbird possessed powers he had never expected. It seemed Storm had the ability to travel between realms, bypassing portals entirely. Maybe this was why the Spellbreakers had been such formidable warriors, with their ability to appear from the sky like some other-worldly avenging angels, soaring down on the backs of ferocious winged beasts. He imagined it must have been quite the sight from the battlefield.

Storm had slowed to an ordinary pace, and though Alex's heart was pounding and he was struggling to wrap his head around what he had just experienced, he couldn't help but think about what other uses there might be for such a talent as Storm's. Could she punch through the border between the normal, outside world and the magical realms, or would that be too much for her? He wasn't even sure she could exist in the real world, being what she was, and yet he couldn't erase the thought from his mind.

First things first, he told himself, returning to the task at hand. The beacon was still flashing north, but it was blinking more rapidly now, the dampened shrieks coming louder. An idea came to him, as he fed his anti-magic into the device, forcing the mechanism to silence the sound, not wanting it to draw any attention, leaving only the comfort of the light. Wherever Lintz and his friends were, Alex was close now.

Ahead of him lay the perimeter of a large, dense forest. It was a familiar scene, vividly remembered from the portal to Falleaf House he had watched Lintz build, but Alex had no idea whether they were near the same spot where that portal had opened. It all looked so similar, the bronzed leaves falling to the ground beneath the warm haze of afternoon sun.

Thinking back to what Caius had told him, about how to find Hadrian, Alex looked across the canopy of the forest, searching for the glint of something golden in the distance. As hard as it was, Alex knew he had to try to trust in the sliver of goodness Caius had possessed, when he had spoken of Falleaf, though, after what had happened between himself and Caius, he wasn't exactly sure he'd see anything—perhaps, Caius had been lying about the way to reach Hadrian.

But, as the sunlight glanced down onto the forest, something glitzy caught his eye. It lay in the center of the trees, but Alex couldn't gauge the distance between the tree-line and the glimmering object, which he hoped was the golden top of the pagoda he sought. Keeping the direction of it in his mind, he knew he would simply have to walk until he found it. With Storm being the size she was, and not being exactly discreet, he knew he couldn't just fly there. He just hoped the others were already inside.

Storm landed softly on a pile of decaying leaves, folding her wings, and Alex dismounted. Realizing she might be a little out in the open if he left her there, he gestured for her to follow as he made his way into the dimmed light of the trees, pausing beside the shelter of an overgrown willow.

"Stay here," he said. "And if anything comes for you, come and find me," he added, still feeling foolish about speaking to a bird. Once again, she defied his expectations as she chirped in understanding, walking behind the curtain of leaves and settling down beside the trunk of the tree. From beyond the willow, it was nearly impossible to make her out beneath the camouflage. Alex smiled in wonderment; she was truly an incredible specimen.

Reassured that Storm would have plenty to eat in the forest, he set off into the trees, heeding Caius's warning about the traps and soldiers that filled these seemingly innocuous woods. The beetle was flashing like mad, restoring his courage—they were nearby, he could sense it.

The forest itself was more oppressive than it had appeared from the portal, and though the canopy was a myriad of gold and scarlet, and everything around him was beautiful to behold, from the tiny wildflowers that grew along the path, to the babbling brooks that cut through the lush green earth, he couldn't help but feel on edge, knowing somebody could sneak up on him at any moment, or he might set off a trap with one misplaced step.

Alex knew he had to travel north to where he had seen the glint of the pagoda's top, but from down on the ground, he could no longer see the beacon of it, telling him where to go. The beetle was still flashing, and he clung to the belief that it would lead him to the others.

CHAPTER 3

T REKKING THROUGH THE WOODS WITH AS MUCH
stealth as he could muster, Alex came across nobody
on his travels. It did nothing to dispel his fears,
however, and his nerves remained on edge. The soldiers
Caius had spoken about could be anywhere, and he wasn't
about to let them surprise him.

As he walked, he saw something strange in a copse up
ahead. It was a toad, resting out in the open, its slick back
glistening. It basked in a spot of sunlight filtering through
the canopy, but, as Alex neared it, something seemed amiss.
He realized it almost a moment too late, as several barbs shot

from the toad's mouth. Alex dove to one side, out of the way of the small darts, which thudded into the tree behind him.

Turning in astonishment, he saw hundreds of tiny holes in the bark, where previous darts had hit home. They had singed the wood, clearly laced in a poison or chemical of some sort, which Alex was certain would have led to a series of very painful injuries, if not death. It was a close call—too close for comfort, and the near miss left Alex even more cautious, as he ventured as near as he dared to the toad. Upon closer inspection, he could see that it was a costumed piece of intricate clockwork, the whirring of the cogs barely audible.

Shaking off his fear, Alex moved onward, scrutinizing his surroundings for anything out of the ordinary. He just had to hope that the flashing beetle meant that Lintz and the others weren't dead, or caught up in the jaws of some grisly snare.

Ahead, blooming in the glowing light, a line of cherry trees appeared, standing out from the maples around them. Their flowers' petals were tinged with pink, and though they seemed innocuous enough, Alex had a bad feeling about their presence within the forest. They were out of place, and yet it was evident he had to walk through them in order to move forward. To either side, the line of blossoming trees stretched, offering no alternative route.

He stepped tentatively up to one of the trees, and noticed immediately that it wasn't shedding its delicate petals, as the ones next to it were, though the illusion was a convincing one. In fact, as he looked up the line, he realized that every alternate tree wasn't showering petals as it should.

A harsh buzzing sound filled his ears, and impulse made him take a quick step backward, just in time to see a shielding trap snap closed around the periphery of the tree. He gasped, realizing how close he had come to being caught within it. It became clear that only the shedding trees were safe to pass near, but the others would trap an intruder inside, until a soldier could find them. Alex shuddered, glad of the escape, but the sound he had heard gave him an idea. If he listened for it, he might just be able to avoid more traps—these kinds of snares, at any rate.

Skirting around the dark trunk of a shedding cherry tree, relieved not to hear the nerve-wracking buzz, he pressed on, undeterred by his near misses. The beetle was going insane now, and his only thoughts were of his friends, and making it safely to them.

Beyond the cherry trees, the beautiful scenery gave way to a more cramped section of the forest, where the trees loomed inwards, their trunks gnarled and twisted, like something from a Grimm tale. He was about to set his foot down when an image popped into his mind, freezing him in mid-motion. It was a picture of a golden leaf, and, as he looked down to the spot where he had been about to stand, he saw the exact same leaf, lying on the ground. It looked more golden than any leaf Alex had ever seen, but it was so small he had nearly missed it. A short distance from it crouched a mouse, though it could only be seen if someone was really looking for it, and Alex knew his concentration must have slipped for a moment.

Another vivid image appeared in his mind, zooming in on the ground where the leaf and the mouse lay. It wasn't exactly a sensation that sat well with him, and each one caused a ripple of confusion in his brain, knowing they definitely weren't pinging in from his own mind. Alex didn't like it one bit, but he was painfully aware that he was stuck with this new slideshow of visions. He frowned, trying to figure out what this fresh image meant. The mouse seemed so out of place. He paused, not knowing how to proceed.

Suddenly, the mouse darted forwards, stepping across the golden leaf. Alex stepped backwards hurriedly, ducking behind a tree as a blinding flash of light shot up from the ground. He peered around the trunk, and in the fading luminescence, he saw the mouse curled up on the grass, dead.

Looking up at the spot where the flash had risen from, his face morphed into a mask of horror as he watched a great, golden beast, looking distinctly bear-like, spring from the tiny leaf. It paused for a moment, its sharp teeth gnashing as it sniffed the air for intruders, but it didn't seem as if the creature could smell Alex. It turned its head this way and that, its nostrils flaring. Alex pressed himself flat against the trunk, listening as the beast sniffed a while longer. He peered out just in time to see the golden bear disappearing back into the leaf, apparently satisfied there was nobody untoward in the immediate area.

It seemed the images being fed into his mind needed closer examination than he'd realized, with this particular one. The danger wasn't always the most obvious aspect in the picture. He exhaled deeply, knowing he'd had a very close call. Though he had managed to dodge the golden bear, the sight of it retreating did nothing to allay Alex's fears for his friends. They were in real danger here, and he knew he had to find them before anything bad happened—if it hadn't already.

He pressed on, picking up the pace, though he began to worry when the beetle's flashing started to slow. He wasn't sure if that meant he was heading in the wrong direction, or if the owner of the magic within was starting to weaken. Not knowing which way to turn, he kept walking, heading farther and farther into the forest.

Without warning, the forest gave way to a large clearing. It made Alex anxious, knowing he should probably avoid clearings, in case somebody caught sight of him, but this one was different, he could tell. In the very center of it was an imposing, artfully crafted pagoda with six tiers, the golden top that had shown him the way curving upward in the shape of a bird. From the central pagoda, various connecting buildings branched off, running into the darkness of the trees beyond, built like elaborately carved treehouses, their roofs painted red and green, following the same aesthetic as the pagoda. Alex peered toward the trees on the far side, certain he could see people moving along suspended walkways hidden among the boughs.

He had reached Falleaf House, by the looks of it, and it was impossible to escape the Japanese flavor of the place. Around the base of the pagoda lay a glorious water garden, with a multitude of exquisite bridges crisscrossing the streams and pools that rippled in the gentle breeze, nudging the lilies that floated on the surface. There were waterfalls too, the sound of running water soothing to Alex's ears as he watched the twist and turn of koi carp in striking colors he had never seen before.

There were blossoming cherry trees around the pools too, though these ones were undeniably real, their blushing petals falling like pink snow into the water, sinking slowly to the bottom. In any other circumstance, Alex knew this place would have been the epitome of serenity and calm, but it wasn't. Instead of pilgrims and visitors, there were soldiers wandering everywhere—and a lot of them to boot, marching in small gangs. They were dressed in a uniform of gold and white, with what looked like a crest emblazoned on the pocket, in the shape of a horse's head with two crossed swords beneath it. Alex wondered if this was the royal crest, what with these being royal guards.

No matter where they came from, Alex couldn't get over just how many there were, and wondered how he had managed to avoid them thus far. Maybe they had simply become too reliant on the efficiency of the forest traps, checking them every so often instead of patrolling, as they probably ought to have been doing.

Soldiers becoming lazy out of wartime—wouldn't be the first time, Alex mused.

He ducked back, staying perfectly still in the shadow of the tree-line, as two walked past, right in front of where he stood. His heart thundered, and though they hadn't seen him, Alex didn't particularly want to push his luck. He retreated back into the woods. He needed to figure out a way to bypass the guards, get into the pagoda, and find Hadrian. With the high level of security, it seemed like a near impossible task. And yet, Alex knew there had to be a way to outfox them. To come all this way for nothing was not an option.

Looking down at the beetle in his hand, he saw that the

flashing had slowed, but as he stepped back into the forest, it blinked faster again, renewing his hope that something awful hadn't yet happened to his friends. Perhaps they were still hiding in the forest, waiting to sneak inside the pagoda, just as he was.

With each step, the beetle flashed quicker, leading the way. Alex followed it, using it as a rudimentary kind of compass, until the blinking light was flashing so fast that it had become a steady light.

Peering ahead, Alex could make out the shape of something in the trees, though it was too dark to see clearly. The figure lumbered around in the shadows, staggering here and there as if injured. It looked human, but for all Alex knew, it could be a trap, meant to ensnare him.

Friend or foe, he couldn't be sure, but there was only one way to find out. Taking a deep breath, he moved closer.

CHAPTER 4

ALEX APPROACHED CAUTIOUSLY, TRYING TO GET A better look at the shadow to see if it was one of the gold-and-white soldiers. The foliage kept obscuring his view, making it impossible to discern the shape of the person ahead. He skirted around the trees for a clearer vantage point, but as he neared, something made him pause. Close to his foot was a toadstool, with another nearby, and another and another, forming a very large ring around the space before him. It reminded him of an old fairytale his grandmother used to tell him, about never setting foot in a fairy circle made of toadstools in the deepest part of the woods because the fairies would trap any intruders and take them to the fairy world, never to be heard from again.

A familiar buzz surrounded him, the same he'd heard beside the cherry trees, and Alex knew it was indeed a trap, just not one laid by any fairies. This was a trap laid by soldiers, and there was someone caught inside.

"Who's there?" he whispered.

The lumbering figure froze, the shaded face turning in Alex's direction.

"Alex, is that you?" a familiar voice replied.

"Professor?"

"Indeed, it's me!" Lintz cried. "Oh goodness, Alex, I am simply ecstatic to hear your voice! We didn't know what had happened to you! Where did you go?"

"It's a long story. I'll tell you everything once we've gotten you out of here." Alex strained his eyes to see the faint glimmer of a barrier in front of him, keeping Lintz within. "How did you get caught, anyway?"

"I missed the signs," Lintz replied grimly. "It's the toadstools—they're clockwork inside, filled to the brim with barrier magic. One false step and here I am, stuck!"

"No soldiers?"

Lintz shook his head, coming closer to the edge of the trap, where Alex stood. "Not yet... though I don't know for how much longer."

Alex analyzed the fairy ring, brainstorming how he was going to get the professor out of this mess. If the toadstools were forged from clockwork, as Lintz said, he knew they should be relatively easy to break.

"I'm going to try and bust you out," Alex said, glancing down at the toadstools once more.

"Goodness, no, you mustn't try something so risky just for little old me!" Lintz protested, but Alex was already kneeling in the grass beside the first one, trying to figure out the mechanisms he would have to break in order to bring the trap's barrier down.

Alex glanced up. "I can't just leave you here, Professor. Those soldiers could be along at any moment, and if they find you, they'll know there are intruders among them."

"Well… if you must try, be very careful. These traps are well made, and I wouldn't want anything happening to you."

Alex held out his hands a short distance from the first toadstool and weaved his anti-magic toward the small piece of clockwork. It was dainty and convincing, the red cap with the white spots painted in a hyper-realistic fashion.

Pulling back on his anti-magic, he felt some resistance as he tried to disrupt the source of the trap's barrier, reversing the cogs in order to break them. However, he found he couldn't grasp all the pieces at once; when he'd just about managed to stall one section, another would take over, defying his anti-magical instructions. Eventually, he realized that a delicate approach wasn't going to work.

Pressing his hands on the cap of the toadstool, he forced a wave of energy through the mechanism, flooding it with anti-magic until he heard the satisfying clunk of the whole system breaking down. There was a whiny whirring sound as the last few cogs tried their best to keep the flow going, before they too gave up. As soon as the high-pitched noise ceased, the shimmering veil fell, setting Lintz free.

"You did it!" the professor bellowed as he stepped out of the circle, clapping Alex hard on the back.

He smiled. "It was nothing a little anti-magic couldn't fix."

"It's so wonderful to see you, my dear boy," Lintz said, a perplexed look on his brow. "We were so worried. One minute, the portal was there, and the next, it was gone. You have to believe I had nothing to do with it—I kept it open, and we were all waiting down by the forest's edge for your return, but then there was a snap, and the next thing we know, the portal is gone, and you with it. A moment later, a troop of soldiers walked past, doing a search of the perimeter, so we had to escape into the forest itself. I'm so sorry, Alex."

Alex got to his feet. "It was Caius who closed the portal. It seems the warden's hatred of mages ran a lot deeper than we thought. He saw me as some kind of savior to their kind.

Needless to say, he didn't want me running off here to get the book, because he doesn't want anyone doing the spell that could save mage-kind from the Great Evil." Alex sighed. "He tried to kill me."

"He *what*?" Lintz yelped, an expression of fury morphing his features.

"Vincent helped hold Caius off… and I escaped before I could see what happened to him, though I know it wasn't good," said Alex, his eyes downcast.

"If I know Vincent, he'll have found a way to pull through," Lintz said reassuringly. "Goodness, I'm sorry I wasn't there to protect you, Alex—I ought to have stayed and kept an eye out. Are you hurt? Is Caius dead?"

Alex shook his head. "I can't be one hundred percent sure on the Caius front, but I'm in one piece, more or less. What about the others? Where are Ellabell and Aamir?"

"Ah, fear not! The pair of them are safely within the walls of the pagoda," Lintz explained. "I caused something of a diversion—I have been known to be quite diverting." He chuckled. "I set off some of these here traps, which have monsters within them, to distract the soldiers while the other two climbed up the side of the pagoda and disappeared through a sixth-floor window. I planned to retreat until things had calmed down, but got myself caught in the process."

"Do you think we've been detected?" Alex asked, worried.

Lintz shook his head. "I'm offended, Alex Webber! I'm a professional at stealth."

Alex stifled a laugh, knowing the professor was anything but stealthy, with his large, rotund build and booming voice.

Lintz flashed him a look. "The soldiers suspected nothing. As they were walking away, I heard one of them say something about the traps here getting more temperamental, given their age. It would appear nobody can be bothered to repair them. Such a shame. These pieces are exquisitely crafted."

It reminded Alex of Caius's sentiments, where the keep was concerned. As long as the inmates were scared enough, it didn't matter if the tools and resources were faulty. It was the fear that kept everyone in line, and Alex wondered if that was the main method of control here, too, only delivered at the hands of soldiers instead of the haven's ruler.

"So how are *we* going to get into the pagoda?" Alex asked.

"I've had a good few hours to think about this, sitting on my tree trunk," Lintz replied, pointing back toward the stub of a tree where he had apparently been whiling away his entrapment. "I think I know another way in that thankfully won't involve any lofty climbing! These creaky old legs weren't built for such active pursuits... not anymore." He smiled wistfully, his moustache turning upward.

"What is it?" asked Alex.

"I'll show you. Hopefully, if we're very smart—which I know we are—we'll evade any sort of detection. Those soldiers won't even know we've been there—we'll pass right under their noses!" Lintz cried, triumphant.

Alex let the professor's enthusiasm feed his own as he followed Lintz back through the forest toward the perilously beautiful scenery of Falleaf House, avoiding the buzz and thrum of traps as they walked. There were toadstools and leaves, now instantly recognizable as dangers, and small forest creatures that hid deadly secrets within their clockwork innards.

Before long, they arrived at the edge of the forest, where the trees opened out into the vast clearing that held the pagoda at its center. They paused, Alex's eyes scanning the area for soldiers. There were no fewer than six groups of six, strolling around the grounds, laughing and joking with one another, barely keeping an eye on what was going on around them. If they had bothered to look, Alex knew they would have been able to make out the shapes of two intruders lurking at the tree-line. As it was, he and Lintz were able to sneak along the outskirts, keeping to the shadows.

Finally, they emerged at a narrow passageway between

the pagoda and the woods, and ran across the grass, keeping low to the ground, until they reached the back of the intricately carved building. There were dragon's heads and pillars shaped like monkeys, with open-winged birds screeching silently atop twisting posts sculpted to look like snakes.

Just ahead, Alex could see a doorway in the back of the building, a hidden entrance of sorts, the way down to it overgrown with winding vines and tumbling weeds. If he hadn't been looking closely, he knew he would have missed it entirely.

"Is this it?" he whispered, pushing back the fronds and spiny branches that were clawing at his face and arms.

Lintz nodded. "I think it leads to the cellar."

Reaching the door, Alex could see that there was a lock on it. It was only to be expected, with so many guards around, but it seemed like it hadn't been used for a long time. The metal had fused together, so even a key would have been useless. However, Alex had something better than a key at his disposal. Confidently, he grasped the lock in his hands and fed his anti-magic through the keyhole, forcing the mechanism within to crack and give way, breaking apart the fused metal, until the whole thing fell off into his hand.

He seized the handle and heaved himself against the door, willing it to open. It groaned in displeasure, having remained shut for such a long time, but with a splinter of wood, it lurched forward, sending Alex stumbling in after it. Hoping the sound wouldn't bring any unwanted visitors, Alex stepped into the unknown of the cellar beyond and closed the door firmly behind him. It was dark and musty, but Alex could make out a light in the distance, leading up to the brighter floors of the pagoda.

Lintz followed him in, and Alex pushed the door closed behind them. They hurried toward the light, Alex's footfalls making splashes as he crept toward it, the ground underfoot clearly drenched. He wasn't sure he'd want the lights on in here, even if he had the option; he just hoped it was water and nothing more sinister.

Like the blood of innocents, he thought wryly, knowing it was what the royals loved best.

A slippery, narrow set of stone steps led up to the crack of light peeping through another old-looking door, but this one was thankfully unlocked, and the hinges creaked only slightly as Alex pushed it open. It led to an empty corridor, the windows looking out at the serene image of a water garden, with lilies swaying in the breeze.

He could hear the domestic sounds of a kitchen somewhere nearby—clinking cutlery and the sizzle of something delicious cooking on a stove. He could smell it, too, the spicy scent making his mouth water. It seemed they had emerged in the servants' quarters, with no obvious signs of any soldiers in the vicinity. Through the window, he could see guards outside, wandering about, but there didn't seem to be any on this floor. It didn't mean they wouldn't be waiting around the next corner, however, and Alex didn't want to take any chances.

"How are we going to get up to the sixth floor without being spotted?" Alex asked, turning to Lintz.

The professor frowned. "That, my dear boy, is a very good question."

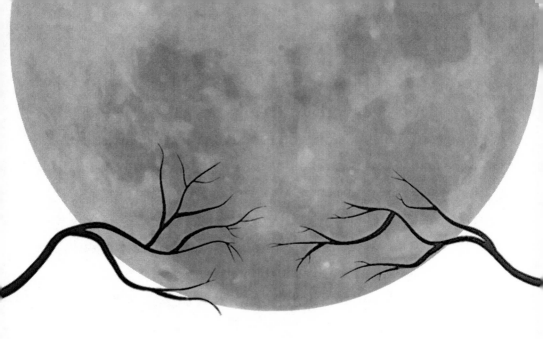

CHAPTER 5

T
HEY HURRIED ALONG THE CORRIDOR TO THE
kitchens, the steam meeting Alex's cold face as
they snuck in through a half-open doorway. Ahead
of them lay a storage annex of sorts, with several scarlet
uniforms hung up on a rack, crisp white shirts folded beside
them. Alex hadn't yet seen anyone wearing this kind of
uniform, but he guessed they were for the serving staff. With
so many military mouths to feed, he knew there had to be
workers somewhere. The Falleaf students, he assumed, were
housed in the treehouse buildings that branched off from the
pagoda, kept separate from the goings on within the central

structure. He pondered whether they were privy to the same delicious smells that wafted toward his nostrils—knowing the usual way in which these places were run, with the exception of Stillwater, he doubted it. They were more likely to be eating the same grim fare he'd eaten at Spellshadow and Kingstone, with the good stuff reserved only for those deemed worthy.

"We could put these on and pretend we're staff?" Alex suggested.

Lintz grinned. "You took the words right out of my mouth!"

With that, Alex plucked a fresh uniform from the rack and shoved it over his clothes. It was made from a sleek red material, buttoning right up to the throat, and though it was clearly intended to be worn by the lower echelons of society, it looked expensive. To Alex's surprise, the clothes fit him remarkably well, making him look decidedly professional. Lintz, however, was having far less luck. There didn't seem to be a uniform big enough for him, which meant he had to squeeze into a smaller size that looked like it was about to cut off his circulation. Red-cheeked and sweating, the professor forced the buttons closed, though as soon as he had them in place, they were straining to burst apart. Walking like a robot seemed to be the only way to stop the fastenings from springing free, and as hard as Alex tried to keep a straight face, the sight was just too funny.

"Enough of that," Lintz sulked. "It'll do for now."

"Sorry, Professor—I think it looks good on you." The last word came out as a laugh.

"Very funny, Webber, very funny," muttered Lintz. "Let's just go, shall we, before this whole thing explodes off me?"

Alex nodded, hoping the sight of the professor wouldn't draw too much unwanted attention, as they slunk back out into the corridor and made their way toward the end of it. Alex peered around the corner, checking for danger, but the coast was clear.

Moving as fast as they could, given Lintz's unfortunate state, they reached a staircase at the end of another hallway. Two monkey heads stared from the banister posts, their mouths open in a snarl Alex found slightly disturbing. The stairs proved particularly difficult, with the professor unable to bend his legs properly, but, somehow, they managed the ascent without anything tearing too badly. There was one particularly worrying ripping sound about halfway up, but nothing appeared to have torn off, and they arrived at the top of the first floor. Here, the military presence was much more noticeable. Soldiers wandered the corridors with ab- sent expressions, pausing to pick at the stunning paintings that adorned the walls, running their hands casually over the countless statues that lined the hallways, clearly not appreciative of the beauty that lay before them.

Alex knew getting to the upper floors was going to be a test of his acting ability. He grasped Lintz by the arm and led him through the corridor, right into the path of a group of soldiers. There was no avoiding them, if they wanted to go up the stairs, but the guards barely seemed to notice they were there. A few cast them cursory glances, but the rest simply ignored the duo as they made their way through the floors of the pagoda, keeping their heads down.

That was, until they came to the fourth floor.

"You there!" a voice called.

Alex cringed, turning slowly to meet the caller. "Sir?" he said, seeing a great hulking beast of a man, dressed in the now-familiar gold-and-white uniform of a soldier, storming toward him. Alex had a feeling that this was it—they had been caught out in their lie.

"Just what do you think you're doing?" the man asked.

Alex gulped. "I'm not sure what you mean, sir?"

The man glowered, reaching a meaty fist toward Alex's throat. Alex braced for the feel of the huge man's fat fingers closing around his windpipe, crushing it with ease, but the sensation never came. Instead, he felt those fingers fumbling at his top button.

"Don't ever let me catch you walking these halls with your top button undone!" the man barked. "It's slovenly, and it brings disgrace on this house. You are in a position of great privilege—act like it, or I'll personally see to it that you end up on latrine duty for the rest of your sorry days. Is that clear?"

Alex nodded rapidly. "Clear as crystal, sir. I'm sorry for my appearance, sir. It won't happen again, sir."

"It had better not," the man growled, before turning and walking away.

Alex let out a sigh of relief as the huge soldier disappeared around a corner. He couldn't help feeling a little unfairly criticized. Lintz was clearly in a worse state of slovenliness than he was, yet the soldier hadn't said a word to the professor.

"I imagine he dislikes the young," Lintz murmured, flashing a knowing grin in Alex's direction.

Lintz's explanation made sense, but it did nothing to ease Alex's feeling that a grave injustice had been done to him. He'd thought he looked pretty smart, but apparently not smart enough for everyone's liking.

With Lintz chuckling to himself, they made their way to the staircase that would lead them to the next floor of the pagoda, moving slowly past the groups of soldiers that filled the hallways, careful to be polite and to seem as lowly as possible. At the fifth floor, the soldierly presence stopped abruptly. It seemed a little strange, but perhaps it meant they were getting closer to Hadrian's domain. Even as a less-than-beloved royal, Alex assumed that Hadrian would still enjoy certain freedoms, such as privacy.

Maybe the top two floors belong only to him? Alex thought, looking around. This floor was certainly more lavish than the ones beneath it, with gold leaf embossed into the floral wallpaper, and bigger pieces of artwork hanging from the walls. The statues also seemed to be made of far more valuable materials—monkeys carved from solid gold, a strange turtle-like creature cut from what looked like pure diamond that glittered in the glow of the torchlight, and coiling dragons with bejeweled scales. It made Alex curious as to whether there was another reason for the heightened military presence at Falleaf House. Perhaps they were also there to protect these priceless artifacts from thieves. If this place was some sort of gallery, or vault, or treasure trove for ancient magical trophies, he could certainly see why they'd need so many guards on duty.

The doorways that led off from the main hallways intrigued him, but he didn't want to pause and see what was inside—not until he could be sure that the other two were safe and sound with Hadrian, somewhere above him.

"Do you think they're up on the top floor?" Alex asked, uncertain.

Lintz nodded. "If you were Hadrian, I'm sure you'd want

to be as far away from everything as possible, wouldn't you?"

They took the last set of stairs up to the top floor. Reaching the landing, they were met by a single, long corridor with a doorway at the very end of it. They made their way toward the door. Clearing his throat, Alex knocked lightly, using the brass knocker shaped like a fish with a ring in its mouth.

"Come in," a voice spoke softly from the other side.

Needing no further encouragement, Alex turned the handle and stepped inside. The room beyond was an apartment, by the look of it, with plush furnishings and elegant watercolors adorning every wall, some pale imitations of the water garden that could be seen from the window. There were doors branching off from the central space, where large pillows had been placed on the floor, around a low table. Three figures sat around it.

"Alex!" cried Ellabell, jumping to her feet and racing over to him. Aamir followed at a more leisurely pace, though his face showed how pleased he was to see his friend again.

"Ellabell," Alex murmured, wrapping his arms around her and pulling her into a tight embrace.

"We thought we'd lost you," she whispered. "We didn't know what happened. We wanted to wait, but then the soldiers came. I'm so glad you're okay! I don't know what I would have done if… Never mind that now. You're safe, and that's all that matters." She squeezed him tightly.

"It's so good to see you too." He smiled, kissing her softly on the cheek, not wanting to embarrass her in front of the others. Reluctantly, she pulled away, her eyes glittering.

"You had us worried there for a moment," said Aamir warmly, stepping up to hug Alex.

Alex grinned. "I had myself worried."

"Don't forget about me!" Lintz bellowed from the doorway. The other two shook the professor's hand as he recounted the journey through the pagoda.

"Ah, you must be the famous Alex Webber?" the third figure spoke, rising from his cushion and turning to face Alex.

Hadrian had the same pale eyes and shock of white hair to be expected from any royal, but he wasn't wearing his hair in the longer fashion he'd seen from some of the others. Instead, he'd combed it into a bold sort of swoop on top of his head, the front section curling backward onto itself in a quaint fifties style that suited him, making him look like a white-haired Elvis. His voice was similar too, with a deep, musical tone to it that made Alex imagine this new royal to be an accomplished singer. He almost expected to see a guitar hanging from one of the walls.

"I wouldn't go that far," said Alex, taking Hadrian's proffered hand and shaking it firmly.

Hadrian smiled, though there was a nervousness to the white-haired man that made him seem perpetually uneasy. "Well, from what I've been hearing from your friends, you are quite the man! Adventurer, maverick, troublemaker—you've done it all," he teased. Hadrian seemed to be exactly as Elias had described him—a pleasant, genuinely nice man. However, Alex wasn't quick to forget how he had been let down by apparently benevolent royals before, and he wouldn't let himself be duped again.

"I've heard a fair bit about you too," Alex replied carefully.

"All good, I hope?" Hadrian grinned, making it harder for Alex to maintain his cool exterior.

He shrugged. "I don't really trust the words of others. I'd like to see for myself," he said, scrutinizing the latest royal. There was something bugging him that he could not let go of. "I'm just wondering why you left my friend out there in the forest, to fend for himself. I'm pretty sure Aamir and Ellabell told you what happened—why didn't you go and set him free?"

The two friends in question exchanged an awkward look, matched only by the discomfort that appeared on Hadrian's face. Lintz turned to the royal, clearly wondering the same thing.

"I would have come to your f-friend's aid, I assure you,"

Hadrian began, tremulously. "The thing is… with so many soldiers around, and my haven under such close inspection by my uncle, J-Julius, I thought it best to keep up appearances. As much as it pains me to say it, I can't just w-wander around, doing as I please, though I did have the idea of coming to fetch him after nightfall. I would not have left him there indefinitely," he promised, a stutter emerging, as he scratched his beardless chin in what Alex presumed to be some sort of nervous tic.

Alex let the excuse sink in, and though he wasn't completely satisfied, part of him could see things from the royal's point of view. Julius was a terrifying man, and with his eyes and ears all over this haven, Alex could understand how the stakes might be higher.

Alex shrugged. "I suppose I'll have to take your word for it, though you probably already know I don't give much standing to the word of a royal."

Hadrian twisted his hands together. "I did learn about your previous run-ins with my c-cousins. Your wariness is understandable, but you won't find me quite as unpalatable as them, I hope," he said, flashing a nervous smile. "I'm intrigued to learn more about you and your mission, but how about some coffee first?"

"Coffee?"

"Yes, would you like s-some?"

"I thought you were all obsessed with tea?" Alex chuckled, though he realized he was the only one laughing. "Sorry, private joke," he added quickly.

"Laughter is the world's panacea. Come, r-refresh yourself," Hadrian replied, gesturing toward the low table, which was covered in a veritable feast of goodies that made Alex's stomach grumble in anticipation. "Perhaps, you w-would like to change first?" the royal suggested, catching sight of Lintz's ill-fitting scarlet uniform.

Flashing a glance at one another, Alex and Lintz nodded. They were eager to be out of the formal attire. With a polite bow, Hadrian led them to their separate chambers, showing them the wardrobes of clothes they might choose from, before leaving them to their selections. Alex chose plain black trousers and a pale t-shirt, while Lintz had gone for something a little more daring, emerging in taupe trousers and a mustard-yellow knitted sweater.

Dressed more comfortably, Alex and Lintz joined the others on the soft cushions dotted around the table. Unable to wait, Alex grabbed a handful of rice balls, shoving them into his mouth as fast as he could pick them up, until his cheeks were puffed out like a hamster's. The morsels were sweet, with a sour berry filling that made him want to eat a thousand of them. Realizing just how ravenous he was, after prison meals and a day of no food, he scooped up eight more, gulping them down.

"Sorry... I'm just... so hungry... Sorry," he said through mouthfuls, knowing he'd forgotten his table manners in his rush to stuff his face.

Hadrian laughed heartily, his stutter fading as his manner relaxed. "No, no, you eat your fill! We must n-nourish ourselves at any available opportunity, to keep mind and body in total harmony," he said. "And when you're satisfied, we shall settle down to the business of your presence here, and what I might do to assist in your future endeavors."

Alex did just that, wolfing the food down, while the others stared on with mixed expressions of bemusement and horror. Only when his pace slowed did he get back to business.

"We've come for the book," explained Alex, wiping his mouth.

"We have many books here," Hadrian teased.

"You know the one I mean," Alex said, not intending the words to come out as harshly as they did. He was still on edge after his encounter with Caius, and he wasn't quite sure what to make of Hadrian yet. After all, he had thought Caius was a good guy, and he had turned out to be a psychopath with a hundred years of vengeance built up inside him. In all honesty, Hadrian reminded him an awful lot of Caius in the way he spoke, despite the nervous tics, and Alex had a feeling this had something to do with the hint of mistrust he felt toward Hadrian.

"Indeed, I d-do," Hadrian responded curtly, his stutter returning. "Your f-friends here already told me."

Alex sighed, knowing he was in the wrong. "I'm sorry, Hadrian, I didn't mean to snap like that. I've been through a lot, and it's going to be tough for me to trust another royal after what just happened," he said, turning to the others as he began to relay the tale of what had taken place between himself and Caius, after they had gone through the portal.

They all looked at him in shock as he came to the end of the story, describing what had triggered Caius's madness, Vincent's selfless act with the specters, and his own escape on a Thunderbird. It was a hard story to recount, considering he still didn't know the outcome of that otherworldly battle, but it had to be told for everyone to fully understand what had happened, Hadrian more than anyone.

"So, you're a Spellbreaker?" Hadrian asked solemnly.

Alex nodded. "I am, and that's why I need the book."

"I did not dare to b-believe you could exist," Hadrian murmured. "You are an impossible c-creature."

Aamir chimed in. "Improbable, but definitely not impossible."

"I can't believe my father would be capable of such terrible things." Hadrian sighed, looking anxiously at the ground.

"No... I tell a lie. I c-can imagine it of him, though it is not an easy thing for a s-son to admit. I have not seen my father in a long time, and though he would have liked to p-pretend our relationship was a good one, I can assure you it was not. There were d-demons eating away at him every day, and I could do nothing to stop their c-consumption of him—I used to try, but there was an argument, and he told me never to r-return. I have feared for a long time that the keep finally got to him, d-devouring what remained of his soul." There was a sorrow in the pale eyes of the royal that spurred Alex's pity.

"An argument?" Ellabell asked.

Hadrian nodded, wringing his hands. "The last time we m-met, I knew his obsession was getting the better of him. He wouldn't stop talking about his lost love—that Spellbreaker woman—and when I suggested he try to move on, my father g-grew angry and told me to leave. I did... and I haven't seen him since. I should have t-tried again, but it felt as if there was too much water under the bridge. Do you believe he is still alive?" The sadness in Hadrian's voice tugged at Alex's heartstrings. No matter what Caius had done, he was still Hadrian's father.

"I think he might be, but I can't promise anything," Alex said quietly, not wanting to encourage any false hope.

"No, I suppose not," Hadrian murmured.

"Caius didn't want to help the rest of mage-kind, but we do. And to do that, we really need that book. Would you be able to give it to us?" Alex ventured, knowing it wasn't the most polite time to ask, but unable to hold the request back.

Hadrian smiled sadly. "Unfortunately, it is not that s-simple."

CHAPTER 6

I T BECAME CLEAR WHAT HADRIAN MEANT AS HE LED Alex and the others to the back of the room, through an archway decorated with vibrant paintings of pastoral life that were etched onto the walls. They seemed to shift as Alex and his friends walked past, the inhabitants of the drawings moving subtly. In the center of the archway stood a statue of a silver fox. With a clockwise turn of the statue's head, a door slid away, revealing a hidden staircase.

The group trekked down the steps, following Hadrian's lead. Torchlight flickered against the wooden structure of the spiral staircase as they descended into the darkness, walking farther and farther, until Alex was certain they had to be below ground. Alex's stomach twisted at the memory of Caius leading him down a similar set of stairs to meet the Great Evil.

Stepping down the last of the steps, they entered the eerie silence of a subterranean vault. At the end of it, there stood a solitary door, exquisitely carved with oriental patterns that coiled along the surface, inlaid with gold leaf and twinkling jewels, with engravings of lotus flowers and billowing clouds flowing around the outside edges. At the very bottom of the door was another depiction of the turtle-like creature Alex had seen in one of the statues lining the halls of the pagoda. Just above the head of the creature, in the very center of the doorway, lay a bright gold disc. It reminded Alex of the sun, with golden threads of metal glancing off the sides.

"What is this place?" Ellabell asked, her voice filled with awe.

Hadrian stepped toward the ornate door and turned to face the others, an expression of barely suppressed fear on his face. "This is why it is not so simple," he explained. "You see, I cannot simply give you the b-book—it has to be earned."

"Earned?" Alex repeated, curious as to what lay behind the door.

"Yes, earned. There are twelve tasks to complete, when you step through this door," Hadrian replied, his tone jittery. It was clear he had no love for this place. "There are t-twelve, in homage to the great mage philosopher Orpheus, to c-commemorate the twelve labors of Hercules, and also to symbolize the twelve years it takes for Jupiter to orbit the sun."

"That is a lot of twelves," Aamir remarked drily.

Hadrian winked. "It is something of a lucky number."

"And where does Jupiter come into this?" Lintz chimed in, his brow furrowed.

"The book you are seeking is called the Book of J-Jupiter, but as for the whys, hows, and whats, I cannot elaborate, I'm afraid. I can't shed any m-more light on the tasks ahead of you; they are for you to d-discover, and you alone, should you choose to continue on your search," Hadrian said.

Alex glanced at the door again. "You can't tell us anything?"

Hadrian shook his head. "I c-cannot. While I am the guardian of this place, and the artifacts within the pagoda, I did not put the book here, and I am s-sad to say that I have never been beyond this door. What lies ahead of you is a secret journey, one which you must walk without aid from outside influence," he said, his voice heavy with remorse. "All I can tell you is that it will not be easy. There will be very real d-dangers, and you must complete all twelve tasks to achieve your mission."

Alex leveled his gaze at Hadrian, wondering what the royal knew about the tasks but wasn't saying, or wasn't able to say. The man looked terrified, his eyes darting around at the shadows of the cavern, as if something might spring out at a moment's notice. But there was more to it than just a general fear of the vault—of that Alex was certain. Whatever Hadrian was holding back, the white-haired man had at least confirmed Alex's suspicions that certain areas of Falleaf House were used to protect valuable artifacts. However, he questioned where all these precious objects had come from, and who they had belonged to before. The pagoda itself didn't seem to belong to the usual style of the royals; it wouldn't surprise him if they were prone to taking from others and using these sites and belongings for their own purposes. Alex was particularly curious about the book itself—had it belonged to the Spellbreakers, considering what lay within its pages? If it had, then he knew it was a stolen artifact, procured by the royals and buried somewhere beyond the ornately carved door. The idea didn't sit well with him. What else had the royals taken that wasn't theirs?

"What if we change our minds and want to come back?" Lintz asked.

"Impossible, I'm afraid. Once through this door, you can

only move forward. You cannot come back out this way," Hadrian explained.

"Do I have to go through alone?" Alex asked, his mind racing.

"No, which I suppose is the one b-blessing in all of this," said Hadrian. "The tasks are designed to ensure that only the worthiest of h-heroes can attain the book, but in doing so, teamwork and loyalty must be t-tested too. If you are still intent on retrieving the book, you must go through with others, to assist in the tasks."

"How come the book is here?" Ellabell asked, voicing Alex's own question.

Hadrian crossed his arms. "The book was taken from the home of Leander Wyvern, and has b-been here ever since. There are many valuable creations locked away in this vault, but only one g-group has run the gauntlet of what lies ahead, in pursuit of the book you seek."

"Was the Head one of that group?" said Aamir thoughtfully.

"If you mean my cousin Virgil, then yes. He was the last to undertake these t-tasks, with two others m-making up the n-numbers, though that was many decades ago now."

"But Virgil didn't manage to do the spell—why is the book still here?" Alex asked.

"The book will return itself to the v-vault after three

failed attempts, by all accounts. That is how it was b-before," Hadrian stated. "And the book must be physically present in order for one to perform any spell, so it cannot be a case of writing it down and l-leaving it here. I know that much."

Alex realized that Alypia must have been planning for him to complete these tasks, in order to retrieve the book. No doubt she would have forced him using one of his friends as collateral, or something equally cold and calculated. In hearing Hadrian's explanation, Alex was also surer than ever that Virgil had intentionally flubbed the spell. Even if the Head had been coerced into memorizing it, that didn't mean he had followed the instructions to the letter. It was likely, Alex knew, that Virgil had tried to weasel his way out using any loophole at his disposal. This time, Alex would ensure that the intricate workings of the incantation, or whatever it was, were obeyed down to the last detail.

"So the others have to come with me?" Alex asked.

Hadrian nodded. "There must be a g-group of at least three, yes. As a quartet, you may f-find it easier, or you may not… I couldn't say."

Alex thought the white-haired man *could* say, but was bound by something that prevented him. It wouldn't be the first time. Glancing around at the others, he saw their anxious expressions, and felt a wave of guilt ripple through him, at having brought them here.

"I don't expect you all to come with me," he said quietly.

"We have come this far, Alex Webber. We are not giving up now!" Lintz boomed.

Aamir murmured in agreement. "You can't get rid of us now. Our choice was made before we even stepped through the portal from Kingstone."

"We're not leaving your side," added Ellabell, grasping his hand.

Their confidence reassured him, and yet he wished he didn't have to drag them all through the dangers that lay ahead; there had already been so much peril, and he hated that he was adding to it. However, he knew his friends well enough by now to know that there was no way of changing their stubborn minds.

"Then, I guess we're all going through," he said, turning to Hadrian for further instruction.

Hadrian bowed his head. "Very well, though I would not w-wish it upon any of you. It is never p-pleasant to see such fine young people heading into unknown dangers."

"I'm glad you think I'm young!" Lintz chuckled, lightening the somber mood.

Hadrian grinned. "There's still life in the old dog yet, am I right?"

"You bet! I'm as lively as a spring chick," said Lintz, punching the air with unexpected enthusiasm.

"In that case, I would ask that each of you s-step up to the disc you see before you, place your palm flat against it, and feed a small amount of your respective energies into the golden plate," Hadrian instructed. "Once the last person has stepped up, you must wait for the d-disc to flash a bright orange. Only then will the door open."

"Why is that?" Alex asked.

"It reads your abilities, to get a b-better sense of the tasks it needs to set." Hadrian gave a reluctant shrug. "You may find that certain aspects of your magical powers become limited within some of the tests, forcing you to rely on other means. You will understand once you are inside, but I can say no more on the s-subject... Please forgive me," he added, sighing heavily. "I dearly wish you did not have to d-do this."

Alex met the man's gaze. "We need that book, Hadrian. There is no other option."

"I see I cannot change your m-minds," said Hadrian sadly, once again scratching at his chin. "Then I suppose there is nothing more to say—step up and see what the v-vault has in store for you."

They did as instructed. Alex went first, placing his palm flat against the cold metal plate, before feeding strands of silver and black into the disc. It shone dimly for a second, then faded to its original sheen. Ellabell went second, followed by Aamir, and then Lintz.

Stepping back, they watched with nervous anticipation, waiting for the disc to flash orange, as Hadrian had promised it would. A few minutes passed, and still the disc hadn't flashed.

Are we unworthy? Alex wondered.

As if answering his thought, the golden disc lit up bright orange, and a loud creak split the silence of the subterranean vault. With a rush of fusty air, the heavy vault door opened. Alex stepped through first, feeling the creep of a cold breeze on his face, as he steeled himself against the unknown. The others followed, and he glanced back, seeing the concerned expressions that rested upon their brows. Nobody knew what lay ahead for them, and that knowledge was petrifying. There were real dangers in this vault—Hadrian had said so himself.

Alex just prayed they weren't walking straight into the jaws of death.

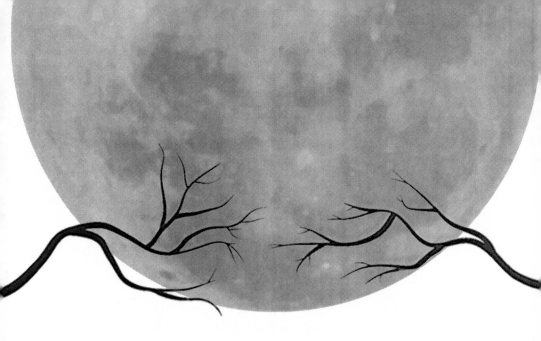

CHAPTER 7

THE VAULT DOOR CLOSED BEHIND THEM WITH A heavy slam that felt bone-chillingly final. Alex tried hard not to shudder, knowing they couldn't turn back. It was onward or nothing, from here on.

As the entrance thudded shut, Alex expected it to take the light with it, leaving the group in a dimly lit room. However, the room seemed to be illuminated by a huge yellow crystal that hung from the center of the cavernous ceiling. With its light casting a hazy glow upon everything below, he could get a good idea of the volume and shape of the place. They appeared to be in an enormous room, not dissimilar to the one Caius had shown Alex, where the ominous pit lay—in fact, it was very much like that cavern, though Alex couldn't sense the swell and roar of anything sinister flowing beneath the ground. The only thing missing was the pit itself, but Alex could sense something strange in the echoes their footsteps were making on the rock beneath their feet. There were echoes that shouldn't be there. He moved forward tentatively, feeling his way with the toe of his shoe, not knowing how sure his footing was. Although he could see solid ground ahead of him, he knew he couldn't trust anything in this place, least of all his own eyes.

He paused, trying to peer into the middle of the room in case he could make out the glimmer of a barrier, or something peculiar that might give them more information. Aamir walked slowly past him. Suddenly, he realized why the echoes were so strange, and reached out desperately for the older boy's arm, yanking him backward, just in time to stop him from going over the edge of a vast ravine that gaped open before them. It was covered in an illusion, made to look like solid ground, much like the glamors Esmerelda had taught them so long ago that would make an object or an image appear to be something it wasn't.

"Watch out, there's a pit ahead of us!" Alex called back to the others, his hand still firmly gripping Aamir's arm. He had found his pit after all, and he speculated that the tests were somehow playing on his fears.

"I didn't even see it!" Aamir shuddered. "You saved me."

"I barely saw it myself—we're going to have to be really careful where we walk in this place," Alex replied, pushing down a surge of fear. They were less than five minutes into the tasks, and already they had almost lost someone.

Aamir nodded. "We must keep our eyes peeled."

"Yeah, I'm not sure we can even trust them," said Alex, trying to slow his racing heartbeat.

With that in mind, Alex and the others began to creep along the lip of the pit. It was easy to see where the rock ended and the illusion began, once they knew it was there, but trying to make out anything they could use to cross it was proving tricky. It was impossible to see the other side, or even to see how far the illusion stretched, and yet Alex knew there had to be a way to get over.

Ellabell stood at the edge, beginning to forge the threads of her golden magic beneath her hands. As she did so, the glittering ribbons crackled, before sputtering out completely. She tried again, only to get the same results.

"My magic isn't working," she said, a puzzled look on her face.

Aamir nodded. "Hadrian said it would take some of our power from us," he reminded them. He too attempted a spell, resulting in the same failed crackle. "Does yours work?" he asked, looking to Alex.

Curious, Alex began to feed the black and silver fronds of his anti-magic between his fingers, only to watch them wither and die with the same pathetic crackle. It seemed they would not be able to use their supernatural talents to find a way out.

We're at task number one, and already we're failing, he thought glumly, not wanting to voice his feelings in case it lowered morale.

"Mine isn't working either," Alex said, as Lintz's voice echoed across the cavern.

"Eureka! I found something!" the professor cried with delight.

Alex and the others hurried over to where he was crouched, almost in the center of the ravine's ridge, his arm reaching down for something below the hazy surface of the illusion. As Alex's eyes adjusted to the shift in what was real and what was not, he could see a metal bar running across the jagged stone, pressed deep into the rock in a perfectly straight line, gleaming beneath Lintz's hand. It was wide, several feet across, and looked distinctly promising, though how they were supposed to get it to do something useful was another matter entirely.

"What is it?" Alex asked, bending for a closer look.

Lintz furrowed his brow in contemplation. "I believe

it's some form of clockwork, or there is some sort of clock-work involved, at the very least. You know I love my mech-anisms!" he said brightly, running his skilled fingers across the various pieces that made up the strange construction.

"Can you get it to work?" Ellabell asked.

"There is a release mechanism here, sticking out of the rock face next to this bar, but there appear to be some pieces missing. If we can find those pieces, it should make whatever is being held back—a bridge, perhaps—shoot out over to the other side of the pit," Lintz explained, showing them a cir-cular clockwork arm with a handle that evidently had to be turned once all the pieces were in place. "The only problem is, where might these pieces be?"

"It's impossible to know how far down this pit goes, or if there even is a way down," muttered Alex, sticking his head below the surface of the illusion to see the gaping void of the pit below. Although it was lit with the same glowing light as above, it eventually gave way to a darkness that prevented him from seeing the bottom. "Besides, it's too steep down there—how are we going to find anything?"

"Wait, there's something written here," Aamir said, lean-ing precariously over the edge.

Alex stepped beside him. "What does it say?"

"'Courage.'"

"What does that even mean?" Alex asked, realizing how

much the vagueness of these words was going to annoy him, if it was going to be a recurring theme throughout the tasks.

"I imagine it means we have to have courage," Ellabell replied, half teasing.

Lintz shook his head. "No, no, it is the first virtue of the great philosopher Orpheus—courage."

The knowledge of its origin didn't make the task any easier as the group set about trying to find some sort of clue as to where the missing pieces might be hiding. All there seemed to be was cold, damp rock and a sheer drop into unknown depths, hidden by the illusion of solid ground.

"There's something over here," Ellabell shouted, her voice reverberating around the cavernous room.

Alex wandered over to where she was sitting, her legs dangling over the edge. Lintz and Aamir followed, gathering around Ellabell to see what she had found.

"I think there's a handhold down here, and I'm pretty sure there are more, disappearing down into the cavern," she said eagerly, showing the deep groove she had discovered in the sheer rock face. "I think it might be possible to climb down. I'm going to go—I'll see what's down there." She chewed her lip nervously, but there was a determination on her face that concerned Alex. The prospect of seeing her clamber down the side of a pit, into the unknown, wasn't exactly a comforting one, given that they didn't know what might be at the bottom. Descending into unfathomable depths wasn't exactly his favorite thing either, but that didn't mean he was about to let her go in his place.

"No, I'll go," said Alex firmly, resting his hand on Ellabell's arm.

She turned, flashing him a look of annoyance. "It's fine. I'm good at climbing," she insisted. "I'll go. I've been rock-climbing all my life."

"No, it's okay. I'll go. Besides, it might be dark down there, and we don't know what could be lurking. I'll do it," Alex replied. The only things he'd ever climbed were the beams of the railway bridge at home, and a motorized climbing wall at a friend's birthday party when he was eleven. Still, he was happy to do it, if it meant Ellabell didn't have to.

"Alex, I've got this, honestly," Ellabell said sternly. "I'm not trying to be a hero—I'm being pragmatic. I can climb. I'm the best equipped for this."

"Let me," Alex implored, still unable to bear the idea of her disappearing down into the ravine, in case she never came out again.

Ellabell let out an exasperated sigh. "Fine, but if you get stuck or you slip, don't say I didn't warn you."

She got up, brushing off her legs in a gesture of irritation, and Alex sat down in the spot where she had been sitting. Taking a deep breath, he shuffled toward the ravine edge, before turning around and dropping his legs down, feeling around with his toes for the deep grooves he knew were there. His heart was thundering in his chest, knowing he could slip at any moment, but his grip remained steady, and the grooves seemed strong enough to hold him as he began the slow descent into the void below.

Gathering confidence, he climbed quickly downward, using the handholds. The light prevailed, guiding his way. However, as he got farther down, he discovered the years of grime and neglect had made the walls slippery, the rock covered in slick moisture and damp patches of slimy moss.

"Whoa!" he yelped, losing his grip with one hand as his body lurched backward. The other hand held fast, to his relief.

He took a moment, allowing his heart rate to slow, before continuing the descent into the abyss, the light fading with every step he took downward. It wasn't the last time he would slip, and his voice rang out in surprise with each misplaced hand and foot. The slimy rocks were perilous, and it was all Alex could do not to think of himself being squashed flat after falling from such a height.

"How are you doing?" Ellabell shouted.

"I'm fine!" he lied, not wishing to alarm anyone, and definitely not wishing to prove her right. The lower he got, the slimier the walls became.

Suddenly, the handholds stopped, and so did the light, but he still hadn't reached the bottom—well, as far as he could see, he hadn't. The undetermined depth of the pit still yawning below him sent a tremor of fear through his body.

I'm going to have to jump, Alex realized, as the meaning of the word written on the golden bar began to make horrifying sense. He was going to have to make a leap of courage, and jump from the side of the rock into whatever lay underneath.

Here goes nothing, he thought, trying to steady his nerves as he prepared to push off. It wasn't easy, forcing himself to make the jump, and yet he knew it was the only option he had. Praying he wasn't about to end up as human mulch, he took a deep breath and sprang backwards, away from the safety of the handholds.

Anticipating a long fall into the darkness, he was surprised when the ground met him relatively quickly, after a split second in fact. Landing awkwardly, his knees buckling with the unexpectedly instant impact, he realized he was at the bottom, and no worse for it. No broken bones, no human pulp, nothing.

Looking around at where he stood, he found that he could make out some shapes by the light of tiny, luminescent lichens that were growing all along the basin. Where he had landed, the lichens branched out beneath his feet, glowing brighter each time he pressed his foot into the ground, sending shockwaves of light across the basin floor. They pulsed with a dim blue light, which cast an eerie shadow on everything it touched, but Alex was glad of at least something to see by.

In the center of the cavern floor was the distinct cuboid shape of a box, too deliberately placed to be anything else, though there were some disturbing white shapes scattered around it that he didn't wish to know the origins of. They looked alarmingly like bones, left to rot and decay. Picking his way around the piles of nasty detritus, Alex made his way toward the box.

Suddenly, a figure rose up from the glow of a nearby lichen, its body transparent, its ghostly skin a thin, gauzy gray. Alex's heart sank. His mother stood before him, her eyes black and unseeing, her phantom arms trailing out toward him. There was an expression of such sadness on her face that Alex could hardly breathe. It hurt to look at her.

"Don't open the box, my darling boy," she whispered, her voice a ghostly echo.

"Mom?" Alex gasped, holding his chest.

"Don't open the box, my darling boy," she repeated, raising her arms to him once more.

"Mom, is that really you?" he asked, his voice choked with emotion. *Did you die? Did you die while I wasn't there to help you?* Tears sprang to his eyes, and he reached out for her, but his hand passed through her body, the image flickering for a moment. She was just an illusion, like the ground that covered the pit.

"Don't open the box, my darling boy," the mirage wailed, the image wavering out of focus again.

"You aren't my mother," said Alex quietly. "And I will open this box."

With a piercing scream, the phantom rushed through Alex and disappeared into the wall of the cavern.

Shaking off the tears, trying not to let it cloud his mind, he stepped toward the box. There was no lock, only a lid, which Alex lifted easily to reveal the contents within. Inside, several pieces of golden clockwork gleamed, though they were half covered by tangled masses of damp black moss. Thrilled by the sight, Alex picked up the gears and bolts, careful not to miss any, before putting them into his pockets for safe-keeping. They clinked against the mouse he always kept about his person as something of a lucky charm, and the beetle beacon he'd more recently added to his clockwork collection. He hoped he had all that he needed to complete task one.

After taking a second look in the box, just to be sure, Alex ran back toward the spot on the wall where the handholds were, and saw that there was a stone plinth just beneath them to assist in the ascent back up the rock face. He jumped up onto it, and reached for the lowest groove, hauling himself up with as much strength as he could muster.

Once he was comfortable with his handholds and footholds, he began to climb back up to the top of the ravine, making good time, as the lip soon appeared ahead of him. The faces of his friends peered down, and the sight made him smile, helping him forget the miserable scene replaying in his mind. In his heart, he knew she was still alive—if she had passed on, something deep inside him would know about it, he was sure. Grasping for the edge, he let Ellabell and Aamir drag him back onto solid ground, where he lay for a moment, catching his breath.

"Did you find anything?" Aamir asked.

"I got these," Alex said, retrieving the clockwork pieces from his pocket.

"You found them?" Lintz cried, holding out his hand for the missing parts.

"They were in a box at the bottom of the pit," replied Alex, saying nothing of the ghost.

"Excellent!" Lintz scurried off toward the golden bar, the pieces clutched in his plump fingers.

Once Alex's breathing had returned to normal, he got up and followed the others to where Lintz was beavering away, making quick work of the clockwork puzzle. With a deft efficiency that still surprised Alex, the professor fitted the cogs and parts into place on the clockwork arm that stuck out of the rock face. With the last piece tucked into place, Lintz turned the small handle that protruded from it. A whirring sound emanated from the clockwork, gathering speed, until finally, with a loud scrape of metal on metal, a golden bridge shot out across the crevasse, slamming hard into the adjoining slot on the other side.

"Task one complete!" Lintz bellowed.

Alex patted the professor on the shoulder. "Nice work, Professor."

"A team effort, I'd say," the professor said brightly, returning to his feet.

"Yes, if you regard a close call and sheer serendipity as a team effort," Aamir muttered.

With that, Alex and the others ran over the newly forged bridge, feeling only a slight shiver of trepidation that it might be a trick. They let out a collective sigh of relief as they reached the other side. Another door lay within the rocks. It didn't appear to have any lock on it, and they walked into the space beyond.

The room that met them was brightly lit, stinging their eyes after the hazy luminosity of the previous room, as they glanced around at their new surroundings. Ahead was an exotic water garden, with a deep, azure pool fed by a waterfall tumbling from a cluster of stalagmites above. There were brightly colored flowers rising up from the lush green grass that carpeted the cavern, and a wooden bridge, painted a vivid red, that traversed the pool, the stream flowing away from it. Alex found the pretty garden to be a strange sight, considering how far below ground they were, but it was here, and no doubt it contained the key to task number two's completion.

A splash broke the surface of the serene pool. Something was emerging from the water.

A creature dragged itself from the depths, clawing at the arc of the bridge with long fingers until it was fully out of the pool and lying across the wooden slats. It unfurled into a standing position, and Alex was surprised to see that the creature looked remarkably similar to the carving on the vault door, and the statue he had seen within the pagoda. The odd being looked like a kind of reptile, with the beak of a turtle and the shell too, and pale brown scales dotting its green body. Strangest of all, however, was the deep recess in the creature's skull; it looked almost like a bowl, with water sloshing around inside.

Alex wasn't sure what to make of the creepy thing as it ambled toward the bottom of the bridge, blocking the way from one side to the other. It was small in stature, but Alex knew not to judge an evil by its size.

"What is it?" Ellabell whispered.

"I think it's called a kappa," replied Aamir.

Alex looked at him. "A kappa?"

"Yes, it's a mythical Japanese creature—my grandmother was big on myths and legends, and used to tell me all sorts, from all over the world," Aamir explained. "I always loved the Japanese stories the best, and she told me about this being once or twice. I never forgot it. The dent in its skull gives it away… but I can't remember what she said about them." A look of frustration crossed the older boy's face.

"I guess we'll have to move it by force," Alex said. Lifting his hands, he inched closer to the bridge, keeping his gaze on the reptilian eyes that seemed to be watching him with the utmost curiosity, a warped smile curving up the sides of its blunt beak.

"Are you going to fight me?" it said, its voice raspy and otherworldly. The sound took Alex by surprise; he hadn't been expecting it to be able to speak. "I should warn you: I abhor rudeness, and I find fighting to be the height of rudeness," it added, blinking slowly. "But do what you must do, and I will do what I must do…"

CHAPTER 8

ALEX MOVED TOWARD THE KAPPA, HIS MIND focused on forging anti-magic from his raised hands. After a moment, he realized that his energy wasn't exactly playing ball, the anti-magic fizzling and spitting, refusing to create smooth threads. It was like he was back at Spellshadow again, in those first few days, unable to conjure anything. He tried again, but still the anti-magic fizzed and crackled. Without it to aid him, he was going to have to fight the kappa in hand-to-hand combat.

Frowning, he took another step toward the reptilian creature.

"So, it is to be a battle?" the creature rasped.

"We only want to cross this bridge," replied Alex.

"I will stand in your way," the turtle hybrid croaked.

Alex raised his fists. "Then you leave us no choice."

The creature's face twisted in displeasure. "Such impertinence!"

Aamir stepped up beside him, resting a hand on Alex's arm. "Wait, I think there's another way," he whispered.

"You remembered something?" Alex asked.

"I think so—let me deal with this one."

"Be careful." Alex let Aamir move ahead of him, until he was standing face-to-face with the kappa.

"Excuse me, eminent guardian of this bridge, but I believe it is you who is the rude one," said Aamir, with easy confidence.

The creature's face morphed into an expression of horror. "How *dare* you."

"How dare I?" Aamir countered. "You are the one blocking our way, when you know we desire to cross the bridge. That doesn't seem particularly generous, does it?"

"It is my duty, intruder," the kappa said, flashing a warning look from its wet, reptilian eyes.

"Have we done anything to make you suspect our intentions are anything but good? Have we sought to steal or destroy anything in your beautiful garden?" Aamir asked. "No, honored guardian, we have not. Our intentions are pure, and we wish only to cross the bridge. But you stand there, telling us you will not move. Surely, that breaks the bonds of guest welcome?"

The kappa smiled. "You are not guests."

"Is a visitor not a guest?"

The kappa raised a scaly eyebrow. "I suppose, in a manner of speaking, they could be considered to be of similar origin, but you are no guests of mine. Nobody enters this place with altruistic intention—you wish to take something, and so you are intruders."

"Be that as it may, our intentions are good. Surely, that makes us anything but intruders?"

It wasn't yet clear to Alex what the older boy was trying to achieve with this battle of wits, but whatever Aamir's goal, he was putting his silver tongue to good use.

"You have entered my domain without permission, and wish to cross without my permission, and so your manners bely your impertinence," the kappa remarked.

"Then, please, may we cross your bridge, honored guardian?" Aamir asked.

The kappa shook his scaly head. "Certainly not. As long as I stand here, you shall not reach the other side."

"Even if you were not here, we would not be able to cross it," Aamir mused.

Alex glanced at his friend, understanding that Aamir was preparing to maneuver into his final play.

"I never leave my post," the kappa countered.

Aamir smiled. "I am merely talking hypothetically. You see, you have deliberately made the bridge dangerous."

"I have done no such thing!" said the kappa, clearly affronted by the accusation.

"You have. Your wet feet have made the wood slippery, no doubt as a means to trick us into falling into the water, should you lose at hand-to-hand combat. Once we fall in, you will simply pull us under, and do away with us," Aamir replied, his eyes gleaming.

The kappa howled in outrage. "What proof do you have? You think me a lowly thing, to resort to tricks, simply because I dwell beneath the water?"

"No, my proof is far more logical than that. I can only use my eyes for such evidence," Aamir insisted. "We would slip the moment we set foot on the bridge. Just look at the slick pools of water all around your feet."

The kappa looked down to inspect its feet, and as soon as its head tilted, the water sloshing around in the bowl of its skull emptied out onto the grass. The kappa froze the moment the last few drops had fallen, its power source drained. It stood, statue-like, perched on the edge of the bridge, unmoving.

"What did you do?" Alex asked.

Aamir grinned. "Outwitted it. But we should get going in case it doesn't stay like that."

Lintz and Ellabell followed them over the bridge, leaving the kappa standing there, motionless. As they ran across, Alex noticed the word "Wit" carved into the wooden balustrade at the end of the bridge.

Task two completed, he thought.

Pushing through another door, they entered a small chamber. It looked like a shrine, with two statues of twin gods, and a solitary goddess, set back into a recess that glowed with the luminescence of countless candles. Set up on tall candlesticks, facing the effigies, were four unlit candles, the wicks untouched, the wax unmelted.

Above the female statue, Alex could make out the word "Aletheia," and above the male statues were the words "Phobos and Deimos." They meant nothing to Alex, but Lintz looked thoughtful, the professor muttering the names over and over.

"Do you know who they are?" Ellabell asked.

Lintz nodded. "I believe the woman is the Greek equivalent of the Roman deity Veritas, the goddess of truth. There is a similar statue in the teachers' quarters at Spellshadow. The other two, I'm not sure—my Greek mythology isn't as good as my Roman."

Ellabell wandered up to the shrine, where a book lay open in front of the deities. Alex watched as she leaned closer to the flames of the already-burning candles, the flickering light reflected in her eyes.

"I think it's like a prayer," she said. "These candles all have words carved into them... 'death,' 'old age,' 'loneliness.'" She moved toward the book, reading it, as the others watched and waited for her verdict. "The female statue is the Greek goddess of truth, and the two twins beside her are the Greek gods of fear and terror. There's a riddle here too. It says, 'In order to uncover the secrets here, you must first unveil your greatest fear.' I suppose we have to make an offering of our greatest fear to these deities, and light the candles as we say what it is."

"Do you think we should carve the words into the candles?" Aamir asked.

Ellabell shook her head. "I think they're there to serve as a guide."

Alex had a feeling she was right. They were clues to the task, the lettering neat and impossibly uniform. Picking up a taper, Ellabell went first, moving toward the unlit candle closest to the door they had come through. She paused for a moment, her expression thoughtful.

"The dark," she said, lighting the wick and blowing out the taper.

Alex went next, taking a minute to think of what he feared most. "Losing loved ones," he murmured, envisioning his mother and Ellabell and all his friends, and the pain he would feel if anything were to happen to them. It was truly his greatest fear.

Aamir stepped up third. "Losing control."

"Failing to reach the real world," said Lintz, lighting the final candle.

As the flame of the fourth candle burst into life, the eyes of the deities flashed gold, and a narrow doorway creaked open on the opposite side of the room. The offerings had been accepted, and task three had been completed.

Moving into the next room, Alex saw the word "Unity" written above the door. Inside, it was pitch black, so dark he couldn't see his hand in front of his face. The room was steeped in wall-to-wall, impenetrable darkness, and they couldn't see each other, let alone anything farther ahead.

Alex heard the sharp inhale of frightened breath from somewhere close by him, and he reached his hand out instinctively, brushing skin.

"Ellabell?" he whispered.

"It's me," she replied, her voice trembling.

Suddenly, he became aware of scraping sounds, filling the room. Soft, weird noises, like fingernails dragging across stone, and Alex knew they weren't alone in here. He grasped what he hoped was Ellabell's hand, and pulled her closer to him, trying to calm her panicked breathing.

Something else reached out for him, brushing the base of his neck. He shuddered, trying not to shout out in alarm. No matter where he moved in the black room, he could feel things trying to grab him with unseen hands, and from the shrieks and cries of Lintz and Aamir, and the tremble of Ellabell in his arms, he knew he wasn't the only one feeling terrified.

"Aamir, Professor, follow my voice!" he whispered, painfully aware of drawing attention to himself.

He needed everyone to be closer together, so they could figure out how to defeat this task. He heard the scuffle of shoes on stone as the others followed his instruction. They bumped into him, forming a cluster in their unknown spot in the room. All the while, he could hear low groans and rattling chains, and the scrape of something clawing along the floor. It was intended to unnerve them, he knew, and it was doing just that.

"What do you think we have to do?" Lintz asked, from somewhere close at hand.

"A teamwork exercise, maybe?" Aamir suggested.

Alex nodded, though he realized immediately that he couldn't be seen. "The word above the door said 'Unity,' so the way out of here must have something to do with us working together."

"Maybe we could start by figuring out the shape of the room, to figure out where the exit is?" Ellabell said. He could feel her chin turning up to look at him, even though they couldn't see one another.

"Let's form a chain and map out the space," Lintz suggested.

It seemed like a good plan, but Alex wanted to make sure Ellabell was close to him at all times. In the previous room, she had admitted her greatest fear was the dark, and she was shaking like a leaf. It was the first time he had sensed true terror in her.

"Ellabell, if you'll be the lynchpin, the rest of us will stretch out from you, and see if we can touch the walls. See if we can't find a door in this place," Alex said.

Everyone moved into position, with Ellabell in the center, her palm clammy as she gripped Alex's hand. Lintz was in the center too, with Alex and Aamir on the outer edges, encumbered with the task of feeling out the walls. Slowly, they began to turn, Alex snatching his hand back every time it made contact with something fleshy. The chains rattled harder whenever he came near, but he refused to let it put him off. They *had* to find the exit—there was no time for meekness.

Pretty soon, Alex realized that the room itself was only

as wide as the four of them stretched out to their full capacity, as they rotated to feel out the shape. From this, they garnered that it was a perfect square. The stone walls were moist with something unpleasant, but Alex pushed away his disgust as he called back to the others what he had found. Aamir did the same, until they had a complete idea of what the room looked like. However, they had found no door on any of the walls.

"Any luck?" Alex asked.

"No door here," Aamir replied.

"What if there isn't one?" said Ellabell, her voice fearful.

"In the famous words of Sherlock Holmes: at a crime scene, always look up... or, in this case, down," suggested Lintz.

It was a good idea. Following the professor's lead, Alex and the others began to search the floor, keeping close to one another as they made their sweep of the terrain. There was a thick mulch of something on the floor, and Alex didn't dare imagine what disgusting things he would see on his hands when they reached some form of light again.

"I've found something!" Aamir shouted. "It feels like a trapdoor."

Alex's heart pounded faster. "Really?"

"Yeah, but there seems to be a padlock on it," replied Aamir regretfully.

"Is there a key?" Ellabell asked.

"Sadly not."

Just then, Alex thought he heard a furtive whispering. It was nearby, too close to be from the chain-rattlers and groaning ghouls, and it didn't sound particularly monstrous. It sounded human. Stranger still, Ellabell's hand had stopped shaking.

"I think I know where the key is," she said a moment later. A skittering sound followed her announcement, as if something metallic had been kicked across the ground.

"Ellabell?" whispered Alex as she let go of his hand, stooping to pick something up.

"I have it here," she said. "Aamir, where are you?"

"Over here."

Alex felt Ellabell move away from him, clumsily picking her way toward the spot where Aamir had found the trap-door. Alex held his breath when he heard the sound of a key turning in a lock, followed by a satisfying click.

"It's open!" said Aamir, delighted.

Alex exhaled, grateful it had worked, but still curious as to where Ellabell had found the key. He figured he'd ask her in a moment, when they weren't in a room chock full of unknown creatures. There was no time to lose. He moved to where he thought Aamir to be, and found the empty gap of an opening in the ground. A rope ladder was attached to the side, and Alex clung to it as he made his fumbling way down, following the light that shone from below.

Task four completed; we're a third of the way through, he told himself, dropping into the next room. They'd been lucky so far, moving through the challenges with relative ease, but, from here on, he had a feeling the tasks were only going to get harder.

CHAPTER 9

WITH EVERYONE ASSEMBLED, ALEX WAS ABOUT to ask Ellabell how she had known about the key, but he had barely gotten through the first two words when she lifted her finger quickly to her lips and shook her head in warning.

At least she doesn't look scared anymore, he noted.

Following her gaze, he saw why she had silenced him. The room was brightly lit, enough for Alex and the others to see the black dirt and reddish grime on their hands, but he barely had time to notice it. At the far end of the room stood an enormous mechanical Minotaur, flanked by two mechanical lions, their golden manes gleaming in the torchlight.

The whir of cogs springing to life had a similar effect on Alex, as he jumped into action mode. Throwing up his hands, he weaved anti-magic between his fingers, only to find his powers stunted again by the energies of the vault. Hadrian had warned them this would happen, but Alex hadn't thought it would feel so frustrating. It seemed the others were having trouble too, as the golden glint of their magic fell flat, dissipating uselessly into the atmosphere. Alex had hoped their abilities might be returned to their full capacity as they progressed through the vault, but it seemed he was wrong.

Looking around, he saw that there were various medieval-looking weapons hanging from the walls, most likely intended for their use.

"Grab a weapon, my dears!" Lintz bellowed, his voice like a war cry.

The professor lunged for a hefty double-sided axe, tearing it from its fittings. He looked truly terrifying as he wielded the vast blade, preparing for the fight ahead. Ellabell followed straight after, pulling a trident down, alongside a net. It reminded Alex of the retiarius gladiators, who had fought in grand arenas with the same weapons she had chosen. Aamir sprinted toward a mace and shield, grappling with them, until he too looked the part of vicious warrior. Alex moved toward a curved saber, lifting it off its bracket. The solid silver handle was scarred with the wounds of past battles, and the blade glinted with a deadly sharpness. It felt heavy in his hands, but, after a few practice swings, he knew he could do some real damage with this thing—and he intended to.

As a unit, they circled the mechanical creatures, who had come to life, moving with surprising fluidity toward them. Proper combat wasn't a natural state for any of them, and Alex was nervous about making the first strike, even as one of the lions snapped its jaws at him.

Within seconds, the creatures had snatched away any choice they might have had in the matter. One of the lions pounced, coming within inches of Alex's shoulder. He ducked out of the way, rallying against the automaton as he sliced his blade down onto its back. It made a dent, but the lion was unperturbed, wheeling back around to have another go. Again, Alex brought his sword down onto the creature's back, wanting to crack the metal, but the beast swung out of the way at the last minute, unscathed.

At the far end of the room, Aamir smashed his mace down onto the Minotaur's chest plate, not seeing the second lion as it approached. Aamir raised his arm to swing the mace again, and the lion pounced, clamping its metal jaws down on his hand. Aamir cried out and dropped the mace, trickles of blood meandering down his forearm. Ellabell ran to him while Lintz distracted the Minotaur. She was fending it off, jabbing at its golden eyes trying to get it to let go, when Alex raced up to assist. With a great leap, Alex drove the sword down into the spot between the lion's shoulder blades, using all his forward momentum to shatter the mechanism within. The creature let out a robotic roar, opening its jaws. Aamir snatched his hand away just as Ellabell forced her spear down into the open mouth of the golden beast. With a heavy clunk, the lion slumped to the floor, the clockwork broken.

"You okay?" asked Alex, looking at the blood trickling down Aamir's arm.

Aamir clutched his wound, breathing hard. "Nothing I can't handle."

Ellabell turned to Alex. "I had it covered," she said, her eyes glinting with irritation.

"I was just trying to help," Alex replied, brow furrowed. "Two weapons are better than one, right?"

Ellabell whirled around in time to smack the remaining lion hard in the face, forcing it to run toward the far wall. "Aamir, are you going to be okay?" she asked, and Alex noticed that she had ignored his question.

He nodded. "As long as you cover me."

There wasn't time to patch him up now, but the older boy didn't seem too bothered by the injury, dropping the shield to the ground and picking up his mace again. With only one usable hand, he returned to the fray. Alex and Ellabell joined him, though Alex had to take a moment to pause at the sight before him. Lintz, in a feat of athleticism, had jumped off the back of the remaining lion and was soaring through the air toward the Minotaur, crashing his double-sided axe down on the monster's neck, beheading it in one fell swoop. The head arced through the air, sparking from the point of its beheading. Its body crumpled. Alex dove out of the way as the head came rushing in his direction and hit the wall behind him.

"Nice, Professor!" he whooped.

Lintz grinned. "It's good to stretch your legs once in a while!"

The others looked at the professor in awe, before remembering they still had another beast to dispense with. They approached the final lion, backing it into a corner. Bombarding it with blows from their various weapons, they had it lying defunct on the ground within a matter of minutes. Looking closely at the unmoving metal body, Alex saw that it had the word "Strength" written down its spine. The fifth virtue of Orpheus, no doubt.

"Well, that was refreshing," boomed the professor,

propping his axe against the wall.

"Where did you learn to do that?" Ellabell asked.

Lintz wiped sweat from his forehead. "I was young once, remember?"

Aamir was still bleeding, and the flesh of his hand was torn up pretty badly. Walking up to him, Alex ripped a strip of fabric from the edge of his shirt, and helped to bind the wound with the rudimentary bandage in an attempt to staunch the bleeding. Aamir winced as Alex tied it into place, but said nothing of the pain.

The door to the next room lay just beyond the crumpled form of the headless Minotaur, but Alex paused for a moment, realizing this might be the only opportunity they'd have to take a breather. Looking at the others, he could see that they were beginning to tire, though their optimism had yet to wane. Alex felt it too, tugging at his muscles.

After a brief respite, they moved on through to task number six.

Almost halfway, thought Alex, with a sigh of tentative relief.

A set of stairs took the group down, deeper into the earth. Alex thought of the pagoda and pictured the vault like a reverse version, with the floors going down instead of up, though it served to make him anxious about what might lie at the very end.

He was the last to descend the steps and enter the next room, which was lit by a central spotlight that illuminated only a small section of the space, the rest shrouded in darkness. He froze, as he saw the others standing stock still, clearly perturbed. As he reached them, the whole room flooded with bright light. They were standing in the middle of a large chamber, crowded with figures wearing Japanese Noh masks, some in basic white with red lips, some smiling, some sad, but others wearing more demonic versions, adorned with horns and sharp teeth. Alex's pulse quickened in fear as all the blank eyes lifted at once, focusing on the new arrivals.

They shifted toward the quartet, swaying to an unheard rhythm, closing in. The room was silent except for the faint padding of footsteps as the figures glided closer.

The group huddled together in a square, lifting their hands as if to conjure, not knowing if it would work in this particular part of the vault. To Alex's delight, he found that he could weave his anti-magic around his fingers, and saw the familiar golden glisten of the others' magic, though Aamir seemed to be having a bit of difficulty, with his hand the way it was.

However, as they fed their energies into their hands, the masked people began to move more quickly toward them. The more fear and retaliation they showed, the swifter the masked beings stepped. Alex suspected that if he released his anti-magic upon them, they would swarm the group.

"There are some masks over there," said Ellabell, gesturing toward several Noh figures at the back of the crowd holding spare masks aloft. "Maybe if we take those masks and wear them, we might be safe," she suggested, but Alex had already darted away from the group.

"Alex!" Ellabell shouted, which only served to bring the masked crowd closer.

Snaking through the heaving throng, Alex could feel that something had changed. Turning ever-so slightly, he saw that the Noh-faced people had turned to watch him, following his movements. The room began to split into two, with half of the masked individuals creeping toward Ellabell, Aamir, and Lintz, and the other half slinking toward Alex, who was watching them out of the corner of his eye.

Alex bowed in front of the masked people at the back of the room, then reached up to pluck the spares from their outstretched hands. He lifted one to his own face before moving a short way back into the crowd. Once he was sure he was close enough, he threw the remaining masks one after the other in the direction of the other three. Though they reached up to catch them, one fell to the ground with a sickening crack, the clay face splitting almost in half. Lintz picked up the broken mask, holding the sides together across his face, as Ellabell and Aamir grasped the other two.

"Sorry about that," said Alex, running back.

Ellabell shook her head. "Why did you do that?"

"Do what?"

"I could have sent them back using my magic—one broke, Alex." She sighed. "You just ran off before I could finish what I was saying. You keep doing that!"

"Doing what?" Alex repeated, bewildered.

"Whenever I try to do something, you keep—never mind, we need to get moving." She strapped on her mask, hiding her face from sight and leaving Alex unable to read her expression.

Alex frowned. "Okay… I didn't mean to…" He trailed off, not knowing what had caused Ellabell's sudden outburst. He was going to have to ask her later, once they were away from this claustrophobic vault. Maybe the strain of the tasks was getting to her.

Aamir donned his mask quickly and joined the others. They moved through the crowd of masked faces, pretending to be unafraid, though Alex's heartrate was through the roof. He looked at Aamir and Lintz between the restricted eyeholes, and saw that their masks were smiling. He hoped his was too.

Immediately, the figures came to a standstill.

Half certain they weren't going to start approaching

again, Alex and the others moved to pass through the crowd, toward the doorway that was just visible, near where Ellabell was standing. The masked individuals stepped aside, granting passage. Even as they moved through the crowd, however, Alex felt a shiver of trepidation. As if sensing it, a few of the Noh-faced people moved toward him again, but he couldn't suppress the fear he felt. He just had to hope he could reach the door before they got to him.

He did, but despite the threat, he paused and turned back around. The creepy hands froze in mid-stretch, like a terrifying game of "red light, green light." Something was drawing him back into the room, but he couldn't put his finger on what it was. It was a need, a feeling like they had forgotten something.

It all seemed too easy, as if they were missing a piece of the puzzle. Looking around for inspiration, Alex's eyes settled on two words, written above the heads of the people he had taken the masks from. The words were barely visible on the wall, only showing when the light danced upon it in a certain way. One said "Adapt" and the other said "Kindness." It made sense now; they had only completed one of the tests in this room, and this was a two-task stage.

"Stop!" he called to the others, who had already gone through the door. They turned to him. "We've missed something."

"What?" Ellabell asked.

"There are two tasks in here. See?" he said, pointing to the two words on the wall.

Lintz frowned. "Well, what the blazes is the other one? 'Kindness?'"

Alex nodded. "It's in here somewhere, whatever it is."

In the silence, the sound of sobbing found its way to Alex's ears. With the shuffle of feet from the marching Noh-faced crowd, he hadn't been able to hear it before, but now it was clear as day. It filled him with anxiety, but there was something compelling about it too, something that made him think it was linked to the second test. It was too out of place not to be.

All the blank eyes were staring at him, the hands still frozen in a mid-air grasp, and the sound of crying was growing louder.

"We need to go," said Lintz.

"I can't ignore it, Professor," Alex insisted. Though he was still fearful, he knew he had to find the source of the crying. The tone of it was heartbreaking, driven from the depths of a tormented sadness. Taking a deep breath, he moved back through the crowd, following the sound of sorrow.

The others hovered in the doorway, evidently believing him to be out of his mind for wanting to weave back through the crowd of Noh masks. Alex didn't blame them; he felt as if he must be mad too.

"Alex, come back!" Ellabell hissed. "It could be a trap!"

"I'll be careful!" Alex replied, scanning the crowd of figures for anything unusual.

The sobs grew louder as he reached a particular individual, whose mask was unlike any of the others. This mask was painted in a bright red lacquer that shone like blood in the torchlight, with pointed demon horns that curved upward and sharp teeth painted around the twisted mouth. Head on, it looked terrifying, but as the wearer dipped their head upon Alex's arrival, he saw that the mask took on a sorrowful expression instead. It was a trick of the eye, and one that made Alex feel slightly calmer.

He had found the person who was in such pain.

CHAPTER 10

"ARE YOU OKAY?" ALEX ASKED THE RED-MASKED individual.

The wearer dipped their head again, showing the sad expression. Not knowing what else to do, Alex removed his own mask, in the hopes it might encourage the crying person to remove theirs. He asked again if they were all right, and again the wearer dipped their head.

Does that mean they're not okay? he wondered. It didn't sound as if they were.

Hoping it wouldn't result in terrible repercussions, Alex reached forward and removed the mask from the person's face, lifting it gently off.

Beneath the mask was a ghostly woman, her eyes red with tears. She might once have been beautiful, but time had not been kind. There was a translucence to her body that made Alex think she was an actual ghost, and her sorrowful expression had him transfixed.

"I'm sorry," he said, handing the mask back. In some defiance of physics, she took it from him, keeping hold of it in her faded hands. "Are you okay?" he asked again.

For a second, it seemed as if she wouldn't speak, her voice lost after death. And then she did, in a tone so haunting it made tears spring to Alex's eyes.

"Have you come to help me?" she breathed.

"I'll try," Alex replied solemnly.

"Kind boy, I am lost, and my child is starving," she whispered. "Could you spare a coin so I might return to him? He is so hungry, and I have left him all alone. I need only a gift from the world beyond this place, and we shall be reunited. A simple coin. A token of value."

Alex turned to see that the others had followed him and were standing nearby. Their faces reflected his own, after listening to the hauntingly sad voice of the phantom woman.

"Do you have a coin, or something valuable?" he asked the group. They checked their pockets, patting them down for stray treasures, but because the clothes were not their own, they didn't carry any currency. They had nothing they could give. "I'm sorry," said Alex, turning back to the woman.

She began to weep again, the sound undulating with an extra layer of hopelessness.

"All is not lost. You'll see," Alex said comfortingly as he checked his own pockets. All he had were the clockwork objects he had obtained on his travels. A thought occurred to him, and he removed the mouse, wondering if the gold-and-silver inlay might be a valuable enough token to buy food for her child, and to reunite them. He held it out to her, and her sad eyes went wide in surprise. Her spectral hands closed over it. With a whoosh of cold air, she disappeared, the red mask clattering to the ground.

On the air, Alex could swear he heard the whispered sound of "Thank you."

Stooping low, he scooped the red mask from the ground and turned it over in his hands. Written on the inside was the word "Kindness."

Lintz smiled. "The seventh virtue of Orpheus. That was a generous thing you did there, dear boy."

"It was the least I could do," replied Alex, knowing her face would haunt him for a long time to come.

As he turned, with his mask and the ghost's mask in his hands, the rest of the Noh-masked people swept aside, bowing in a sort of reverence as the group passed on their way to the doorway.

Entering a passageway with a cavernous roof, dripping with stalactites, they saw two entrances ahead of them, though only one was open. The other had a heavy stone door blocking the way, with no obvious means of opening it. There was no lock, no keyhole, nothing, only the half-eroded face of an ancient bust, most of the features worn away.

"I guess we have to go this way, then?" said Alex, gesturing to the open passageway.

"Why don't we scope it out first, you and I?" suggested Aamir.

Alex nodded. "We'll be back in a second," he promised Ellabell and Lintz. "Once we know the coast is clear."

They headed through the open entrance, and as they paused at the lip where the tunnel stopped, Alex could sense something was wrong. The cavern beyond was filled with water, but it was not the kind of pool anyone would have wanted to swim in. Dark shapes weaved along the surface, pointed fins emerging and disappearing beneath the water. With a splash, a school of flying fish covered in barbs soared through the air, gnashing rows upon rows of vicious teeth. Alex could bet there was a moat creature in there somewhere, ready to lunge.

An enormous bird-like monster with vast, leathery

wings swooped close to the cave's entrance, sending the two young men staggering back from the edge. It was a hybrid of sorts, somewhere between a dragon and a bird, with a face that looked more like a skull than a living head. There was no way they could go in that direction, not if they wanted to live.

With shocked looks on their faces, the duo hurried back to where Ellabell and Lintz were patiently waiting.

"Yeah, we can't go that way," Alex said, catching his breath.

"So how do we get this one open?" Ellabell asked, tapping the stone doorway.

A vision flashed into Alex's mind. He moved toward the eroded bust that stood just to the side of the doorway, looking more closely at the worn features. Standing nose-to-nose with the masonry, Alex was glad he had stopped for the ghostly woman. Upon further inspection, the features, though worn down, were remarkably similar to those of the ghost he had met. Alex was still holding her mask in his hand. Carefully, he placed the mask over the face. It fit perfectly, and as it locked into place around the sculpted features, a loud rumble shook the passageway. The entrance to the second tunnel was sliding upward, revealing a safer path—or so Alex hoped.

With no time to lose, they moved through the newly

opened passage, praying it would prove kinder than the alternative route.

After following a dim, torch-lit tunnel for what seemed like an age, they emerged into a grand room, decked out with tapestries and fine furnishings. All around the walls were elegantly painted urns, depicting friezes of Grecian battles and ancient deities, but most intriguing of all was the magnificent feast laid out on a long table in the center of the room. Mountains of food rose up from silver platters and golden sauce jugs, from clusters of plump, ripe fruit, to desserts piled high with cream and chocolate. Alex's stomach rumbled. He hadn't realized just how hungry he still was, until he saw the beautiful spread that had been laid out.

"Do you think this is for us?" Aamir asked cautiously.

Lintz licked his lips. "I don't know, but it sure looks good!"

The professor was right: it did look good, and Alex had a feeling it might be some sort of reward for having come this far through the vault. He reached out to grasp a glistening slice of fruit-filled pie, but Aamir's hand shot out to stop him, snatching his arm away.

"Hey! We've earned this," insisted Alex, none too pleased by Aamir's intervention.

"We shouldn't trust anything we see," Aamir said. As he removed his hand from Alex's arm, a strip of his bloodied bandage fell onto the table below, making impact with the slice of pie. As soon as it touched the enticing pastry, a swarm of vile-looking bugs with jagged pincers surged upward and engulfed the food in a writhing mass. When they receded, nothing was left of pie or bandage.

Alex shuddered, thinking about what would have happened if he'd actually made contact with the slice.

"I guess my stomach got the better of me," Alex murmured.

Upon closer inspection, he realized that the whole inner core of the feast was rotten, everything decaying, covered in a forest of gray and black mold. It was an illusion. Only the outer layer was fresh and glistening, designed to entice gluttonous hands, to encourage the flesh-eating bugs to come out of hiding. Alex understood that this was test number eight as he read the word embroidered on the purple velvet tablecloth: "Temperance."

Alex glanced toward the beautifully decorated urns, and felt suddenly nervous. If this was a task, then what were the urns for? For the first time since entering the vault, Alex wasn't even sure he wanted to get the book anymore, but the thought of Virgil, and the promise of destroying the Great Evil, of setting everyone free, pressed him on.

"We should go to the next room," Ellabell said, urgency clear in her voice. "I don't like this place."

The others nodded and made their way toward the door at the other end of the room. However, as they neared, it became clear that the doorway was a trompe l'oeil, a deceptive painting, made to look realistic. There was no door.

Panic flooded Alex's veins as all the torches were blown out. From the sudden darkness, a glowing, unnerving light filled the room. A split second later, frightening specters, very like the ones Alex had seen around Vincent, floated upward from the urns, their wispy forms twisting into being.

"Close your eyes!" Alex yelled. "Don't look them in the eye! Whatever you do, do NOT open your eyes until we are out of this room, under any circumstances!"

"What? Why?" asked Ellabell.

"You have to! Close your eyes now, and don't open them again until I say!" he insisted, his panicked voice making them obey.

Even with his eyes closed, Alex could feel the cold prickle of the specters all around him, brushing at his skin with their vaporous hands. Goosebumps rose on his flesh.

"*We are the Gaki, the starving ghosts of the greedy,*" some whispered, passing close to his ear.

"*We are the Goryo, vengeful spirits of the dead,*" said the others.

Alex didn't know whether they were the same species of specter as the ones that had surrounded Vincent, or simply an illusion, but he wasn't willing to risk an incident, regardless of where they had sprung from. They were creatures of dread, made all the more terrifying by the fact that they could not be fought in the conventional way.

"They're telling me I have to open my eyes!" Aamir shouted. "I can feel them trying to lift my eyelids… I am not sure I can fight them," he added, his voice strained.

"Don't listen to them!" Alex instructed. He, too, could feel the spirits physically trying to lift his eyelids, their ice-cold hands making his eyes dry and itchy, compelling him to want to open his eyes and blink away the discomfort. He held fast, keeping them squeezed shut. He didn't want to experience what Caius had.

Thinking fast, Alex wondered if there might be a key or a lever within the moldering buffet, but he couldn't bring himself to plunge his hand into the mess, just to have his flesh gnawed off by disgusting bugs.

"Professor, what is the ninth virtue of Orpheus?" Alex asked.

"Honor!" Lintz replied.

Honor? thought Alex. *What is that supposed to mean here?*

Feeling the tug of vaporous fingers pulling at his eyelids again, he thought about how he could get the specters back into their urns. What might entice them back in? He had seen them in his encounter with Vincent, but they were not something he had fully delved into—he knew he wasn't supposed to look them in the eyes, but that was about it. Wracking his brains, he considered holding the urns and asking them to return, perhaps saying a few words or a prayer, in order to honor the dead. That would fit the bill, Alex reasoned, but the idea seemed a little too easy.

He thought about performing a necromantic incantation, but he was painfully aware that he didn't know any. It made him wonder if he was entirely equipped for this series of tasks after all, or if he was missing an ability. Perhaps the golden disc had read his talents wrong.

His only link to necromancy was walking the spirit lines, and the way he was able to incorporate mind control, to manipulate memories, but he had no idea whether any of that would work on these beings. Before, he had used those talents to make people feel happy, and to restore their minds, but he didn't think these specters could be made to feel happiness.

Going back to plan A, he clumsily made his way toward one of the urns and reached out to pick it up, almost knocking it off its plinth in the process. He held it steady, realizing it was a stupid idea, but knowing he had to at least try it out.

"Please go back inside, honored spirits," he said.

"You think we will obey the words of a feeble human?"

one of the specters cackled, making Alex feel foolish.

That left only the spirit lines as the sole valid idea he had. Dubious of its success, he fed his anti-magic out into the space of the room, seeking out the pulse of the spirits. To his surprise, he could almost see them as clearly as if he'd had his eyes open, though there was a more human quality to them when he viewed them through a necromantic lens. Where before there had been hollow eyes and gaping mouths, he could make out the echoes of their previous faces shifting beneath the surface. With an almost magnetic pull, he drew the spirits to him, letting his anti-magic flow into the wells of their former minds.

Pushing his energy into the mind of the first specter he encountered, he saw a flash of her history. She had been a young girl, no older than Alex himself, running through an empty house, her head turning fearfully backward over her shoulder as she mounted the rickety steps of a spiral staircase. There was somebody behind her, Alex could feel it, and the adrenaline pulsing in her veins pulsed in his. There was fear and dread as she hurried across a landing into a room where everything was draped in dustsheets. Panicking, she realized she had nowhere to run, the sound of footsteps gaining on her. Standing in front of a stained glass window, a shadow fell across her. Alex couldn't make out the face of her attacker, but he heard the girl's scream. A firm hand shoved her hard in the chest, sending her careening backward with such force that she sailed straight through the bright glass pane, shattering it with her body, before plummeting to the ground. Everything hurt, her broken form lying twisted on the stone below. Death did not come instantly, however, her eyes managing to glance upward one last time to see a handsome man standing in the shattered window, looking down upon her, a cruel smile on his lips.

With her dying breath, she whispered, "My love."

This was not a happy spirit, but searching deeper into her memories, he found a small pocket of warmth. She was sitting by a fire, reading a book to a smaller girl, who looked up at her with loving eyes and an awestruck smile. Alex fed the memory to the forefront of the spirit's mind, and felt a shift in the specter's emotions. The vaporous being pulled away.

"I am remembered," she whispered, before disappearing into the urn she had risen from.

Moving from spirit to spirit, Alex did the same for each, though some had minds crowded with dark remembrances, making it all the harder to find a lightness with which to make the specter return to its urn. When he came across such a mind, he manipulated the memories he did find, altering them until they could be skewed as happy. It took longer, and he was forever conscious of the struggling cries of his friends as he forced these false memories into the forefront of the specters' consciousness. At least this way, Alex thought, these ghosts would be able to rest awhile in peace.

As the last specter returned to its urn, Alex heard something clatter onto the floor. Nervously, half expecting it to be a trick and to see a hollow-eyed spirit swooping toward him, he opened his eyes. The room was clear of ghosts, and on the floor, beside the painted door, lay a key.

Alex picked it up off the flagstones, noticing for the first time a small keyhole in the ground beside it. With a hopeful heart, he twisted the key in the lock. There was a quiet click, followed by the grating sound of stone on stone as a section of the floor moved away, revealing another downward spiral staircase.

Almost there, thought Alex triumphantly. *Almost there.*

CHAPTER II

"We should get out of here," Alex said, glancing at the others. Their faces were pale, and they were reluctant to open their eyes, though Alex had promised them it was safe to do so.

"Are you sure they're gone?" asked Ellabell.

Alex smiled. "I promise they're gone."

Tentatively, the group's eyes opened in one collective movement. There was more fear written on their faces than Alex had ever seen before, and he could understand why; the specters were worrying creatures to come up against.

Feeling a pang of terror, Alex addressed the others. "Do

you swear the specters didn't open your eyes?"

"They tried, but I managed to fight them," said Aamir.

"I kept them squeezed tight, I swear," replied Ellabell.

Only Lintz did not answer right away, his face drained of color.

"Professor?" prompted Alex.

Lintz shook his head as if shaking off something unpleasant. "I didn't look at them," he answered at last, bringing Alex a small measure of relief.

"Good, then we should get going," he said, pointing toward the spiral staircase leading down into the floor.

They descended toward the next task, but the mood had taken a drastic turn. Nobody spoke, the only sound being the scuff of their shoes on the stone steps as they headed down, the atmosphere growing hotter the farther into the earth they walked.

At the bottom of the steps stood a vast iron door, with a depiction of Theseus and the Minotaur carved into the metal surface. It didn't bode well, bringing to Alex's mind a remembrance of the task with the mechanical beasts. A relatively easy challenge, in hindsight, but no less frightening at the time.

"Abandon hope, all ye who enter," said Lintz ominously, smoothing his hand over the frieze.

Alex gave a tight chuckle. "No need to be pessimistic—it

can't be any worse than the last room," he said, immediately wishing he hadn't tempted fate. The others seemed to share his feeling, as they flashed him worried looks.

The door opened by itself with a force that shook the walls, making dust fall from the roof above their heads. As it slid to one side, it revealed two corridors that split off in either direction, instantly clarifying the depiction on the door. Theseus and the Minotaur—it could only mean one thing: they were heading into a labyrinth.

On the side of each entrance were two tiles. On the right-hand tile were the letters "M" and "N," and on the left were the letters "L" and "W." In the center, above both tiles, was an inscription, reading, "Here is where your paths diverge. Pray they cross again."

"What do you think it means?" Alex asked, taking a closer look.

"I think it means we have to split up," replied Aamir, gesturing toward the letters with a trembling hand. His injury had become worse, his hand flopping limply, the bandage drenched in scarlet.

"Yes, you see, the tiles—I don't think the letters are arbitrary," Lintz agreed.

Ellabell's eyes widened. "You're right, Professor! 'N' and 'M'—Aamir's last name is Nagi. Mine is Magri. So, the two of us must go this way. Alex, that means you and Lintz need to go that way," she said, with an apologetic look. "It's probably for the best; I can change Aamir's bandage on the way. It's starting to look a bit nasty," she added, with forced brightness.

Alex didn't feel positive about the decision in any way, though he knew better than to argue with the vault's demands. If he were to argue and insist on going with Ellabell, who knew what retribution the challenge might take? It seemed to him that the vault was doing this on purpose, splitting Alex and Ellabell up, to test them separately. Perhaps it was also meant to test his resolve in putting the tasks before any personal feelings. It wasn't fair, and he feared the reasoning behind it, but he wasn't about to defy the rules of the game. Not with so few tasks left to undertake.

"Our paths *will* cross again," she said, evidently seeing his discomfort. "If we move quickly, and follow the rules, we'll see each other again soon."

Alex smiled, pulling Ellabell into a tight embrace and planting a gentle kiss on her forehead. He still didn't feel comfortable kissing her properly in front of the watchful eyes of Aamir and Lintz, but he desperately longed to.

"I'll see you on the other side," he whispered close to her ear.

"You better." She smiled, melting Alex's heart a little.

After a more casual farewell to Aamir, the group parted

ways. Alex watched as Aamir and Ellabell disappeared down the right-hand passageway, before following Lintz down the left. It became clear within minutes that this place was definitely a labyrinth, as Alex had suspected, but what purpose it was intended to serve wasn't yet apparent. It was just plain stone, no traps, no tricks, just an ever-winding walkway.

"How are we supposed to know which way to go?" Alex asked, brushing his hand against the blank wall.

Lintz smiled. "There's a mathematical knack to these things. You stick with me, and I won't lead you far wrong!" he explained, charging off through the maze. Alex followed confidently, knowing the professor had as good a chance as anyone of getting them through it.

Turning a corner, Alex spotted the first clue. A giant glass bubble of water, tinted blue, sat perched on a plinth. Nearing it, Alex could see a golden letter trapped inside, about the size of his palm—the letter "P." However, the bubble was enclosed in its entirety; there was no lid to lift, no gap through which to attain the letter. It was truly trapped in there, with no easy way out.

"We could try smashing it?" Alex suggested, as he approached the glass orb. Trying to pick it up, he felt his muscles twinge under the strain; it was much too heavy to lift.

Lintz twisted the ends of his moustache in thought. "It

must certainly be smashed," he said. "The question is, how?"

The pair of them stalked around the orb for several minutes, inspecting every curve, in the vain hope that they might have missed something. Alex investigated the plinth too, wanting to seek out a secret lever, or a button, or another clue as to how to break open the glass orb. No such clue appeared, the stone plinth devoid of anything useful.

"In the study of physics, and it has been many years since I've studied such ordinary sciences, vibration is often a good means of shattering glass," Lintz said, having walked around the glass globe for a tenth time.

Alex looked at the professor with excitement. "Vibrations! Of course! If we put our powers to use on both sides of the glass, we might be able to shatter it." He thought back to his high school physics classes, the teacher explaining how it was possible for an opera singer to break a champagne glass with only their voice.

"Shall we?" Lintz grinned.

Alex nodded enthusiastically, approaching one side of the orb, while Lintz approached the opposite side. They stood, facing each other, and rested their palms on the cold glass. Taking a deep breath, Alex wove his anti-magic through the glass, letting it flow within the molecular structure of the orb. He felt his energy touch that of Lintz's, and held his anti-magic back from it until the globe was alight—half gold and white, half black and silver.

"Ready?" Alex asked.

Lintz beamed. "Let's science this thing into submission!"

Alex vibrated the molecules within the glass, feeling the pressure build. It pushed harder and harder, the anti-magic expanding the very fabric of the orb until, with one triumphant crack of breaking glass, the globe shattered, water surging over the edge of the plinth like a waterfall, cascading to the floor. Now that it was drained, the golden letter lay in the center. Alex plucked it out, careful not to touch the jagged edges of the broken glass.

"Good job, Webber," said Lintz.

"Good job, Professor," he countered, with a small smile. There were undoubtedly more mini-challenges ahead; it wasn't yet the time for patting each other on the back.

Clutching the letter tightly, Alex and Lintz carried on through the labyrinth, peering nervously around corners, in case there was anything unpleasant lurking in the tunnels beyond. As they walked, they kept their eyes peeled for whatever might come next. It turned out to be a riddle, etched on the wall.

"What comes once in a minute, twice in a moment, but never in a thousand years?" Alex read aloud, his eyes glancing over the pattern of alphabet letters that had been pressed into the stone.

"Easy!" cried Lintz. "This one was around when I was a child!"

Alex frowned. "You know the answer?"

"Yes, it's the letter 'M'—get it?"

"I'll have to remember that one." Even though he knew the professor must be right, Alex felt a shiver of trepidation as Lintz approached the board of alphabet letters and pressed down hard on the letter "M." As it was pushed inwards, the letter "Y" popped out of the board and fell to the ground. Alex picked it up.

As they carried on, Alex's mind turned to Ellabell and Aamir. Were they collecting letters too? How far along were they in the labyrinth? He glanced over at Lintz and saw his own worry reflected back at him in the professor's expression.

They hurried onwards, having to turn back a few times after taking the wrong fork in the road and coming to a dead end. The labyrinth had low visibility, lit only by the flicker of torches and the glow of some unknown substance lurking in the walls, and Alex and Lintz kept missing entrances in the stone that were shrouded by shadow.

Eventually, after a lot of missed turns, a burst of inspiration seared into his mind—the forced image of a small statue with a tangle of vines above, camouflaging a letter hidden in the wall, zinging into his brain, vivid and unexpected. Knowing what it meant, he insisted they go back.

"It's this way. I know it is," he promised.

"How do you know?" asked Lintz, his tone dubious.

Alex shrugged. "I can't explain it. I just feel like we missed something."

Lintz said nothing else, seeming to go along with the plan, as Alex led the way. At a small statue, Alex paused, and looked up to find the intertwined curtain of dark green vines that he had seen in his mind's eye. Delving into the thorny weeds, the barbed points scratching his forearms, he found what he was looking for, buried within the center. With a great heave, he tugged the letter free of the wall and removed it from the spiny bushel.

Lintz eyed him curiously. "How did you know that was there?"

"I just... knew," he replied. To try and explain that Elias was somehow in his brain, without yet having confirmation of the fact, wasn't a conversation he felt like having at that particular moment. It was still something he was trying to come to terms with.

In his hand, he held the letter "H," though it meant little to him. Together, they had the letters "P," "Y," and "H," but he couldn't picture the word they might make.

"Any idea what it means?" Alex asked.

Lintz shook his head. "Afraid not, dear boy, though I have been wracking my brains a good long while. I'm sure it will come to us, with a few more clues."

"Let's hope so," said Alex, decidedly less optimistic.

With the three letters gathered, they headed back through the tunnels, treading carefully. Alex was still convinced there were going to be traps set around every corner, but so far, they had come across none. Much of the labyrinth looked the same, and so it came as quite a surprise when they abruptly found themselves at the end of it, arriving at a door with six blank squares on the wall beside it. Above the squares were the words "The Goddess of Lost Souls." Sticking out of the wall beneath the squares was a demonic head, sculpted from pure silver, its savage mouth agape. It reminded Alex of a guardian to the gates of Hell, ready to snap its jaws at anyone unworthy. Wasn't that what Hadrian had said? Only the truly worthy would be able to attain the prize. He could only pray he'd done enough to prove himself.

"Any idea who the goddess of lost souls is?" Alex asked, glancing at Lintz.

Lintz toyed with his moustache. "I believe it to be Psyche, if memory serves—though it's something of a sieve these days," he murmured.

The sound of footsteps nearby distracted Alex. There was a scuffling in the second passageway that led to the end of the labyrinth, followed by the joyful emergence of Ellabell and Aamir, who looked no worse for wear, aside from the fact that Aamir was drenched from head to foot and a pool of red had begun to emerge again from the bandage on his hand. In Ellabell's hands were three letters, letting Alex know that the task had been successfully completed, provided that they were in fact the right letters.

"What happened to you?" Alex asked Aamir, trying not to laugh.

Aamir frowned. "There was a waterfall," he explained, giving little else away.

"He was very valiant," Ellabell chimed in, making Alex feel a slight pinch of jealousy.

"You're too kind." Aamir smiled, not seeing the look Alex was giving him.

Lintz cut in, in his usual, oblivious manner. "Please tell us you've got 'S,' 'C,' and 'E?'"

"How did you know?" Ellabell marveled.

"Well, we have 'P,' 'Y,' and 'H,' and I believe we need to spell out the word 'Psyche.'"

"She's the goddess of lost souls?" Ellabell asked.

Lintz nodded. "She certainly is—a protector of sorts, in ancient mythology."

Ellabell handed over her letters, and Lintz fixed all six into place within the blank squares. They waited in anticipation for the sound of the door grating, or the creak of it swinging open, but nothing happened.

"Did you put them in right?" Alex asked, casting a glance toward the spelled-out word.

"I could have sworn I did," Lintz replied, pressing the letters in deeper. Still, nothing happened. He tried spelling it backwards, jumbling up the letters, spelling it forwards again, but still, nothing.

"Do we have to say something, maybe?" Alex suggested. It being the only idea they had, they began to shout, "The goddess of lost souls" at the letters, followed by "Psyche," but again, nothing happened.

Did we miss something? Alex wondered to himself.

It seemed this task wasn't so simple after all.

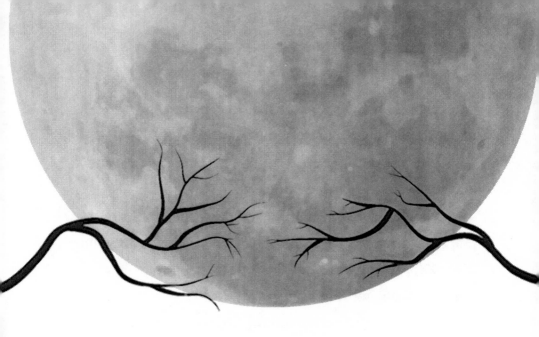

CHAPTER 12

As THEIR VOICES DIED DOWN, AND ALEX BEGAN TO feel a little foolish, something wispy swept down from above the door. For a moment, he thought it was Elias, but the vapor was a misty white instead of Elias's trademark black.

"Quick, close your eyes!" Alex cried, believing it to be a specter.

From behind the darkness of his own eyelids, he heard a voice. "I am a messenger. I come with a warning," the voice whispered, with an eerie, musical lilt.

"It might be a trick. Keep them closed!" Alex insisted.

"It is no trick. I am no specter. I am a messenger—I come with a warning," the voice repeated.

Anxiously, Alex opened one lid partway. Ahead of him, he saw the ghostly form of an old man, the features shifting in and out of clarity. He didn't look like a specter, but more like the crying woman he had helped in the room full of masks. In fact, he seemed to be waiting for somebody to acknowledge him.

"And what is your warning?" Alex asked with trepidation.

"You have been penalized for receiving outside assistance, and, as such, one of your number is required to pull the lever inside the mouth of the demon," the apparition spoke. "Be warned, this person must stay behind. The rest will go on ahead, with only a slight chance of reunion once the trials are complete."

"What? What outside help?" said Alex gruffly.

The apparition whorled in the air, revealing an image of the dark room with the jangling chains on the walls. Inside the vision were Alex and his friends, but there was something else, too: a flash moved across the image, just for a moment, pausing beside Ellabell. Although the shape and face were impossible to make out, Alex knew what he was seeing in the vision being played back to him. Elias *had* been following them through the vault, and it looked as if the shadow-man had genuinely intended to help, though it had been misguided.

Alex was of two minds as to whether this warning was real, or simply part of the test. If they hadn't received assistance, would they still be required to leave someone behind? Alex guessed they would. This place was intended to challenge them, doing whatever was necessary to push them, and prove Alex, in particular, a worthy recipient of the book.

The vision vanished, the messenger disappearing with it.

"I'll stay," said Alex, before anyone else could speak.

Ellabell shook her head. "You can't stay—you're the one who needs to go and get the book. It has to be one of us. You don't get to step in this time."

Alex knew she was right, but didn't like it one bit. "There has to be another way."

Lintz stepped up. "I'm afraid Ellabell is right, dear boy. It has to be one of us. You heard what the warning said."

"I'll do it," Aamir insisted.

"No way," said Ellabell. "I don't mind doing it."

"As the oldest among you, I believe it should be me who does the deed," Lintz added, moving closer to the demon's gaping mouth.

Before Alex could process what had happened, Ellabell had darted past the professor and shoved her hand into the mouth, pulling hard on the lever inside. With a metallic clank, the jaws snapped shut, locking her hand in place. It didn't appear to hurt her at all, though she winced as the teeth crashed down, but it worked like a large cuff, trapping her there.

"What did you do that for?" Alex gaped, unable to believe his eyes.

She gave a half smile. "I don't want us wasting any more time discussing who should take the fall."

"What if we can't get you out?" Alex ran a panicked hand through his hair. "What if I can't get the book, and you—"

"You're worthy, Alex. You will complete the trials, and I'll be there to meet you at the end," she murmured, no trace of fear on her face.

"I can't believe you—" His words were cut off by the sound of the door opening.

"Just go, Alex. Hurry up and get this thing, so we can all get out of here!" she urged, silencing any further attempt of his to tell her she'd done something stupid.

"Come on, Alex. The sooner we go, the sooner we can come back for Ellabell," Aamir said, grabbing Alex by the arm.

Lintz helped Aamir, though there was reluctance on both their faces as they dragged Alex through the door. Somehow, even with the two of them holding him, he managed to wrestle free, turning back and running for the doorway, only to have it slam in his face just as he reached it. The last thing he saw was Ellabell's face, her blue eyes wide as she disappeared from sight.

"Why did you do that?" he shouted, turning on the other two.

"Alex, you have a task here, and that is where your priority lies. Ellabell will be fine, but only if we can succeed in this task. If we don't, who knows what might happen to her?" Lintz reasoned.

Alex shook his head in disbelief. "So we have to go on without her."

Aamir rested a hand on Alex's shoulder. "This is not easy for any of us."

Alex knew they were right, and yet her face haunted him as they pressed on down a long, narrow corridor. Part of him felt angry with her for doing something so reckless, and he found he couldn't stop thinking about what she had begun to say in the mask room. It made him wonder if that was why she'd done it, to prove a point, to get him to see something he didn't understand. All he knew was that he couldn't get the image of her, trapped all alone, waiting back there, out of his head. It was hard to keep his mind focused. His thoughts were brought back from the brink of distraction by the sight that beheld him as they stepped through the plain-looking door at the far end of the corridor and entered the room beyond.

It made Alex's stomach plummet.

They were standing in the biggest library he had ever seen, bigger than the one at Stillwater, bigger than the one at Spellshadow, bigger than he had thought a library could be.

This has got to be some kind of joke, he thought bitterly. There were more books in this library than they could ever scope out in a lifetime, much less a few hours. The shelves seemed to stretch into infinity, each one several stories high.

"Should we just start looking?" Aamir suggested.

Alex shrugged. "What else can we do?" he muttered. "Just remember, we're looking for the Book of Jupiter."

Splitting up, the trio wandered into the stacks. It was hopeless, and Alex knew it, but he tried to stick with the plan, riffling through the rows upon rows of dusty tomes. There were some books of interest, which he'd have liked to look over if he'd had more time, but none of them were the Book of Jupiter. Despite the subject sections within the library, giving it a vague organizational set-up, he knew it would take forever to find the book—if they were even looking in the right place. There didn't seem to be a section for 'Spellbreaker' or even 'Spells'.

Thinking there must be a method to the madness, Alex tried to narrow down the search, looking for books on planets, and Spellbreakers, and anything else he thought might be related to the book, but it all came up empty. Aamir had headed toward the very back of the library, and was making his way back up to where Alex was, a defeated look upon his face.

"Anything?" Alex asked.

Aamir shook his head. "Nothing, unless you're a big fan of… let's say, Renaissance art?"

Alex smiled, catching Aamir's meaning, but it quickly faded in the face of the task at hand. In a library so big, it seemed impossible. Just then, he passed a large green book with the words *A Gentleman's Honor* embossed on the spine. It gave him an idea, or part of one, at any rate.

"We need to look for Orpheus's book," Alex said excitedly.

Aamir nodded. "Of course, the book containing the twelve virtues!"

"You found something?" Lintz called, from a squat stack he was investigating.

"We need to find Orpheus's book," Alex repeated.

"Goodness, of course!" Lintz bellowed, following the others into the stacks.

Alex clambered up one of the ladders that leant against the vast stacks, and found it up on one of the top rows, under the section marked "Philosophy." It wasn't nearly as impressive as he'd expected it to be, taking up only a slim space on the shelf, the cover a dull, dusty brown. He reached out to pull it from the shelf, only to find it stuck. He tugged harder, determined to free it, but it simply wouldn't budge.

"Alex, you might want to come and see this!" Aamir yelled from way below.

"I've found the book, but it's stuck on something!" he called back.

"Forget about the book—I think you've done what you were intended to do," Aamir shouted up.

Puzzled, Alex clambered back down the stacks and headed for the front of the library, where Aamir was gazing up at something that hadn't been there before. A big clockwork diorama of the solar system had emerged from a false wall beside the huge marble fireplace. The planets, forged from smoothed precious stones, rotated slowly around the central sun. Lintz was gazing at it too, though his eyes had grown so large Alex feared they might fall out.

"What is it?" Alex asked.

"My dear boy, this is our solar system," Lintz gaped, his eyes following the tick of the clockwork.

Alex smiled. "No, I know that, but what does it have to do with what we're looking for?"

"Darned if I know," Lintz murmured. He began tinkering with the mechanisms, smoothing his hands over the shiny components like they were rare jewels.

"Professor, can you move Jupiter to the highest point on the clock-face?" Alex asked, an idea blossoming in his mind.

With a bemused expression, Lintz followed the instruction, pushing the large red orb that symbolized Jupiter up to the twelve o'clock point. With a loud click, a secret compartment opened at the base of the structure. Inside the tray lay a book—a big, ancient thing.

The title was emblazoned on the front in bronze lettering: *The Book of Jupiter*.

At the very bottom of the compartment was the word "Success" beside the number eleven. *Eleven?* Alex frowned. *That means there is still one task to go.* It was a blow. Alex had thought that finding the book would be the last step, but it appeared that the vault had other ideas.

As Alex reached for the book, the same ghostly apparition that had appeared at the door where they'd left Ellabell floated into existence once more. Alex knew it couldn't be a good sign, considering what this ghost had told them last time.

"I come with your final challenge," the ghost spoke, in that same lilting voice.

"And what is our final challenge?" Alex asked, fearful of the answer.

"In order to receive the prize you desire, one of your own

must vouch for the one who will use it. This person must give up their life and remain within the vault. Death will not be immediate, but shall come when there is no nourishment left," the ghost explained. "There will be no way out, and no hope of salvation. This is the price."

Alex flashed a worried look at his friends. "It can't be me?"

"If you are the one who seeks the prize, then you cannot vouch for your own worthiness," the ghost replied curtly. "Whoever is going to give their life in return, you must reach up to the orb of Jupiter and say, 'I vouch for this person. They are worthy of the prize.' You shall remain within the orb until the others have departed, when you will be returned to the library. Now, you do not have the luxury of time to decide—you have only until the time runs out, or the vault will take a life that will not be returned, as you will have failed your final task."

The ghost whirled in the air, showing an image of Ellabell, trapped by the mouth of the demon. All around her, the walls were beginning to close in, moving closer and closer to her. Though Alex couldn't hear the sound of her scream, he could see her mouth opening wide in silent panic.

"No!" Alex said, wishing he could reach through the vision and free Ellabell from her prison.

"It has to be one of us," Aamir said somberly.

Lintz shook his head. "No, dear boy, it has to be me."

"We need to talk about this!" Aamir insisted.

"I am already on borrowed time, Aamir Nagi." Lintz sighed. "I lied back there, Alex, when I told you I didn't look the specters in the eye. I did. I did, and I-I know what that means. I know that they will come for me. It has to be me who gives myself. I will die, one way or the other—in truth, I am already dead. I was dead the moment I looked into their eyes. I cannot cheat the specters, and I cannot cheat death," he said, his voice laced with sorrow. "At long last, I will be reunited with all those I have lost."

"You won't need to die, Professor. I'll make sure this spell gets done as quickly as possible, and I'll come back and set you free when it is," Alex promised. "We'll find a way to keep the specters at bay, I swear it."

"A noble thought, and one I hope comes true, but I don't think there is time." Lintz smiled. "Now, Ellabell needs you, so I'll tell you all you need to know as quickly as I can. Hadrian can help to open any portals you might need opened. Make sure you read the spell carefully, and don't be duped by any tricks the other royals might throw at you. Oh, and if you get your chance to be free, all of you… take it. Promise me you'll take it?"

Alex nodded slowly, unable to process what was

happening. "You'll be coming with us, Professor."

He grinned, but it did not quite reach his eyes. "I'll wait."

With a quick shake of hands and a pat on the back for his dear students, Lintz darted toward the red orb of Jupiter and clasped his hand around it.

"I vouch for this person. They are worthy of the prize," he said.

With a sickening whoosh, Lintz began to disintegrate, his body being sucked into the mechanism. Alex watched with open-mouthed horror as the diorama absorbed him. First his hands, then his arms, then his torso, followed by his head, his stomach, his legs, and, at last, his feet. The orb glowed orange for a moment before dimming to a simple planet again.

Slowly, the clock began to tick, sounding Lintz's death knell.

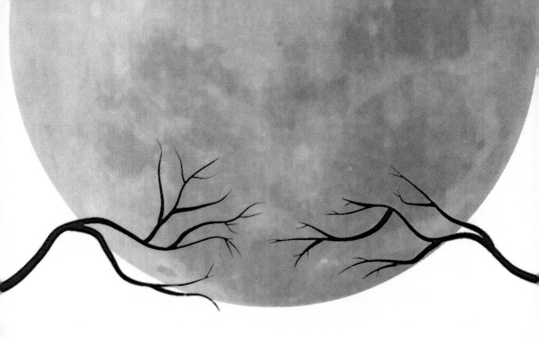

CHAPTER 13

ALEX PLUCKED THE BOOK OUT OF THE compartment, his eyes snapping to the vision of Ellabell. The walls had ceased closing in on her, and relief flooded her expression. A moment later, the jaws of the demon sprang open, releasing her.

Alex watched on the gauzy screen until she had ducked through the now-open door and made her way back to them. He could hear her footsteps running along the narrow corridor leading toward the library, and his arms were open and waiting as she sprinted into the room. She ran to him, wrapping her arms around his waist.

"I was so sure that I was going to—" She paused, breathing sharply.

He leveled his gaze at her. "If I had known that was going to happen—" he began, still a little mad at her.

"Then someone else would have had to stay," she cut him off, her determined expression showing she was still satisfied with the choice she'd made. "I did what I had to do. That's as much as any of us can do here, to get through this. It can't always be up to you, Alex," she added, not unkindly. There was a soft affection in her voice, laced with a steely undercurrent.

"I didn't say it was always up to me," he replied quietly.

"Of course not, but I know what you're like. You want to protect, but you forget that others can protect too, and sometimes you're the one who needs saving." She smiled.

"I just... I worry about you, that's all." He sighed, his shoulders slumping.

She squeezed his hand tightly. "And that is what I love about you," she said, the word "love" flowing easily from her mouth. "It's also what irritates the hell out of me. You just need to know I'm no damsel, and you're no hero—we're a team, a partnership, shouldering equal responsibility. Once you see that, you won't worry so much."

"I think I'll always worry too much about you," he said softly.

"Alex, look," Aamir said, shattering the moment. He was

pointing toward the side of the room, where a doorway had appeared. It hadn't been there before, and Alex could feel the chill of a breeze wafting through.

Putting his arm around Ellabell, he walked toward the newly opened door, with Aamir bringing up the rear. It led out into the depths of the forest, the air growing still around them. It had started to rain, and a light drizzle met their faces as they rose from the underground tomb. As soon as Aamir was through, the side door slammed shut, closing the vault.

Ellabell glanced back, startled. "Where's Lintz?"

"He sacrificed himself so we could have the book," Alex explained sadly.

"He's dead?" she gasped.

Alex shook his head. "No, not dead... Well, not exactly. He told us he looked the specters in the eye—I guess they don't leave you alone once you've done that. Now, he has to stay in the vault, as the price for us taking the book, but I'm hoping we can free him, if we're quick with the spell, and get the book back as soon as possible. I'm sure he can survive long enough," he said, though he wasn't convinced in the slightest. It stung to admit it, but he had a sinking feeling that Lintz was already dead. Even if they could return to the vault in time, he knew the specters wouldn't rest until they dragged Lintz down with them.

It did little to comfort Ellabell, though Alex could tell she was trying to put on a brave face. It was what they were all trying to do, silently sharing the knowledge that the professor was likely lost to them.

"You three!" A familiar voice called to them from the trees. Hadrian crept from the darkness, his expression anxious. "You made it? Where is the professor?"

Alex gave another quick rundown of what had happened, and watched as Hadrian's face fell. It seemed the royal had known it might have been the case, from the weary weight that made his shoulders sag and his brow crease.

"I'm sorry for that," he said kindly. "The p-price is always high."

"Did you know this would happen?" Alex asked, his tone accusatory.

Hadrian gave a slight nod, wringing his hands. "I had an inkling. It has happened before, but the game often changes, so I couldn't be certain."

"You didn't think to tell us?"

Hadrian winced. "I couldn't, Alex. The vault knows when assistance has been given. B-besides, what would you have done if you *had* known? Would you h-have given up the book?" the royal scrutinized him with nervously darting eyes, and Alex found he didn't have an answer. In truth, no matter what the price, they would have had to pay it. It wasn't just their own lives at stake—the whole picture was so much bigger than them, and as much as he hated to admit it, Alex knew they probably still would have had to go through, even if they'd known beforehand.

"I guess not," Alex finally replied, though his eyes glanced back toward the vault door. "Are you sure I can't just write down the spell and put the book back?"

Hadrian shook his head. "With this p-particular counter-spell, the book must bear witness—the book must gauge the s-sincerity of the performer."

Alex clutched the book tighter in his hands. He would have to make sure he didn't lose it, or let it fall into the wrong hands. If the book had to be present at the counter-spell performance, he was determined to keep it safe, leaving it under the watch of trustworthy guardians when it wasn't safe for him to have it by his side.

"Will we have to return here when the spell is done?" Alex asked, reluctant to step away. It was stupid, but part of him felt like he was abandoning Lintz, and the pull of those ties was unbearably painful.

"Since it has never been successfully completed, it is not known. The book may need to be returned by h-hand, or it may disappear by itself, as it does when the spell f-fails three times," Hadrian said, his eyes flitting toward the tree-line. "Come, we must get you to safety,"

Alex still felt reluctant to go, but the book was calling his name as the group followed Hadrian. It was a slow trek through the damp woods, the exit to the vault having popped up a long way from the pagoda, but eventually the grand structure appeared in the distance. Hadrian carried a small device, shaped like a long, slender pen, with him that seemed to scope out any traps or devices lurking in the dingy forest, its presence leading them safely back, without incident.

It didn't deal with guards, however. That's what Hadrian was for. Ensuring the coast was clear by sending several troops off to see to broken-down traps, the royal ushered them into the pagoda and up the stairs, to the very top floor, where he had had chambers prepared for them. It was a kindness Alex had not expected, and the thought behind the act made him thaw slightly toward the man.

On the low table in the central space, another feast had been laid out for them. Alex eyed it with suspicion, his mind still dwelling on the moldering, bug-infested fare that the vault had offered them. The others didn't seem too keen either, though everyone sat dutifully, at Hadrian's behest. Alex put the book on the floor next to him, desperate to delve into its pages, but not wanting to appear rude to his host. After the others had helped themselves, he reached for one of the sour, berry-filled rice balls. It tasted good, but his mind lay with the book beside him.

With a shiver of anticipation, he slyly lifted the cover. To his surprise, the inner page was filled with the same glyphs and markings that had been in Leander Wyvern's notebook. There were no complete words, only code. The sight thrilled him, making him feel as if it contained a secret solely for his eyes. He didn't feel right opening it while the others were around, not when he knew it was of true Spellbreaker origin. In addition, he felt he ought to at least look at the pages on his own first, to make sure there was nothing dangerous within. After the loss of Lintz, he didn't want to put anyone else in harm's way if he didn't have to. He would tell them what it contained later, but first, he wanted to take time to pore over the text.

"I'm not that hungry," he announced. "I think I'm just going to have a look at this book, then hit the hay."

Hadrian looked up, a stern expression on his noble face. "It can wait, Alex. You must properly honor the sacrifice that Professor Lintz made by giving thanks and sparing a silent moment for his courage. It would not be right to continue without having done so. Given the amount you still must do, the truth is…you might not get back to him in time. I believe we must honor the Professor as if he were already gone, though the flicker of hope may remain."

Alex felt a pang of guilt. "Sorry, Hadrian, you're right,"

he murmured. It wasn't simply his secret—it was theirs too, and he needed to show the proper respect. Picking up a glass of lurid green liquid, he raised it across the table. "To Professor Lintz, who gave us so much—the bravest man I've ever met."

Alex's use of the past tense didn't go unnoticed. A solemn, heavy air hung low over the feast, as the others picked up their glasses and repeated the words, clinking afterwards. Alex lifted the drink to his lips and sipped tentatively. The color of the drink was garish, but it tasted delicious, somewhere between an apple and a kiwi.

As well as food, the group shared their sadness. Tears welled in the eyes of all those present as the hope they'd had for Lintz's return faded by the second. It was clear now that the chance of his release was improbably slim—a couple of days wouldn't be quick enough to avoid the specters, and though Alex couldn't explain it, it felt like the professor had already gone. His spirit soared around them, an almost tangible presence, and Alex knew it would be a long while before the wound of Lintz's loss healed. He had to put it beside the scar Gaze's passing had left, and hope he wouldn't have to add any more to his internal cemetery before their journey was done.

"I shouldn't have let Lintz do it," murmured Aamir, his face crumpling. "I should have insisted."

"We all know Lintz would never have chosen different-ly," said Alex, his tone somber. "He wouldn't have let you do it. Even if he hadn't looked the specters in the eyes, he would still have done what he did."

Aamir nodded, but Alex could see the older boy was plagued by doubt. It wasn't easy to think of outcomes that might have played out, if only one action had been altered.

Tapping the side of the glass absently, Alex's mind turned toward Kingstone. Seeing the specters again made him contemplate the fate of Caius and Vincent, and that of Alypia too. When he had left, they had all been in a bad state, with the exception of Alypia, perhaps, but it troubled him. He had to go back at some point, to relay messages of progress to those at Stillwater, but also to check that everything was still in order. If Vincent had managed to overcome Caius, Alex was sure the necromancer would be holding back any chaos that might have ensued. However, if he hadn't man-aged to overcome Caius, there was no telling what state the prison might be in.

Alypia might have escaped, he thought, the prospect a chilling one. It made a return visit to the keep a necessity.

He knew that he could use the still-open portal at the keep to pass a message through to Natalie, Jari, and Helena, and make sure everything was okay on their side. After ev-erything that had gone on since the two groups parted ways, he felt bad for not having thought more of them, but there had been a lot of other things taking up his headspace. He just hoped they were okay, and were safe at Stillwater, though he wasn't looking forward to telling them about Lintz when he saw them again.

Alex glanced down at the book beside him, and thought of the promises held within its pages. Caius had believed the mages didn't deserve to be saved, what with the genocide they had wrought. But how had the two races come to despise each other in the first place? He had never thought to ask.

"Hadrian, do you know what it was that started the war between the mages and the Spellbreakers?" Alex asked. The others looked at the royal with interest, as if they too had been thinking about it.

Hadrian gave a wan smile. "It's a long story, but I'll tell the short version," he promised, his stutter fading to nothing as he relaxed. "My grandfather, Titus, the king at the time, was a strong believer in equality between the races. The leader of the Spellbreaker Houses was also a strong believer in peace. You see, there were whole towns and cities that were split by race, and though Spellbreakers and mages lived almost side by side, they rarely fraternized. It was frowned upon, but my father and the leaders of the Spellbreaker Houses were keen to see an integration.

"My uncle, Julius, was not. He was the face of those who wanted the integration efforts to fail. There were peace talks going on, and, during one of them, my grandfather was assassinated—at the hand of a Spellbreaker, they said, but I have my own theories on that one. I believe it was made to *look* like it was a Spellbreaker, when really it was done by the hand of a mage.

"Naturally, Julius took control of the throne, and had the leaders of the Houses executed. Both sides were enraged, and it led to war. Spellbreakers fled the supposedly integrated towns and cities, and many mages too—all those who wanted to be as far from the conflict as possible. I helped smuggle many mages out into the non-magical world, which is where you must have come from." Hadrian gestured toward Ellabell and Aamir. "You are their descendants. Their identities were kept secret, to avoid any kind of retribution, but I suppose nobody is able to outrun my uncle forever."

"Is that why Finder was sent for us?" Ellabell asked.

Hadrian nodded. "Julius knew refugees had escaped, and he put it to my cousin, Virgil, to find a way to seek them out, even if it took a generation or two."

"So much death," Alex whispered, more to himself than anyone else.

"That is war," Hadrian replied solemnly. "We saved as many as we could, but the death toll was overwhelming."

"You didn't think the Spellbreakers might have needed refuge?" Alex muttered.

Hadrian winced. "A fair p-point. We did not do enough, and for that, I am sorry. I can't even b-begin to imagine the loss you must feel," he said, his stutter returning with Alex's confrontation. It seemed that whenever the royal was frightened or felt cornered, the stammer in his voice came back, a tic brought on by his ever-present nervousness.

"It hurts more, the more I find out," Alex admitted. It was a lot to process, thinking how the mages had staged an assassination, leading to a war that wiped out his people. He felt overwhelmed, needing solitude. "I'm sorry, I'm really not hungry. Please, excuse me."

Nobody stopped him as he got up and left the table, heading for the room on the far side that had been designated as his. Sitting down in a chair by the fireplace, he rested the book on his lap, his mind too full of other things to really get into the pages. All he could think about were the executed leaders of his people and the suffering that had ensued. So many people running for their lives, only to be snuffed out at the end of it all.

He sat there, mulling it over, trying to make sense of it, feeling the weight of the book on his knees. Before he opened it, he thought once more of Lintz, and the sacrifice the professor had made for the book Alex held in his hands. Alex would miss the comforting boom of the professor's voice, and knew the world would feel too quiet without it. Lintz had always been warmhearted despite enduring his own share of heartbreak and disappointment. Alex felt sorry that the professor would never get to see the sister he had waited so many years for, in the hope she'd appear at the gates of Spellshadow. He knew that Lintz would continue to wait, at a very different set of gates, until the day they were finally reunited.

Taking a deep breath, he turned the first page.

CHAPTER 14

F LICKING THROUGH THE PAGES, ALEX RAN HIS FINGER
across the glyphs, eager to find out what secrets they
would reveal. Remembering the way he had conjured
the thin veil of anti-magic to read Leander's notebook, he
did the same now, creating a square of gauzy energy that
would unravel the glyphs. The symbols spread out before
his eyes, tumbling into sentences and paragraphs. There
were diagrams, too, though some of them depicted things
Alex didn't even want to look at. Flaying a person, removing
a voice, disintegrating a body from the inside out. That last
one reminded Alex of Julius, and what he'd done to the

laughing prisoner. He shuddered at the memory.

The whole book was packed to the brim with spells, some intriguing, some awful, some downright baffling. Alex wondered if any of these horrible things had been used during wartime, and had a strong feeling they probably had.

It took him until the very end of the book to find the spells he actually wanted to see, not that he didn't enjoy the detour. Anything to do with the Spellbreakers had him hooked. Running the square over the glyphs, he saw that they were twin spells, coming one after the other—the one Leander had used to release the Great Evil, and the one Alex was expected to perform. Reading through it, he wondered if it had been Leander himself, or some other Spellbreaker, who had built the contraption that held the book within, as a means of keeping out prying eyes. Perhaps the writer of the book had created the vault, though there was no name on the cover or inside the tome, as far as Alex could see.

It made him think about who might have sacrificed themselves for Virgil's run of the gauntlet. *Does that mean Virgil is worthy?* Alex mused, trying and failing to see Virgil in another light. It didn't seem possible. Maybe the Head had cheated somehow, or forced somebody to give their life. Alex simply couldn't believe Virgil had enough moral fiber to have won the book on his own merit.

Drawing his focus back to the book, he began to absorb

the words on the page in front of him. The steps themselves were relatively brief, only requiring a few items, but the incantation was long. Surprisingly, it was just one sole object on the list that caused his heart to sink the farthest.

The first was the revelation that the counter-spell had to be performed by consuming more than five drops of blood from the king or queen, and the second was the knowledge that the spell had to be done by someone who was wholly ready to meet their fate. Alex wasn't sure what that meant, but he was beginning to suspect it meant that the spell required voluntary participation. So, he couldn't be coerced into doing it, no matter how much the royals might want to force him. For a moment, he felt a fleeting sense of joy, as he realized that the royals must not know about that aspect. Elias's words began to take on more clarity too; the shadow-man had said it was Alex's battle, nobody else's.

However, he began to have doubts about the implications where Virgil was concerned as he read on. The spell said that the performer must give an honest sacrifice, without selfish intention, with one hand placed on the book, so that the book may gauge the honesty of the spell-caster. Alex hoped he could manipulate Virgil's mind into feeling those things, with enough truth to convince the book of good intention and honest sacrifice, but the blood aspect was a huge wrench in the works. He definitely couldn't fake that.

After all this time trying to evade the upper echelons of royal society, to be told that he now needed their involvement was a real blow to his optimism.

He kept reading, regardless. The incantation covered two whole pages, but there was a rhythmic flow to it. On the back page, where the incantation ended, was another section, written in a box below the spell itself. It told of a loophole, though not in so many words:

Where there are rules, there are always exceptions. Should a Spellbreaker be unable to undertake the task at hand, there is another who will suffice. A mage may take the place of a Spellbreaker sacrifice, should they be of extraordinary power. No simple, everyday mage. The mage must be nearly unique in their potent ability. Failing such a volunteer, the king or queen whose blood is consumed may be used in the completion of this spell, though the sacrifice must be willingly intended, just as the Spellbreaker's should be. If an apology were to be made, with the price of their own life paid, then the powers released would be drawn into the earth again, all ties mended, all lost lives paid for in sorrow.

Alex knew he had little chance of making Julius take on the mantle of martyr, not with what he had learned of the king, and seen with his own eyes. Venus, however, remained something of a mystery, though he was pretty sure she'd have the same reaction as her husband, if the option were put before her. He didn't think one disastrous affair with a Spellbreaker would be enough to make her change her mind, though the more he dwelled on her, the more he wondered what she would make of him, given his origins.

She had loved his ancestor. Did that bind them together, in some strange way?

If it did, he still had zero hope that she would step in and voluntarily take the task of the counter-spell upon her shoulders.

No, it's either you or me, Virgil.

Before he could even think of the Head, however, he had to come up with a way of getting the blood. In the spell, it said he needed the blood of the king or queen, but Alex didn't even know where they lived. He would have to bring Julius or Venus to him, somehow.

His mind raced with possibilities, settling on Venus as the proposed target. Julius was too volatile and too unpredictable, and Alex knew he'd never get close enough to the king to extract any blood. He was, however, more optimistic about the queen; so far he hadn't heard any fearsome tales about her. Alex would just need to get close to her, perhaps visit her as she slept and take some blood without her even knowing.

How hard can it be to get five drops? he thought as the ideas rolled in.

If he could get her to come to Falleaf House, he was positive he could retrieve the blood, one way or another. There were endless methods he could utilize, but it meant enlisting Hadrian's help. The kind royal was scared of his own shadow, and visibly quaked at any mention of Julius, or any other royal for that matter. Alex didn't know where to begin when it came to convincing Hadrian that it'd be a good idea to invite Venus down to Falleaf House. Elias had been right about Hadrian's pacifism, but it was so much more than that—it wasn't pacifism, but an all-out refusal to face conflict of any sort. This was going to take some real effort, and all the charm Alex had at his disposal. He knew it might even take a threat or two, if pushed.

With his mind brimming, he walked toward the door of the chamber and peered out, but the dining table was empty. The others had undoubtedly gone to bed too, after the strain of an arduous, sorrowful day.

For a moment, he pondered going in search of Hadrian, to start convincing him right now, but thought better of it. It didn't seem polite to steal through someone's home and disrupt them in their personal chambers, just to ask a favor that they would no doubt have nightmares over. It would have to wait until morning, and though that frustrated Alex deeply, there was a hint of relief too. He was utterly exhausted; he could wait one evening before putting his plan in action.

CHAPTER 15

IT SEEMED HIS NIGHT WASN'T QUITE YET OVER, however, as the shadows began to shift in the corner of the room, dripping downward in a vaporous waterfall. They slithered along the floor, and Elias burst up out of the darkness. For the first time since Spellshadow, there was no barrier seeking to distort Elias's form; he was as whole as a wispy thing like him could be.

Alex rolled his eyes, turning away from the shadow-man. It had been coming for a while, this appearance, but Alex wasn't ready for it. There was a lot of unspoken rage inside him, where Elias was concerned, and he didn't think another meeting would do much to heal the wound. No amount of good intention could ever bring his father back, nor could Elias be forgiven for his kidnapping of Ellabell. Even if it had been Elias helping her in the vault, trying to ease her fear of the dark by handing her the key, it didn't make up for the act that had probably made her afraid of the dark in the first place.

"The fun has arrived!" Elias grinned.

"The fun should go away," Alex remarked sourly.

"Is that any way to speak to your new partner? We're linked now, kiddo—there's no escaping me this time, so you might as well get used to having me around," Elias purred.

Alex flashed the shadow-man a dirty look. "I've been trying to 'get used' to you since the moment we met," he said curtly, his expression changing as he processed the words Elias had said. "Wait, what do you mean 'linked'? What have you done to me?" Whatever it was, he knew it had some-thing to do with the visions he'd been having.

Elias pulled a face. "It's not what I have done to you, but what you've done to *me*. You tore off a little piece of my soul, and now we're linked *forever*—whether you like it or not." He chuckled. "There's a funny sort of irony in it, wouldn't you say? You try so hard to keep me away, then go and do something stupid like get yourself mentally joined to me. I do love a delicious slice of comeuppance."

"It's not me who needs the comeuppance, Elias," Alex growled, letting the words sink in. Elias was the last person in the world he wanted to be linked to, in any way, shape or form. Regardless of the reasoning, Elias was the one responsible for the death of his father, and the knowledge of their new bond made Alex feel as if a terrible virus had crept its way into his veins.

A moment of tense silence stretched between the two acquaintances. It was Elias who broke it.

"I know, Alex," he said, with uncharacteristic solemnity. "I'm… sorry for the pain I have put you through, and the things I have done to hurt those you love. I promise I am trying to be a better being, in any way that I can."

Elias hung his head, and Alex felt as if he were in therapy, listening to the words of a recovering addict. It was tricky to gauge whether the sentiment was genuine or purely for show.

"What's brought all this on?" Alex asked. "It's not like you to be so gushy."

The shadow-man gave Alex a withering look. "Here I am, pouring my heart out, and all you can do is mock. Well, I shall take my feelings elsewhere—or, perhaps, I'll feed them into your mind until you beg me to go back to gushing. How about that?"

"So it has been you feeding images into my head?"

asked Alex.

Elias sighed wearily. "You really do need everything spelled out for you, don't you? I'm sure if I whacked you around the face, you'd say, 'Did something just hit me?' How you coped before I came along, I'll never know," he teased. "Yes, it has been me, feeding my thoughts into yours. I'd say I've come in pretty handy, wouldn't you?"

Alex had to admit that he had. If Elias hadn't used their mental link, Alex knew he might still be standing on the edge of a mountainside, trying to figure out how to ride a Thunderbird.

"You've done okay," he said reluctantly, though it didn't make up for all the hurt Elias had caused.

"Ouch—damning me with faint praise." Elias scoffed.

"Was it you who got us into trouble, in the vault?" Alex asked, ignoring Elias's dramatic expression of hurt, one shadowy hand pressed to his vaporous forehead.

Elias lifted his wispy shoulders in a shrug. "Even if I hadn't helped that curly-haired crush of yours, you'd still have had to do what you did. That nosy guardian just decided to throw me under the bus, to make you blame me. He'd have made something else up, even if I hadn't given my assistance. Your little sweetheart would likely do the same again, given the chance. Quite the firebrand, that girl. I'm starting to think I should have started pestering her instead of you," he remarked, with something akin to respect.

Alex had a feeling he was going to prefer it when Elias *hadn't* liked Ellabell, and yet, there was a small part of him that wanted to thank the shadow-man for how he had helped her, in the pitch-black room. Still, he couldn't quite bring himself to say so, after the enormity of what had happened between them. Not yet, anyway.

"Do you think you'll be able to help me collect the blood I need for the spell?" Alex asked, changing the subject.

Elias tilted his head from side to side. "I may come up with something—what did you have in mind?"

"You don't already know?" Alex joked. "I was thinking of asking Hadrian to call Venus to Falleaf. Maybe you could get the blood for me, if you can sneak up to her?"

"Not really in the job description, old pal, but I can certainly provide a suitable distraction while you get close enough to extract what you need. Mind you, I think the harder task will be getting wimpy little Hadrian to get her here in the first place!" He cackled. "You don't feel up to taking on the big dog, then?" He flashed a knowing look at Alex.

Alex shook his head. "I still value my life. I figured Venus would be easier to approach than Julius."

"You're not wrong." Elias nodded. "Have you read over the counter-spell carefully? It may sound obvious, but, knowing you, it may not be—the spell must be performed perfectly. There is no room for any error, however small. There can't be a single flaw, or missed step, otherwise it won't work. More than that, there could be disastrous consequences if it gets messed up. I don't mean a slap on the wrist or a paltry shock or something—I mean *disastrous* consequences."

"I'm aware, Elias. I know what's at stake," Alex grumbled. As ever, Elias was making him feel like a stupid kid, unable to put two and two together.

Elias raised his palms in surrender. "Hey, no need to shoot the messenger. If something does go awry, I'm just covering my ass, making sure you can't blame me."

"I doubt you'd let me blame you anyway—you're always wriggling free of responsibility," Alex remarked tersely. Elias was beginning to get on his nerves again. "What are these disastrous consequences, anyway?"

Elias raised a wispy finger to the place where his lips should have been.

Alex let out a sigh of exasperation. "I thought we were over that?"

"Afraid not. Still only allowed to say snippets, without giving away the whole truth," Elias said. "It's as annoying for me as it is for you."

Alex found that hard to believe, knowing how Elias

reveled in the misery of others. He was fairly sure the shad-ow-man wouldn't lose sleep over not being able to say more, if he even slept at all.

"How come this spell is so complex?" Alex asked.

"Spells are always complex," Elias retorted.

"I know that, but why is this one *so* complex?" Alex explained. "I mean, if the counter-spell is this hard, how did Leander bring the Great Evil into the world with such apparent ease? Like, compared to this, the stories I've heard of how he did it seem pretty simple."

"It's easier to break things than to fix them," Elias replied.

For once, the shadow-man's ambiguity made perfect sense. Alex flipped back through the spell book to the twinned spell that had released the Great Evil, and saw that it was, indeed, much shorter and much simpler. It required a few of the same ingredients, but the spell as a whole was not nearly as involved as the one he was expected to perform.

An idea formed in Alex's mind, and it was definitely not one that had been put there by Elias. It was the makings of a contingency plan, should things get really bad. Reading over the notations at the very bottom of the last page, his eyes were drawn to the mention of somebody with extraordinary power being able to assist with the spell. Although Elias was no longer very human, he was definitely a creature of extraordinary power, who had once been the kind of mage described in the pages of the spell book—a unique individual. He'd heard Derhin mention it too, as well as Elias himself, who was often boastful of his own abilities, now and in the past.

Could a guardian protect a Spellbreaker, if they were strong enough? he pondered, flashing a curious look at Elias, who was busy trying to grasp the tail of an asteroid that was trailing along his arm. Perhaps the shadow-man would prove himself when the time came—it just depended on what Elias was willing to give up, provided his eternal vendetta didn't get the better of him.

"You should probably go. I need to sleep," said Alex. There was a lot to think about, and Elias's presence was clouding his thoughts.

Elias grinned. "I'm taking my guardian duties to heart these days. You won't be sending me away so easily anymore. I plan to watch you, around the clock, until there is no longer anything to protect you from," he said, evidently overjoyed at the prospect of causing Alex more irritation.

Flashing Elias a look of pure loathing, Alex got up and stepped into the bathroom that adjoined the chamber Hadrian had set up for him. Looking at the door through the bathroom mirror, he half expected Elias to come in after him, but, fortunately, the shadow-man kept his distance. After washing himself and dressing in the pajamas that had been provided, he opened the bathroom door a crack and peered out at the room beyond.

Elias was nowhere to be seen.

Even so, as Alex slipped beneath the sheets, he could feel the familiar prickle of eyes on him. He tossed and turned, struggling to drift off. Just as he was about to surrender to the oblivion of sleep, he heard a voice whispering, close to his ear.

"Rock-a-bye baby, on the tree tops, when the wind blows, the cradle will rock. When the bough breaks, the cradle will fall, and down will come baby, cradle and all."

It was the creepiest lullaby Alex had ever heard, and the sound of it being breathed into his ear made his spine tingle in the most unpleasant way. It conjured up every nightmare he'd ever had, of monsters and ghouls hiding beneath his bed, and scary-faced clowns hiding down storm drains.

"Elias!" he yelled.

The shadow-man cackled, clearly delighted. "Just doing my guardian duties, singing you off to a sweet slumber."

"You're not funny!" Alex pressed his pillow down over his face, smothering his eyes and ears. It was going to be a sleepless night.

CHAPTER 16

I N THE COLD LIGHT OF DAWN, THE TRIO REGROUPED IN
the pagoda's communal space. Breakfast had been laid
out, but Hadrian wasn't anywhere to be seen. They ate
in companionable silence, enjoying the good food while
they could; it was a welcome change from the gray gruel at
Kingstone. Alex was exhausted, having gotten little sleep, but
the other two looked more refreshed than he had expected,
given the events of the day before.

"How was your bedtime reading?" Aamir asked as he bit
into a juicy plum.

Alex looked up at his friend. "It's lengthy," he admitted.

"Doable?" Ellabell chimed in.

He nodded. "I think so—definitely, with time to practice."

"What else did it say?" Aamir pressed, brushing a trickle of scarlet juice from his chin.

He gave them the lowdown on the content of the spell, pausing to gauge their expressions as he touched upon the need for royal blood. They carried the same sense of trepidation that his own expression had.

"We could do the same thing we did in the labyrinth," Ellabell suggested.

"Which thing?" said Alex.

She turned to Aamir. "You know, the glass orb with the letter inside? We could do the same thing we did with that, and vibrate it, if we could just get her to hold a glass," she explained. As Alex had suspected, it seemed they'd had to undertake fairly similar tasks to the ones he and Lintz had faced.

Aamir nodded in agreement. "If we pre-fed our magic into the glass, and got her to pick it up, we could distract her and make it shatter in her hand. If we only use thin strands of magic, she hopefully won't notice the glitter of it."

"Then we've got the attack on Spellshadow to consider, once we have the blood," Alex said, not wanting to pile doom on gloom, but knowing it had to be brought up. "I'd like to travel back to Kingstone as soon as possible, to get word through the still-open portal there to the others at Stillwater, and let them know we have the book. If we can get them prepared, we can launch an attack sooner rather than later. I don't want them going through to Spellshadow before we have everything in place to perform the counter-spell. I'd rather we were all there before the fight began, you know?"

Ellabell nodded. "Absolutely—we don't want them arriving before we have a chance to join the party!"

"We'll need essence, too," Aamir added. "We used up most of the Stillwater stash to make the portal here. If the others are going to build a portal back to Spellshadow from Stillwater, and we're going to build one to Spellshadow from Falleaf, we're going to need a lot more."

"Hadrian might be willing to give up some of his store," Alex said. "The Stillwater squad could use some too, and we need it not only for the portal, but for when we come up against the Head. When the time comes, it might be the only thing that can swing the odds in our favor in the fight."

"Hang on a minute—we could use the essence to kidnap Venus," Ellabell said, her eyes bright with the lightbulb-flash of an idea. "The last thing we want is for her to suspect something and tell her husband. If we have some essence to fight with, we can keep her trapped somewhere."

Alex had been worrying about that aspect of the plan. If

anything went wrong with the blood extraction, then Venus would go running to Julius, and that would signal annihilation for them. However, if they could knock her out using a golden monster or two, the way he had done with Alypia, then they might stand a chance. If Venus were coming down to Falleaf for a legitimate purpose, there would be no reason for her husband to suspect anything was wrong when she didn't immediately return. Alex hoped he could get Hadrian to ask that she visit him for several days, which would give them a clean window of opportunity.

"It's a near perfect solution," Alex said enthusiastically.

"So, things to do," Aamir said. "Number one, ask Hadrian if we might borrow some of the essence here."

"Number two, get Hadrian to send word to Venus about a visit," Ellabell added.

"Number three, head back to Kingstone to inform the others of what's going on, through the portal to Stillwater, and pass on some essence to them," Alex continued. "We won't need to worry about building a portal from here to Kingstone, because my Thunderbird will take us."

Aamir and Ellabell flashed each other an excited look.

"Then, we come back here and wait for Venus to arrive, at the specified time," Aamir said. "Once she is here, we take her out."

"After that, we steal some blood from her. Then we head

through to Spellshadow with essence in tow, and we capture the Head, using whatever means necessary. It'll then be up to me to begin the counter-spell, and hopefully end all this madness for good." Alex grinned. It was nice to have a plan, and feel organized for once.

Ellabell smiled back. "There, how much simpler could it be?"

The trio laughed, though there was an undercurrent of nervous anticipation. Below that, a tremor of genuine terror. It didn't sound like a lot, but the struggles that lay ahead were vast. It would take everything they had in order to succeed, but they had come this far. Nobody seemed willing to back down, which added fuel to the fire that burned in the pit of Alex's stomach.

Not for the first time, he found himself wondering what his life would be like if Natalie had never arrived from France. If his mother hadn't offered to take the exchange student, after her first option fell through, where might he be? Would he be up at all hours, trying to balance school and work? Would he be shyly approaching girls at parties, if he had never met Ellabell? It seemed like that life belonged to a different boy. The young man in those memories bore no resemblance to the Alex he had become, and it was a bittersweet realization. He longed for the carefree life he'd had, and knew, with complete certainty, that even if they did manage to get home again, things would never be the same. There was no going back to that previous life. Not now.

"Ah, glad to see you're all awake!" a melodic voice called out. Hadrian appeared in the doorway, his demeanor much calmer than usual. "I trust you slept well? I didn't wish to disturb you before you'd had the opportunity to regather your thoughts."

"Good morning, Hadrian," they chorused.

Alex gestured for Hadrian to join them. "You're just the man we wanted to see."

"Oh? And what makes me so popular on this fine morning?" Hadrian asked, taking a seat at the low table. He reached for one of the copper kettles that had been laid out, and poured a cup of something dark and aromatic.

"We've been discussing our next plan of action," Alex explained, "and we need your help for two parts of what we have in mind."

Hadrian's face fell. "I will try to help where possible, though I can't p-promise anything."

"We need essence. I know it's asking a lot, but if we can't get our hands on more essence, we stand no chance of freeing the mages from the Great Evil. Right now, you're the only person we know who might have access to some— I'm guessing there is some stashed away at Falleaf, as there is at the other havens?" Alex said, leveling his gaze at the white-haired man.

"Indeed, there is essence here at Falleaf House," replied Hadrian, with a touch of reluctance. "I would be more than willing to share s-some with you, though you will not f-find it to be quite what you're expecting."

"Don't tell me—it's too powerful?" Alex pressed, remembering the ferocity of the Kingstone essence.

Hadrian shook his head. "The very opposite, in fact, though I would be willing to g-give whatever quantity you require for your endeavors. It's n-not something I could do, what you want to do, but I can help a little bit, so long as it doesn't b-bring anything bad down upon m-me," he stuttered nervously, his resolve teetering on the brink. "I have never been able to fully bring peace to the s-students under my tutelage, but their b-best chance rests on your shoulders. I know you have struggled to put your f-faith in me, but I w-will help you now."

"That's good to hear, Hadrian," Alex replied. "And though I hate to ask, there is one other favor we need."

Hadrian frowned. "I will d-do what I can."

"We need you to ask Venus to visit Falleaf," he said.

Hadrian's expression morphed into one of alarm, the blood draining from his face. "We shall discuss this f-favor later, though, as I say, I will do what I can for you. I p-put this on hold only because your first favor is a little time sensitive. If we are quick, I can take you to f-fetch the essence now. They will be changing the g-guard, but if we stay here too long, we will miss the gap," Hadrian explained hurriedly, his eyes flitting toward the clock on the wall.

"Okay, it can wait," Alex confirmed. "If we have to go now, we should go now."

Ellabell and Aamir nodded in agreement.

The anxious expression Hadrian had given him left Alex feeling dubious, and not for the first time, about what the latest royal would actually be willing to do with regards to Venus, but he knew that now wasn't the time to apply pressure to the situation. Hadrian was the first royal who had shown willingness to share essence, and Alex wasn't about to ruin that opportunity by hanging around to ask further questions. Plus, he feared that if he asked too intensely, the anxious royal would bolt; he was like a spooked horse at the best of times.

Venus would be coming. It wasn't a matter of if, but when. Even if Alex had to call her down himself, he would get her close enough to retrieve the blood he needed.

But, for now, the hunt for essence was underway. Royal blood could wait.

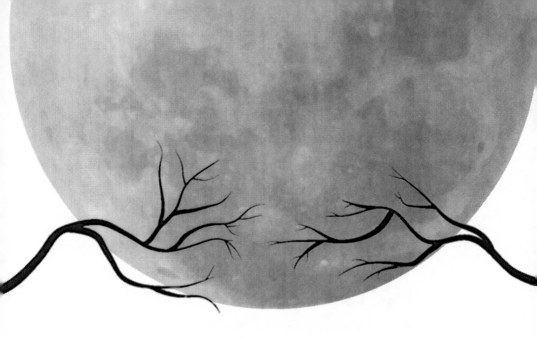

CHAPTER 17

THEY SNUCK OUT OF THE PAGODA WITH AS MUCH
speed as they could muster, rushing down the stairs
and out into the forest. For the first time, there
was no military presence, though Alex could make out the
shapes of people moving in the treetops toward the other
side of the pagoda. They weren't soldiers, but looked to
be young men and women a little older than Alex and his
friends—the students of Falleaf House, the strangers he was
fighting for.

The group wandered through the dripping forest,
Hadrian using his device to ensure they didn't accidentally

trip over any traps, though he muttered to himself the whole way, his mood decidedly on edge. It was a strangely peaceful walk, the only sounds the brush of their feet against the grass and the rustle of the leaves as a breeze wound through the branches. There was the odd *coo*, and flutter of wings, reminding Alex of the Thunderbird he hoped was still waiting for him at the edge of the forest. If he was going back to Kingstone, with essence in his possession, he knew he would need her soon, and could make amends for the couple of days he had spent away from her. He still had to introduce her to his friends, after speaking so highly of her and the manner in which she had delivered him to Falleaf. They had known he was telling the truth when he first spoke of her, but she was a strange thing to wrap one's head around, and he just hoped that seeing would be believing.

They followed a winding stream, the water babbling beside them, and stopped in front of a cluster of stones that rose up from the wet earth, one of them almost three times the size of Alex. It seemed to be their destination.

Rounding the rock cluster, Alex saw a door tucked away in the rock. It had to be approached from a certain angle to see it properly, but it was there, hidden in the shadow of the stone outcrop. It had a large keyhole, and Hadrian pulled out an equally large, ostentatious key. The tense royal took a final, furtive glance at the surrounding trees before opening the door and ushering them inside. Before Alex stepped through, however, he too cast a furtive glance over his shoulder, making sure that Elias wasn't there. To his relief, he found he couldn't sense the shadow-man anywhere in the vicinity. It was a welcome absence.

As he entered the cave, Alex felt a sudden wave of déjà vu. Beneath the rocky ceiling and rough-hewn walls, there were statues of warriors standing in fighting stances and battle poses, as well as some figures who looked peaceful—the antitheses of the warlike sculptures. One was holding a set of scales, and another was holding a book open on her lap. Many of them were female, making Alex curious to know who they were, and if there was anyone buried beneath, like the hideous commemorations at the manor. These were not nearly as frightening; there was a nobility to them that he felt compelled to observe, like he was looking at famous paintings in a gallery.

Moving farther back into the passageway, Alex and his friends emerged into an open, cavern-like space. Filling the huge room were shelves upon shelves, stacked with the familiar black glass bottles. It looked like a wine cellar almost, only decidedly more macabre. Approaching the nearest shelf, Alex could immediately sense the difference in the energy within. Hadrian had been right—the pulsing red glow was much weaker than any he had come across before.

"Why are they so weak?" Alex asked Hadrian.

Hadrian turned, scratching his chin. "I have tried to b-beat the system, to the best of my ability. We only take half of a s-student's essence, and then we send them away to a place where they can be s-safe," he explained, gesturing to the bottles. "As far as the b-bigwigs are concerned, these students are d-dead, their essence extracted—what they don't know can't bother them."

Alex was awestruck by this unexpected news. He hadn't known it was possible to just take half, without ending up with something as strange and unearthly as Elias. Regardless, it sounded like a painful procedure. He imagined it would feel akin to having surgery without any anesthetic.

"Isn't it painful?" he wondered.

"It is very painful, but it is kinder than the alternative." A sharp voice spoke from the shadows at the very back of the cavern, and a figure emerged.

It was a woman. Alex would have urged everyone to run, but Hadrian didn't seem too perturbed by her sudden presence, which was strange for the nervous man who was scared of everything. The woman was fairly youthful in appearance, and beautiful in a frightening, aggressive sort of way, with the same white hair of a royal. However, there were sections of hair that were shaved away, and the cut was short, with longer strands trailing across her right eye, which seemed to have been damaged, the pupil entirely white instead of the usual deep-set black. There were streaks of bright color in her hair too, dyed to look like purple and green zebra stripes.

Beside the damaged right eye, Alex could make out the shape of a tattoo—a circle with nine indents along the periphery and four larger dots inside. He counted them, suddenly very conscious of the fact that he was staring at her. Dropping his gaze, he wondered if the circle was supposed to represent the havens—the ones that had fallen, and the ones that remained.

"Who are you?" Ellabell asked, stepping toward the woman.

She crossed her arms. "I am Ceres, Hadrian's sister. I'm the one who nurses the students back to health, once the deed has been done, and I'm the one who returns those who have come from the non-magical world back to their parents, on the sly." She winked, making it look effortlessly cool. "Those who can't go home, I keep. We work together in our own civilization, far from the prying eyes of Julius and his cretins."

Alex was stunned. Now that he looked for the resemblance, he could see that there was a strong one between Ceres and Hadrian.

"Caius never mentioned a daughter," Alex said,

immediately wishing he could shove the words back into his mouth.

Ceres's eyes flashed darkly. "I don't suppose he would. Selfish, cruel old coot," she growled.

"My sister and our f-father don't exactly have the warmest of relationships," Hadrian said, looking embarrassed.

"Unlike you, I don't put up with betrayal. How can you still have empathy for that man, after the things he did?" Ceres retorted. "I take it you've had the pleasure of meeting my father?" she said, turning to Alex.

"We didn't part on particularly good terms either," Alex admitted.

"Our f-father seems to have lost his mind, Sister—he's a troubled soul. He has been for a long time; you know that." Hadrian sighed.

Ceres glared at her brother. "You think that gives him the right to act however he likes? Mother didn't forgive him, and neither should you. He doesn't deserve forgiveness— that man is selfish to the core, only ever pleasing himself."

"I'm not here to argue with you, not now." Hadrian shook his head; it was clearly a conversation they'd had many times before.

Their discussion intrigued Alex, leading him to wonder what conflict lay between Caius and the mother of these two, who presumably wasn't the Spellbreaker love he'd lost. Perhaps the wife had grown sick of her husband's pining, after what sounded like years of suffering? It seemed like the most likely explanation for Ceres's vehemence toward her father, but Alex didn't like to presume.

"And why are you here?" Ceres snapped. "It's not like you to come and visit, unless you want something."

"That's hardly fair," Hadrian remarked, his expression growing sheepish. "Although, we d-did come here for a reason. I've p-promised some of the Falleaf essence to these brave individuals—they have run the g-gauntlet, and retrieved the Book of Jupiter. Alex here is going to h-help perform the counter-spell."

Alex didn't correct him; none of the royals needed to know what he truly had in mind for the spell, and the vessel through which it would be performed.

"You've promised *what*?" Ceres growled.

"I've p-promised them as much essence as they require, in order to do what they must. They are launching an attack, and they n-need it more than we do," Hadrian countered, though it was clear he wished he were anywhere else but here. It appeared even his sister could make him break out in a cold sweat, and Alex watched the uncomfortable royal begin to wring his hands.

"Well, on your own head be it," Ceres snarled, folding

her arms. "If our uncle decides to make a surprise vis-it, you'll be royally screwed, and I won't dig you out of the mess you've made this time. He's already freaking out about not having enough, and you go giving it away, willy-nilly."

"These young people are the b-best chance our race has, Ceres. I won't waste that opportunity by being cautious—p-prudence never gets anyone anywhere," Hadrian replied, making Alex feel warmer toward the white-haired man, especially as he looked like he might pass out at any moment.

Ceres snorted. "I thought you were Captain Cautious? You telling me you've finally grown a pair? I'll believe it if you can say Julius's name without shaking in your boots."

Hadrian gave his sister a withering look. "Julius! See, no problem," he said, though his knuckles had gone white with the strain.

With that, Hadrian plucked two large drawstring bags from one of the shelves and began to fill them with bottles. Ceres watched with a look of deep displeasure on her face.

Alex picked up one of the nearby bottles, and let the memories come to him. Instead of bursting into his mind, as they usually did, the remembrances of the person these be-longed to trickled into his head, the visions fragmented and missing whole sections. It made sense, given that they con-tained only half a person's energy, but Alex found it more troubling than any other bottle he had previously picked up. These bottles were desperately sad.

"I think you're making a mistake," she remarked as Hadrian shoved the last of the bottles into the second bag.

"You'll see that I'm not," Hadrian replied, his stutter all but gone.

"Where do the Falleaf students come from?" Aamir asked, evidently trying to break the tension between brother and sister.

"Why do you care? You're taking their essence without so much as a second thought," Ceres sniped.

Aamir shook his head. "I assure you, I care deeply about the origins and fates of these individuals. I have been close to being where they are myself. You don't forget something like that," he said softly.

This seemed to stun Ceres for a moment. "You were at a haven?"

"We were students at Spellshadow Manor," Aamir explained.

"You broke out?"

Aamir nodded. "We did, and now we mean to put an end to all of this."

"Well... I suppose it wouldn't hurt to tell you," she said, relenting. "The students come from the non-magical world, and from the ordinary magical folk who still reside in the magical realm. Anyone not lucky enough to be a noble, basically."

"They come from the non-magical world too?" Ellabell cut in, her face showing her keen interest.

"Those who were hunted down and put onto a register—yes, their children come here, though they are picked through a set-out system. It's usually the first-born of the family," Ceres explained. "It's the same with the ordinary mages in the magical world too. Whoever is unlucky enough to be born first gets a death sentence."

"I thought you said they didn't die?" Alex remarked.

Ceres gave a wry smile. "For some, it might be kinder. Recovery from splitting your soul in half is not an easy road, and the result differs from person to person. Some can be as fine as they were before it happened, with the odd pang from time to time, while others never properly heal. They become walking ghosts, always in pain, barely saying a word, a listless look in their eyes. Again, luck of the draw."

Alex was horrified. Even the alternative was no better than death, if recovery failed. He wondered where these people were being held—a safe place had been mentioned, but its location had yet to be disclosed. Alex supposed he could understand that, considering what might happen if anyone found out where the safe place was. He couldn't imagine it would end well for Hadrian and his sister if Julius found out they'd been smuggling mages out for years, taking only half their essence each time.

"Haven't they noticed the essence here is so much weaker?" he enquired, glancing up into the white eye of Ceres.

She scoffed. "They're too arrogant for their own good, especially my uncle. He thinks this is just the potency of underlings. I don't think he's questioned it once—odd, considering he prides himself on his vast intellect." A nasty look passed over her features, as if she'd sniffed something bad. Alex had a feeling Julius garnered that reaction from a lot of people.

"Two bags of essence—will that be enough?" Hadrian asked, holding up the weighty-looking sacks.

Alex nodded. "That should be plenty for what we have in mind. I can't thank you enough."

"Well, now you've come and taken what you wanted, maybe you should all go—take your thanks and leave," Ceres said tartly. "You're keeping me from my work."

"It's fine, Ceres. We're going." Hadrian sighed, passing one of the sacks to Alex, while shouldering the other himself. "And if Julius comes, I promise I won't drag you into my mess," he added, with equal tartness, before moving toward the passageway, and the exit to the cave.

"I hope you don't regret this!" she called, her voice echoing around the rocks.

"I won't," he muttered.

Alex and the others followed Hadrian up to the cave mouth. Unable to help himself, Alex turned back toward the cavernous room, only to find that Ceres had disappeared.

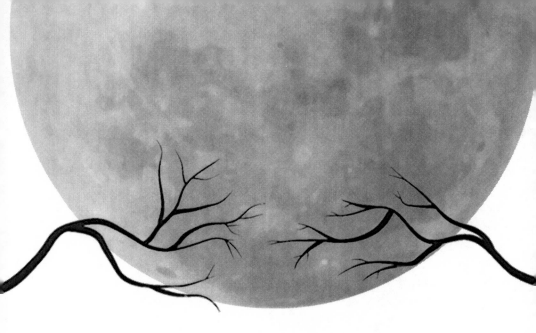

CHAPTER 18

Aftertertertert leaving the cave, Alex paused. With the essence already in his possession, it didn't seem right to waste time heading back to Falleaf House, but there was something that needed to be done before he could make his way to Kingstone, to pass on the message to Stillwater.

"Hadrian?"

The white-haired man turned. "Is everything all right?"

Alex shifted the bag on his shoulder. "I need to ask that other favor of you."

Hadrian grimaced. "You want me to invite Venus to

c-come here?"

"You could summon her on the pretense of discussing how you might go about enrolling more students to collect more essence, or something like that," Alex said. "I'm sure she'll come down and speak with you if you make it sound like she'll benefit."

Hadrian flashed him a dubious look. "Venus and I have always been on g-good terms, but even so, I am not sure how quickly she will respond to my summons. They work on their own t-time, at court, and she will come only when she feels like it. If it seems like something that might b-bore her, she'll stay away longer. If it's something that might give her a much-needed break from J-Julius, she might arrive sooner." He winced as he stumbled over his uncle's name, and Alex couldn't help feeling sorry for the white-haired man.

Alex couldn't imagine anyone wanting to be around the king for longer than was absolutely necessary, but he supposed there was more to Julius and Venus's relationship than met the eye. Perhaps she did love him, though Alex struggled to believe anyone could care for such a vile specimen as Julius.

She'd have to be just as bad, he mused.

"Days or weeks—it doesn't matter, as long as she comes eventually," Alex said. "Once she's here, and we've retrieved the blood from her, we can send a message through to the others, to let them know that we're good to go."

Hadrian glanced at Alex in surprise. "Blood?"

Alex nodded. "We need it for the spell, Hadrian," he urged.

"If I send the call as soon as I return to the p-pagoda, you should still have plenty of time to visit Kingstone," Hadrian promised, punctuated by an anxious gulp.

"I'll come with you," Ellabell insisted, resting her hand on Alex's arm. Alex could see there was no point in objecting; there was a defiance on her face that he knew not to argue with, not anymore. He had learned his lesson.

Aamir chimed in. "I'll stay here, to keep an eye on things—speaking of which, we should arrange a backup plan, just in case. A warning of some sort, to call you back from Kingstone if something happens, or Venus arrives earlier than expected."

"Have you still got the beetle beacon on you?" Ellabell asked.

Alex nodded, retrieving it. "Do you have yours, Aamir?"

The older boy fished around in his pocket for a moment before removing a second beacon. "I knew I'd kept it!" he said, triumphant.

"If we can sync them, we can make it so that when you press the button in the middle, it will set mine off, calling us back," Alex explained, but Aamir was already ahead of the curve. The older boy reached for the beacon in Alex's hands, putting them side by side. A few seconds later, he was twisting his fingers this way and that, weaving golden strands into the two clockwork objects. They both burned brightly for a moment as the magic settled within them.

"They should be twinned now. I'll try it out," Aamir said, handing Alex's back to him.

As soon as the small beacon was in Alex's hand, Aamir pressed the central button on his. A loud siren pierced the air. Alex smothered the clockwork object with his hands in a futile attempt to get it to stop. Eventually, he resorted to anti-magic, pushing enough of it through to silence the eardrum-shattering shriek of the beetle. Once it was quiet, Aamir refilled the mechanism. There would be no missing that sound, if it went off.

"Okay, so you'll definitely summon Venus?" Alex asked, turning his attention back to Hadrian.

The royal nodded, his face pale. "I will d-do it as soon as I return to the pagoda. She can only be called from my study."

"Could you keep hold of one of the bags of essence?" Alex asked Aamir. "We'll only need this one, to give to the others. There's no point carrying both all the way there, just to carry one back again."

Aamir nodded. "No problem."

"Right then, looks like we're good to go," Ellabell said brightly.

After a brief farewell, Alex and Ellabell set off through the forest. All around them, everything was eerily still, with only the odd rustle to make his pulse quicken. It made the whole place seem ominous, the trees looming in on them. He'd become pretty good at spotting the signs of snares hiding among the foliage, his senses on high alert, listening for the buzz and thrum of nearby perils. Pretty soon he could see a gap on the horizon where the forest ended, giving way to rolling fields.

Alex was eager to return to Kingstone. He hadn't really allowed his thoughts to dwell too much on the state he'd left Caius and Vincent in, but the thought of them returned to him in a sudden flood of trepidation. He didn't even know if either of them was alive, and, if they weren't, he had no idea who might be running the show. Alypia had been restrained by her shackles, but the woman was crafty, and Alex knew she'd get out, if given half a chance.

"We're nearly there," he said, flushing as Ellabell reached to take his hand in hers. It was nice, her skin warm and comforting to the touch.

"I've barely had a moment alone with you," she murmured, shyly turning her gaze toward the trees.

He smiled. "I know... We never really had a proper

reunion, what with Lintz and Aamir being there. I didn't think I could kiss you in front of my teacher," he joked.

"I wouldn't have minded," she replied, giving his hand a gentle squeeze.

They came to a halt. "Perhaps I can make up for it now?" he said.

His heart was pounding as he turned her toward him, holding her close. She looked up at him, her blue eyes sparkling. All he wanted to do was kiss her, and let her know how much he had missed her. He longed to tell her that it was the thought of her that had spurred him on, driven him to find a way back to them, but, standing in front of her, he found himself once again tongue-tied.

A kiss tells more than words ever could, he thought to himself. He slowly leaned toward her.

Just as their lips were about to meet, a loud squawk shattered the moment, followed by the thunder of heavy feet as Storm came barreling toward them. Ellabell jumped back, startled, and Alex stood between the charging Thunderbird and the girl he loved.

"Storm, stop!" he yelled. "I'm fine!"

The Thunderbird skidded to a stop, her intelligent eyes flashing toward Ellabell, scrutinizing her. With a loud chirrup, she took a step closer, forcing Alex to move toward her, his hands raised in a gesture of peace. Slowly, he approached her, until he was close enough to stroke the smooth feathers at the side of her face. She chirped again, the sound softer this time.

"Wait, is this the Thunderbird?" Ellabell asked, her mouth agape.

Alex nodded. "She is—her name is Storm."

"And you really flew on her?" Ellabell gasped.

"I did," he said proudly.

"And we're really going to fly to Kingstone? I mean, I knew that was the plan, but I suppose I never really thought she'd exist until I set eyes on her... She's a beauty," Ellabell murmured, awestruck.

Alex grinned. "I figured we may as well save the essence for when it's really necessary. Storm can get us there just fine, no need for the hassle of portal-building."

Ellabell squealed. "I can't believe it! We're really flying there!"

"If you're happy to, and Storm is happy to, then that's what we're going to do," he replied. "What do you think, Storm? You happy to fly us back to Kingstone?"

The bird chirped brightly.

"Does that mean yes?" Ellabell asked, her eyes as wide as saucers.

"I think it might." Alex smiled. "But, first, you have to hold your palm out flat, to allow her to give her permission," he instructed, showing Ellabell what to do. As mad as he was with Storm for ruining their romantic moment, he was pleased to see Ellabell so excited about the trip they were about to take.

Ellabell did as she was told, and waited as Storm examined her. Eventually, the Thunderbird dipped her head and rested her beak in the middle of Ellabell's palm, tapping it gently. Ellabell grinned, taking a moment to stroke the soft feathers of the Thunderbird's head. If Storm minded, she didn't give any indication, only a quiet chirp of satisfaction.

As soon as Alex had done the same, they were ready to depart. Ellabell mounted first, clutching the two bone handles that Alex pointed out to her and scooting her knees up to the base of Storm's neck. Alex hopped on after, putting his arms around Ellabell so that he, too, could reach the two handles. They were sitting very close to one another, with the bag of essence sandwiched between them, and her proximity made him grin like an idiot. It was nice to be so close to her, after so long of having to keep a friendly distance.

As they walked to an open space, Alex realized he'd never actually taken off with Storm from flat ground; it had always been the mountainside. For a moment, he wasn't sure how Storm was going to do it, but, just as he was beginning to doubt his plan, the Thunderbird once again proved her awesome power. She started with a jog, her two strong legs moving steadily under her, her wings spreading out wide. Seconds later, she was sprinting faster than anything Alex had ever experienced, her legs pounding the ground, her wings arched, her head stretched forward to make her more streamlined as Alex and Ellabell hung on for dear life.

Catching a current, she lifted suddenly, like an airplane rising off the tarmac, and the next thing Alex knew, they were soaring. Once they were up high enough, she began to beat her wings, bringing power to their flight.

It was as exhilarating as the first time, if not more so, and Alex couldn't wipe the joy off his face. Ellabell was grinning too, closing her eyes as the wind whipped her face.

"This is amazing!" she cried.

"It really is," Alex replied, yelling to be heard over the sound of the wind rushing past. He knew he might as well enjoy the fun, while he had the chance. "Okay, Storm, to Kingstone!" he whooped, as the Thunderbird rocketed through the sky.

With a whoosh, the world began to bend.

CHAPTER 19

THE FABRIC OF THE REALMS STRETCHED AND strained around the flying form of Storm, before snapping back with a brisk rush of air. They appeared above the open plains, the sparkle of water visible in the distance and the swaying tops of the surrounding forests rustling beneath them. Off to the left, the jagged rise of the strange mountain range was still visible, the spires and towers shining as the golden afternoon light bounced off the metal. Upon a second viewing, Alex was convinced it had something to do with the noble elite, keeping the upper echelons safe, but well out of the way of any riff-raff who inhabited the other parts of the realms.

"What just happened?" Ellabell asked, breathless.

Alex grinned. "Storm just took us through the barrier between realms. Pretty cool, right?"

"Understatement of the century!" she whooped, as Storm settled into a steady rhythm, heading toward the rise of the keep, just visible on the horizon.

They neared the familiar structure, and Alex was pleased to see that very little had changed. It didn't look chaotic, at least not from the outside. A sudden doubt hit him as to where he was going to land Storm, especially if he was going to have to smuggle Ellabell inside. She couldn't simply travel up to the keep, as he could, considering the barrier that smothered the place. The Thunderbird, however, had no such fears, her course never wavering as she swept up onto the turret where Alex had performed his first successful attempt at magical travel. The rusty-colored fog that surrounded the keep didn't seem to faze her in the slightest, her feathered body soaring through it with ease before her sturdy feet touched down on the stone surface of the turret. Alex braced for the release of red fog, but it didn't come. Whatever magical energy Storm possessed, it didn't appear to alert the barrier at all, and had kept Ellabell's from detection too.

"You are quite the creature, aren't you?" he murmured,

patting the side of the Thunderbird's silky neck.

As soon as Alex dismounted and neared the edge of the battlement, he could feel that the magical barrier was even stronger now. It pulsed, almost tangibly, through the air. Glancing down, he saw that it had set the hairs on his forearm on edge.

He knew he was going to have to tread carefully, and he shouldered the drawstring bag of essence. They walked cautiously down the turret stairs, Alex peering out at the bottom to ensure the coast was clear before they pressed on toward Vincent's cell. He figured the necromancer would be their best bet, if he was still alive.

A tense optimism filled his mind as they followed the semi-familiar hallways. So far, nobody had jumped out to surprise them, and the dark glitter of eyes still shone from behind the barred panels in the center of the prison doors.

Somebody is taking care of this place, he mused, *but who? Caius or Vincent?*

Reaching the corridor that held the cells of Agatha and Vincent, and the guard room that had been repurposed for holding Alypia, Alex paused. He knocked, awaiting a response.

"Who goes there?" an anxious voice called.

"Vincent? It's Alex and Ellabell—we come bearing news," Alex replied.

There was a scuffling sound, as if somebody were running inside, before the necromancer finally made his appearance at the door, pulling it open with an over-enthusiastic flourish. To Alex's relief, he saw that there were no specters to be seen, and Vincent seemed to be his usual self, though his eyes were perhaps blacker, and the veins beneath his translucent skin had darkened to a deep, ugly black. His appearance was now closer to that of the other necromancers who lived within the prison walls. Alex felt a pang of guilt, knowing that it was because of him that Vincent had sunk to the darkest realms of necromancy. It was as if the act of summoning the specters, and the attack he had made on Caius, had somehow poisoned Vincent's blood.

His demeanor, however, didn't seem too much changed.

He hurried toward them. "Can it really be you? I must say, it is rather splendid to see both your faces—I feared I might never see them again, after your sharp exit. At least you heeded my warning," he remarked, relief washing over his face.

"We can't stay long," said Alex, feeling the weight of the beetle beacon in his pocket. "We just wanted to check in, and deliver something to the others. It'd be good if we could catch up with them, too, see where they are on their side of the planning table," he added. "Have you heard from them?"

"There will be time enough for shop-talk, but for now

you must both sit," Vincent insisted. "I have refreshments, if you would indulge me in partaking?"

Alex frowned. "We really don't have a lot of time, Vincent."

"Surely you can spare a moment, after everything we have been through?" Vincent replied. Alex shared a look with Ellabell. The necromancer had done a lot for them; it was literally all over his face, and yet the thought of pausing too long here made Alex feel antsy.

"Of course, Vincent, we can sit with you a short while," Ellabell cut in, answering the offer before Alex had the chance to refuse it.

"Excellent! You can tell me all your news, and I would be more than happy to play messenger," Vincent promised, but there was a tightness in the necromancer's voice that made Alex nervous.

It's all in your head, he told himself. *It's just this place, playing tricks with you.*

"How is Caius?" Alex asked, sitting opposite the necromancer.

A grim look passed over Vincent's face, his shoulders sagging. "I could not bring him back from the brink of true existence," he said miserably. "I'm afraid Caius is trapped in the otherworld—his body still breathes, the blood still rushes in his veins, as if he is merely asleep, but it is a lights-on, no-one-home kind of affair. In necromancy, we call it the 'Waking Death.' For all intents and purposes, you are alive, but there is no substance to the life you continue to live. You cannot speak, think, move... You become a breathing husk."

It was a darkly poetic end to the life Caius had lived, and Alex tried his best not to feel responsible. Vincent had done what he had to do, to keep Alex safe, and to give him the time he needed to escape. It was just hard to focus on that fact with the image of a half-dead husk repeating in his mind, haunted by the wide, dead eyes of the specters.

"You got rid of the specters though?" Alex said, glancing around, as if they were about to pop out at any moment.

Vincent inclined his head in an elegant nod. "It took some time, longer than I care to admit, but I succeeded in banishing them back to the underworld. As you see, the exertion of returning them hasn't exactly enhanced my beauty." He smiled tightly, then gave a short, sharp laugh.

"And Alypia?" Ellabell asked.

"She is quite safe—as you may have observed, this place has yet to go to wrack and ruin beneath my leadership," Vincent replied. "I have increased the strength of the barrier, just to be certain of maintaining order, but aside from that, I have had to do little else to retain the control Caius enjoyed." It seemed the necromancer was still haunted by what he had done to Caius, keeping the old warden at the forefront of his mind in his decision-making. There was a repentance in Vincent's actions that wasn't easy to ignore, as if he were trying to make up for what he had done to Caius by being the best replacement he could be.

Ellabell frowned. "Has any news come from Stillwater House yet?"

"No, not as yet, though I will definitely pass on any messages you might have," Vincent replied, though he seemed to change his mind as soon as the words were out of his mouth. "Actually, I tell a lie. There was a note, a day ago, from one of Helena's messengers, if memory serves. It said they were okay, and still working on things on their end, but everything is going smoothly. No alarms have been raised, and they are still working on the Spellshadow aspect of the scheme."

The words were music to Alex's ears. It was precisely what he wanted to hear, but that in itself brought concerns with it: was that why Vincent had changed his story, simply to give Alex the news he thought he wanted to hear? How could Vincent have forgotten something like that?

"I think we'll head through to Stillwater ourselves, just to touch base with everyone," Alex said, trying to keep his tone casual.

Ellabell nodded. "That'd be a good idea, just in case there was anything they forgot to mention in the note," she added, evidently attempting to humor Vincent.

"Nonsense, I won't hear of it—as you already explained to me, you are on something of a tight schedule. I would not keep you from your tasks back at Falleaf House. I shall deliver your message with as much care as if it were a precious jewel," Vincent insisted. "And, I will seek to inform you, as soon as I have better news from the others."

"Not that we don't appreciate your offer, Vincent, but we have some essence to give them too," Ellabell said.

"I can deliver that as well!" Vincent promised.

Alex flashed a sideways glance at Ellabell, and saw the same confused expression on her face that he felt upon his own. There was something amiss. It wasn't that he didn't trust Vincent, because he did, but there was an undercurrent of something uncomfortable that Alex couldn't quite put his finger on. It was a gut feeling that he couldn't push away. Vincent seemed unusually cagey, with an unsettled shift in his eyes.

"Either way, Vincent, we're pretty set on seeing the others ourselves," Alex explained firmly.

A worried look furrowed Vincent's brow. "No, no, there really is no need."

"Regardless, we'd like to see them," Alex repeated. "I'd like to see Alypia too, while I'm at it—if that's okay?" he added, trying not to show his concern.

Vincent nodded. "Of course… I suppose you're wanting to put your mind at ease?" His mouth curved into a strange smile, and an unnatural chuckle bubbled from the back of his throat.

"Something like that," Alex said, giving nothing away.

"This way then," Vincent sighed, rising sharply from his seat. Alex and Ellabell followed Vincent out into the hallway, hurrying after him as he strode toward the door to the old guard room.

The necromancer turned a large key in the lock, opening the door cautiously. Through the crack that appeared, Alex could see the slumped figure of Alypia sitting in the chair by the fireplace, her manacled hands held out on her lap. She appeared to be sleeping, her patchwork face oddly peaceful.

"I've been keeping her under a sleeping spell," Vincent explained. "Have you seen enough?"

Alex nodded, more or less satisfied, though he couldn't push away the dubious feeling that persisted. There was something wrong; he was sure of it. He hoped the others might be able to shed some light on the problem.

With that, Vincent pulled the door shut again, his manner furtive.

"We should probably get to the portal, and make our pit stop to the others," Alex said, turning to walk back in the direction he knew the Stillwater portal to be, out in the open courtyard. Ellabell followed him, walking with conviction.

Vincent hurried after, a perplexed look on his face. "Honestly, I do not mind delivering your wares and wants," he called, but Alex and Ellabell were already farther ahead.

A piercing shriek split the air.

It was the beetle beacon in Alex's pocket, signaling a warning at Falleaf House. Alex flashed a panicked look at Ellabell as he drew it out, seeing the blinding flash of the lights on the tempered carapace. The sound was louder without the cloth of his trousers to smother it, and it was all Alex could do not to cover his ears, to try to protect his eardrums from the deafening siren. Ellabell cupped her own palms over her ears as Alex pushed his anti-magic into the small clockwork device, silencing it to a dull whine.

"What was that?" Vincent asked, catching up to where Alex and Ellabell stood.

"Bad news," Alex muttered. It wasn't ideal. There was more he needed to do here, and yet he knew he had to get back to Falleaf. If Aamir had pressed his beacon, it meant something important was going down. Unfortunately, it took priority over his suspicions of the keep, and whatever Vincent appeared to be hiding.

"It's fine," Ellabell announced. "I'll stay, while you go back to Falleaf House. I'll make sure I get the message to the others." She flashed Alex a knowing look, tilting her head subtly towards Vincent. Alex realized she wanted to stay to get to the root of why Vincent was acting strange, and though he too wanted to figure that out, he wasn't sure about leaving her to it, if something dangerous had taken hold of the necromancer.

He frowned. "I'm not sure that's a good idea."

"Remember what we talked about?" Ellabell said, a warning in her eyes. "It's just for the time being, and you're the only one who can ride Storm. I'll be fine, I just want to make sure everything's okay," she added. Alex knew she was right, even if he didn't like it. He was still getting used to not worrying. "Though you should probably take the essence back, and bring it with you again when you return," she whispered, just out of the earshot of Vincent.

"Good thinking," he murmured. At least then, the essence would be safe if something went awry. He had a feeling he might even need it, to face whatever it was Aamir was warning him about. Two bags were better than one, and right now, Falleaf was in greater need.

Leaving Ellabell behind didn't sit well with him, but there was nothing he could do about it now. If anything dangerous arose, he knew she was more than capable of handling herself. It was the not knowing that plagued him. Until he returned to Kingstone, he wouldn't know if anything bad had happened, or if she was perfectly fine, the message successfully delivered, and everything covered in rainbows and cupcake frosting.

He kissed Ellabell gently on the lips, vowing to come back as soon as he could. With a trail of snowflakes flurrying around him, Alex raced toward the turret. Falleaf was calling, and he was ready to answer.

CHAPTER 20

ARRIVING BACK AT FALLEAF, ALEX JUMPED OFF
Storm's back and ran through the woods, listening
for the sound of traps, his eyes darting this way
and that. He was still concerned for Ellabell's welfare, no
matter what she'd said about being fine, but he knew he
couldn't think about that now. The beacon was still vibrating
weakly in his pocket.

As he reached the tree-line that opened out onto the water garden, at the front of the pagoda, he skidded to a halt.
The place was in chaos. There were soldiers running to and
fro like headless chickens, panicked looks on their faces,

their hands hurriedly fixing parts of their uniforms that had fallen into disarray. Alex realized this could only mean one thing, as his eyes glanced up toward the pagoda itself. It was hard to make out anything from such a distance, but he could see figures rushing around beyond the glass of the windows, too.

Venus must already be there.

It didn't seem possible, considering he'd only been away a short period of time, and yet the sight before him told a different story. There was only one reason the soldiers would be in such a hurry.

Using the confusion to his advantage, Alex dashed across to the broken door of the cellar, letting himself into the pagoda. He hurried upward, reaching the ground floor where the kitchens were. Bustling about were more servants than he had ever seen, though some of them looked too young to be staff. It appeared some of the Falleaf students had been roped into helping, at such short notice.

Coming face-to-face with a few of them, Alex's resolve strengthened; they were just like him. Of the ones he came across, none of them could have been older than sixteen or seventeen, and they moved in deference to the older staff. These kids weren't privileged—they weren't like the elite at Stillwater. They were ordinary. They could have been any of his classmates back in high school. They didn't have striking, otherworldly eyes, or extraordinary beauty. They were just plain kids, exactly like him, brought to this place against their will and making the best of it.

"Here, you don't want to be seen without a uniform!" one of them, a bespectacled boy of around fifteen, shouted from the hallway as he launched a spare uniform at Alex.

Alex caught it. "Thanks, man."

The boy grinned. "No worries. Definitely wouldn't want the big dog to catch you in your skivvies! Hurry up, though, it's all hands on deck!"

Alex frowned, wanting to ask who the "big dog" was, but the boy had already run off. With a sinking feeling, he began to put the scarlet uniform on over his normal clothes, listening to the pound of footsteps on the wooden floors above his head. Everyone was in a rush, it seemed.

Just then, Aamir came careening around the corner, wearing the same scarlet uniform Alex was wearing. His eyes went wide as he saw Alex standing there, buttoning up his shirt.

"Alex! Thank goodness!" he cried.

"What's going on?" Alex asked.

Aamir shook his head. "It's not good, Alex, not good at all."

"Well, what is it?"

"Venus is here," Aamir explained.

"That's good news—that's what we wanted. I didn't think she'd come so quickly, but—"

Aamir sighed heavily, cutting Alex off. "*He* came with her."

"Who?" said Alex, though he already knew the answer.

"Julius, of course—who else?" Aamir remarked. "I don't know what we were thinking."

Alex frowned. "How were we supposed to know Julius would come with her?"

"The stories we've heard, Alex. We should have thought a bit harder… He was never going to let her out of his sight, to visit a haven where she hasn't actually got any family ties. He's insane!"

Alex realized that Aamir was right, but it simply hadn't occurred to him before. He'd never suspected that Julius wouldn't let his wife visit a haven alone, where they didn't have children. Stillwater might have been different, perhaps even Spellshadow, but Falleaf was run by the son of a bitter brother. Julius would never have allowed it, not with how controlling he was.

"It's fine," Alex said, with forced brightness. "We've still got an opportunity in front of us."

Aamir gave Alex a look of disbelief. "You can't be serious."

"I am deadly serious. We carry on with the plan," Alex

insisted. "They're here—if we don't do this now, we may never get the chance again."

"It doesn't seem like a very wise plan," Aamir remarked.

Alex shrugged. "It isn't, but it's the best we've got. Come on, we've muddled through up to now, what's a little more going to do?"

"Get us killed?" Aamir replied.

Alex rolled his eyes. "You're always so negative. Honestly, Aamir, you definitely know how to massacre the mood," he teased.

"I am merely pointing out the obvious," Aamir retorted, a small smile playing upon his lips.

"Shall we?" Alex asked.

"Lead the way."

They made their way up through the floors of the pagoda, passing the unyielding flow of bodies as they went. There were servants of all shapes and sizes, carrying trays piled high with delicious-smelling treats and boxes full of candies. Others were returning empty trays, while the rest barked orders. Nobody seemed to pay much notice to Alex and Aamir, who weaved through the throngs with ease, rising higher and higher up the building.

At last, they reached the top floor. There were guards posted at either side of the door, but Alex approached them boldly, his head bowed in veneration. The two men on duty were enormous, bulky individuals, the buttons of their uniforms straining across their barrel chests. Still, Alex showed no fear as he neared, even when their gaze fell upon him and they stared at him as if he were little more than an unsightly bug.

"What do you want, wretch?" one asked.

"We are here to serve His Royal Highness, King Julius," Alex explained, keeping his head dipped. "Our presence has been commanded by the venerable Hadrian," he added, hoping that the royal would cover for them, if he came to the door.

"No servants are worthy of a King's audience," one guard sneered.

"I assure you, he is expecting us. He will be sorely disappointed if he finds you haven't let us through," Alex countered, hoping he sounded convincing.

The guards looked at one another before the one who had spoken tapped on the door. Hadrian appeared, poking his head out. For a moment, a look of horror flashed across his face at the sight of Alex and Aamir, but he covered it quickly, turning to the guards.

"What appears to be the problem?" Hadrian asked.

"These two say you ordered them to come up?" the guard said gruffly.

Hadrian nodded. "Indeed, I did. Allow them through."

With a shrug, the two huge men stood to one side, letting Alex and Aamir pass with little more than a cursory glance. Once inside the top floor chambers, Alex's heart really began to thunder. Sitting at the low table, where Alex and his friends had shared breakfast that morning, was Julius. Beside him, staring blankly into a cup of something hot and bright red in color, was a woman dressed in a striking violet silk kimono with vivid pink blossoms embroidered upon the fabric. She was of an exquisite beauty that quite literally took Alex's breath away. Even Alypia, beneath the veil of her enhancement spells, paled in comparison. It had to be Venus.

Although it was clear she was of an older age, there was a youthfulness to her face that defied time. Her eyes were a pale, silvery blue that seemed to pierce the soul, and her hair was long and pale, not quite the same shade of white as the other royals. Hers was closer to silver in color, flecked with strands of gold. Alex noted that Helena must take after her grandmother, rather than her mother, where looks were concerned. Venus's face was indescribable. If Alex put together all the most beautiful women in history, he wasn't sure any of them would match up to the beauty he saw in front of him.

Julius rose, prowling around behind his wife. It was clear that, even after so many years of marriage, the king couldn't take his eyes off his queen. He lunged toward her suddenly, and though everyone else in the room flinched, Venus didn't bat an eyelid. Making a charade of it, Julius reached past her shoulder to pick up a candy shaped like a ladybug, his mouth moving as he whispered something in her ear. There was malicious intent in his eyes, his lips curving up in a cruel smile. Whatever it was he'd said, she still refused to react, focusing on the liquid in her cup.

Chuckling to himself, Julius planted a firm kiss on his wife's cheek. It was becoming quickly apparent that Julius and Venus had the kind of twisted relationship in which nobody was ever sure if he was going to kill her or kiss her. It wasn't a comfortable thing to watch.

"Your book collection is terrible, nephew," Julius purred as he moved away from Venus, stalking toward the bookshelves at the back of the room. "You should always replenish your stock," he said, thumbing the spines.

Alex froze as the king came close to the spine of the Book of Jupiter, tucked away where Alex had left it at the far end of the highest bookshelf, under the supervision of Hadrian and Aamir. Having not expected such an honored guest to turn up, Alex had thought it would be safe there. All he could do was watch as Julius made his way down the line of books, mouthing the names as he went. There was only one book left between Julius and the Book of Jupiter, and Alex didn't think he could bear it. He wanted to shout, or throw something, to create a distraction, but he had a feeling it might have the opposite effect. Julius wasn't stupid; he would suspect something.

At the very last moment, Julius turned back to the room, missing the book by mere millimeters.

"It's essential that you read as much as you can; it is the only way to truly understand the world around us," Julius said, his tone brimming with self-importance. "I, myself, always have several miniatures about my person, so that I can read wherever I may be. My dear wife will tell you—I am rarely without a book in my hand. Knowledge is power, and to be truly powerful, you have to have read more than any other man."

As if to prove his point, he removed several small books from various hiding spots all over his body. It was mesmerizing to watch, like seeing clowns emerge from a tiny car.

"Very impressive, my king," Hadrian murmured, wringing his hands furiously.

"You can't just read from your own writers, either. No— how can one get a good grasp of the world if they hear only a portion of its voices?" Julius continued, evidently not caring about his audience's clear disinterest. "I read mage books, non-magical books... I've even been known to dabble in a Spellbreaker book or two, in my time, though they're not easy to come by. I'd say I have the finest collection of literature on the planet, and that is no exaggeration, wouldn't you say, darling?" He placed his hand at the back of Venus's neck, as if to caress it, or snap it like a twig.

"Your collection is the finest of them all," Venus said softly.

"You!" Julius barked, his gaze settling firmly on Alex. "Do you read much?"

Alex gulped. "Not as much as I'd like to, Your Royal Highness."

"You must always make time for books—what are you teaching these wastrels?" Julius scoffed, flashing a withering look in Hadrian's direction.

"They aren't s-students, Uncle. This is Thomas and Leon, two of our non-magical staff," Hadrian lied. "The students have a m-much richer education, with far better access to the literature of which you s-speak."

"You look familiar," Julius murmured, stepping closer to Alex. It seemed the king had no concept of personal space, as he got right up in Alex's face, scrutinizing him closely. "Have we met before?"

Alex shook his head. "No, Your Royal Highness. I don't get out much."

The king burst into a bout of alarming laughter. "I like this one! Perhaps you just have one of those faces?"

"Perhaps, Your Royal Highness." Alex forced a smile

onto his face, though his heart was thundering and his palms were clammy.

"Could be, though it's rare that I forget a face, isn't it, darling?" He turned his attention back to his wife for a moment.

She looked up, smiling falsely. "It is, though I think you're mistaken with this boy. Do leave him alone, dear. Can't you see you're frightening the life out of him?"

Julius flared his nostrils, an angry glint appearing in his eyes. "Did you say something, darling?"

"Come back over here to me—your coffee is getting cold," she replied, her voice sickly sweet. It was clear Julius had heard what she had said, but the power play between them was an interesting one. Alex hadn't expected to hear such boldness from her, and yet she had spoken without fear. After so long suffering under the cruelty of her husband, Alex supposed she didn't feel scared anymore. There was no point.

"Yes, I suppose we should be returning to business anyway," Julius remarked, moving over to the low table again. He sat down beside his wife, pulling her to him in a tense embrace. She wrapped her slender arms about his neck, evidently adept at calming him.

"Business?" Hadrian spoke, biting nervously into a dumpling.

"I can honestly say, I never thought I'd see the day when I could commend the offspring of my brother, but you have truly surprised me," Julius said. "To see such ingenuity from the leader of a haven is utterly refreshing. The others, they coast along, doing the bare minimum, but you—you call me here to discuss how we might work together to increase our yield of essence. Now *that* is the kind of initiative I want to see."

Alex watched as Hadrian steeled himself. "Yes, Uncle, I thought it would be good for us to talk, and for us to perhaps begin something of a partnership. I have so few ideas; thus, any assistance is much appreciated, especially from your f-fine mind."

Julius smiled, the expression lacking warmth. "A partnership, you say?"

"Yes, though perhaps partnership is the wrong word— it'd just be me putting your ideas into action," Hadrian replied, keeping his stutter at bay. It was ill-advised to show weakness in front of a man like Julius, and it was clear that Hadrian was doing his best impression of a brave face.

Julius straightened the high collar of his suit jacket. "Well then, it looks like we have a little something to celebrate!"

With that announcement, the king picked up a narrow glass chalice, and Alex saw his opportunity.

CHAPTER 21

J ULIUS RAISED HIS GLASS UPWARD. HADRIAN PICKED UP his, as did Venus. Grabbing a bottle of some kind of sparkling drink from the sideboard, Alex moved toward the table, eager to get closer to the king, and the glass in his hand. Aamir reached out to grasp the edge of Alex's shirt, evidently trying to stop him, but Alex weaved out of the way. This was a prime opportunity, and he wasn't about to miss it.

"To new beginnings, and a replenishment of our great nation's essence!" Julius toasted.

The others around the low table chorused the sentiment, and Hadrian even managed to look almost pleased with the words tumbling out of his mouth. Alex had to give the man props; he was putting on a very good show. It didn't look like the king suspected anything was amiss, though Alex's eyes were drawn to Venus, who seemed remarkably more curious about the whole thing than her husband. From time to time, she would glance around, clearly absorbing her surroundings. Where Julius was outwardly vocal about his intellect, and undoubtedly had the evidence to back it up, Venus was quiet and stealthy with hers, though Alex could sense there was a deep pool of it within her, ever-ticking behind her serene silver eyes. More potent even, perhaps, than her husband's.

It was Venus who looked at Alex oddly as he stood close to Julius. There was a warning in her eyes, but Alex thought he might be imagining things. She couldn't possibly know what it was he planned to do, could she? He'd never even seen her before; she couldn't know what he was. Still, it threw him for a second. It just so happened that, at that exact moment, he was pouring more drink into Julius's glass while feeding imperceptible slivers of his anti-magic through the sparkling liquid, into the chalice that the king held in his hand. In his distraction, Alex vibrated the particles all wrong. Instead of shattering the glass, he only succeeded in shaking the molecules of the drink, causing it to spurt the fizzy fluid up through the narrow chalice, straight into Julius's face.

The king was less than impressed, whirling around and grasping Alex tightly by the throat. It was all Alex could do to restrain the anti-magic inside himself, stopping it from crackling through his skin in retaliation. Julius oozed magical energy; it radiated from him in tangible waves.

"You little wretch! You did that on purpose!" Julius roared, spittle flying in Alex's face. "Did you shake the bottle? Did you think it would be funny?"

"No... Your... Royal... Highness... I... just..." Alex croaked, unable to finish his sentence as Julius's hand gripped tighter. It was a move Alex had seen the king use before, on the laughing prisoner back at Kingstone Keep. Suddenly, Alex was very aware of his mortality.

"I am your king, you cretin! I talk to you, I welcome you, I engage in polite, intelligent conversation with you, and you choose to repay me with this?" Julius growled. "Let me guess, it was your little friend that put you up to this? Or was it you, Hadrian, you stammering fool? Are you precisely like your father after all?"

Hadrian raised his hands in surrender. "Uncle, this w-was an unfortunate accident—I can assure you, it is no p-practical joke on my part," he insisted, his voice tight.

"Then it must have been you!" Julius snarled, glowering in the direction of Aamir.

Aamir shook his head rapidly. "An innocent error, Your Royal Highness—I believe the bottle got too close to the window, and the sun increased the volume of bubbles within the bottle, due to increased speed of fermentation," he replied hurriedly, the words pouring out of his mouth with such conviction that even Alex nearly believed him, though he was starting to feel like his head might explode.

It was hard to breathe, his cheeks puffing out, the veins at the sides of his head throbbing, and his eyes beginning to bulge as Julius continued to tighten the hand around Alex's throat. With a surge of panic, Alex realized he was close to losing control over his powers. It was like drowning, feeling the pressure of blood pushing through the body, urging the sinking person to take a breath. Alex's anti-magic was his survival instinct, and it was taking every fiber of his being not to use it.

Julius raised his hand, bringing it close to Alex's face with such force that Alex thought he was about to be punched. The king stopped just short of impact, showing exceptional control over his own muscles. It was this kind of strange thought that kept Alex's mind away from the sinking feeling that he was having, knowing he was about to be disintegrated from the inside out, until there was nothing left but a floppy husk.

Alex could feel the pressure building beneath Julius's

hand, the space between the king's palm and Alex's face growing unbearably hot. It was because of this man that the Spellbreakers and the mages had split apart, ripping up a potential treaty of peace in favor of violence and segregation. It was this man's hatred for Alex's kind that had signaled extinction for the Spellbreakers and brought about the Great Evil. In mere seconds, Julius would realize what he was dealing with, would know that the key to his own survival was standing right before him.

"Nobody makes a mockery of me," Julius hissed.

With barely a sound, Venus stood and rested her hand upon her husband's arm. She leaned toward him, her mouth close to his ear, and whispered something soft and soothing. There was a musicality to her voice that had Alex transfixed, even though he could only catch snippets of what she was saying. It sounded like a familiar poem—a sonnet, perhaps.

"Love is not love... that looks on tempests and is never shaken," she whispered.

It was Shakespeare, and a poem Alex knew well—it was one his mother liked.

"Release him, my love," she requested, her hands covering his. As if drawn by the desire of her voice, Julius's hands lifted upward, away from Alex's face. They settled on Venus's face instead, his forehead leaning in toward hers, until they were nose-to-nose. A crackle of energy flitted between them, like static electricity. The way the king's hands rested at the base of her neck still made Alex feel as if Julius could either embrace his wife, or strangle the life from her.

For a long while the couple stood that way, with their eyes closed, breathing rhythmically with one another. It was like a bizarre meditation, a still moment in the middle of a storm. Nobody dared to speak.

With a loud exhale, Julius let go of his wife's face and straightened.

"Apologies for the outburst. I'm not one for practical jokes," he said casually, sitting back down and taking up the glass once more. It was mostly empty after the upward surge, and Julius held it up to Alex, who was still recovering from the shock. "Wouldn't mind a top off now, if it's not too much trouble?"

Alex's hands shook as he attempted to pick up the bottle. Thankfully, before another catastrophic spillage could occur, Aamir swooped in, taking the bottle from Alex's trembling hands and pouring out another full glass for the king.

"Didn't scare you too badly, did I?" Julius scoffed.

Alex shook his head. "No… Your Royal Highness… not at all," he croaked, his throat raw.

"Pity, I love a good scare," the king remarked. If almost killing someone was the way he reacted to a perceived joke,

Alex could only imagine how Julius would react to a real threat.

Venus placed her hand on her husband's. "Now, now, darling, they'll be trembling too hard to hold anything if you continue to terrify them with your terse manner," she chastised. Something hypnotic seemed to have happened to Julius, who smiled lovingly at his wife, no hint of malevolence behind his eyes.

"Whatever you say, my precious sweet pea," he cooed, like a teenager in the first throes of love. It wasn't to last, as he turned to Hadrian, a steely look overwhelming the doe-eyed expression. "You really ought to have learned the proper way to receive guests by now, Hadrian. Honestly, this isn't good enough—I expect you to keep this place spotless, and you turn it into a crass, uncouth dump. It wasn't by chance that you received the finest haven, filled to the brim with all my precious things. I took a chance on you, and you have let me down." He sighed dramatically.

"Come, darling, you were praising him a moment ago," Venus said softly, though Alex could tell her comments weren't appreciated by her husband. She dipped her head, knowing she had gone a fraction too far in her boldness. Alex guessed it was a delicate tightrope she walked, between saying the wrong thing and saying just enough. It was neither right nor fair, but Alex didn't dare speak up.

Julius stared at Hadrian. "No, I really am most disappointed by your upkeep of this place. I won't stay a moment longer," he said, standing sharply.

"Now, darling, we mustn't be rude," Venus said, her tone soothing, but it seemed her charms had worn off for the day.

"We are leaving," he snapped.

She tilted her head toward him, almost like a bow of reverence, as she too stood to go. Alex began to panic, wondering how he was supposed to get his hands on the required amount of royal blood if they left now, and yet he could think of no way to stop them.

While Alex was wracking his brain, Julius was gathering his own servants together by yelling loudly down the hallway. The two married royals seemed to have arrived with an entourage, which Alex supposed was to be expected, given their status.

"Are we ready?" Julius demanded, turning toward his wife.

She smiled pleasantly. "Yes, darling."

"Well, what began with such promise has turned into something of a wasted visit," Julius remarked, pulling up the edges of his high collar. "Nephew, I require… nay, I demand more essence from this place. These havens cannot expect to go on giving the bare minimum, and though you have displeased me, I dare say you have been the one to inspire me. More essence must be collected. You must increase your yield, and I would see you add to the number of children taken in the annual lottery. Let's give first-born *and* last-born a whirl, shall we?"

Hadrian nodded reluctantly. "Whatever you wish, Uncle."

"Well, don't sound too pleased about it." Julius scoffed. "At least I offered you a small sliver of the credit. I am a generous man, let's not forget."

"Of course not, Uncle." Hadrian forced a tight smile onto his face. "You do me a g-great honor, and I will not let you down."

Julius flicked away an invisible dust mote. "Very well, see that you don't. I shall return in a few months' time to check on your progress; I expect to see an entirely new intake among your ranks. The essence here is so puny anyway that you shall have to bolster your numbers, more so than any other havens, though they too will be receiving word from me about what I want from them."

"I shall endeavor to m-make things more pleasant for your next visit, Uncle," said Hadrian, teetering on the edge of what Julius found acceptable, from the flash of warning in the king's eyes. Seeing the expression, Hadrian visibly retreated into himself, clamming up like a startled tortoise.

"See that you do." Julius turned around and left the room

with a dramatic swish of his long, cream-colored coat.

Venus followed, though she cast a strange look back at Alex, Aamir, and Hadrian. There was an apology in her expression, and she mouthed a word at them which looked a lot like "sorry."

"Venus!" Julius barked, from the hallway beyond.

With a captivating smile, she swished the rich fabric of her kimono, and was gone in a haze of sweet-smelling perfume, hurrying after her cantankerous husband. Alex stood, frozen to the spot, as he watched his last hope disappear.

Well, not quite his last hope. A second later, Alex dived for the glass, hoping for some trace of something that he might use. Although he hadn't managed to vibrate the glass properly, he had run some energy through it, though whether it had been enough to break anything, he didn't yet know.

To his delight, he saw a hint of red at the very bottom. There was a chip in the base, and it looked as though Julius had caught his finger on the jagged indent. Gleefully, Alex raised the glass to the light, to get a better look, but his optimism soon died. There couldn't have been more than two drops present on the jagged edge, and extracting what was there was a near impossibility; most of it had already dried up.

"Anything?" Aamir asked, standing over Alex's shoulder.

He shook his head. "Not nearly enough."

"You didn't get what you n-needed?" said Hadrian mournfully, his whole body trembling.

"I got distracted. I missed our chance," Alex confessed.

"But you must hurry on with your p-plan, Alex, before we are all left in r-ruin," Hadrian warned. "You heard what Julius said—he wants *more*. If you don't succeed, I will have to get him m-more. It's in his head now. He won't let it g-go."

Alex frowned, wanting to tell Hadrian how unhelpful his words were, but the royal looked deflated enough as it was. "I know what's at stake, Hadrian, but I can't do it without the blood," Alex said.

"There has to be someone else who can help us," said Aamir.

A smile pulled at the corner of Alex's lips, as it came to him. "I know just the person."

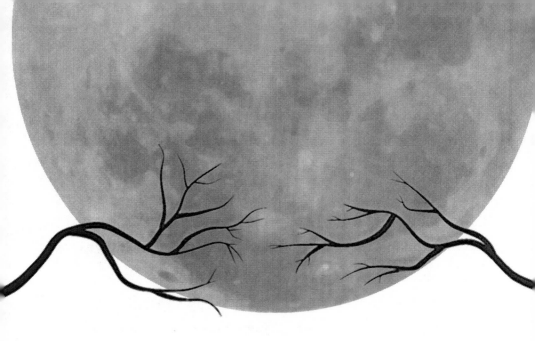

CHAPTER 22

"HELENA MIGHT BE ABLE TO HELP US," SAID Alex, not knowing why he hadn't thought of it before. She was, after all, part of the royal circle herself, so if there was anyone who could get in touch with the other royals, the ones Alex needed, it was her.

"Alypia's daughter?" asked Hadrian dubiously.

Alex nodded. "She has been helpful to us so far. I imagine she'd be one of the only people who could pull it off, if we were to persuade her to go and get some right from the horse's mouth, as it were."

"You've m-met her?" Hadrian frowned.

"We befriended her at Stillwater House. Without her, we would not be here," Aamir explained. "She is very much for our cause, rather than that of her mother," he added with a wry smile.

Hadrian made a strange sound. "Well, I never. You lot are full of s-surprises." He chuckled, but it didn't quite reach his eyes. Alex couldn't blame him; they had been through a lot today.

Without Julius's presence to worry about, Alex's mind turned back to the events that had occurred just before he'd returned to Falleaf. Ellabell was still at Kingstone Keep, hopefully safe, though he was beginning to have serious doubts where that was concerned. Each time he pictured Vincent's anxious face, his own anxiety increased. There had been something terribly amiss back there, and he was eager to return as soon as possible, to figure out what it was.

"I need to go back to Kingstone anyway to get Ellabell, so we might as well go and see Helena at the same time, kill two birds with one stone," Alex suggested.

"I was wondering where she had gone," Hadrian remarked, his stutter easing.

"She's still there, keeping an eye on things. There was something a little strange going on, so she stayed behind to scope it out," Alex said, trying to push the fear out of his voice.

Aamir frowned. "What kind of strange?"

"Hard to explain, just Vincent acting cagey and not very Vincent-like," Alex replied, knowing it sounded like he was making a mountain out of a molehill. Still, his gut was insistent that something was up.

"Would you mind if I tagged along this time?" Aamir asked.

Alex smiled. "I thought you'd never ask," he joked.

"Do you require my assistance as well?" Hadrian asked.

"No, thank you. I imagine you have bigger things to attend to here," Alex replied. In all honesty, he would have loved to have Hadrian there, but he wasn't yet sure how many people Storm could carry on her back, and he didn't fancy overloading the Thunderbird in case she balked.

Hadrian nodded solemnly. "I should say you're right."

With that, they parted ways, Alex picking up one of the two unused bags of essence still at their disposal, and strapping it across his shoulders like a backpack, as Aamir ran more magic through the beacons and handed one to Hadrian, in case of emergency. The royal seemed thrilled by the tiny clockwork creation, marveling at the craftsmanship. It made Alex think sadly of Lintz, the loss still raw. They left the second bag of essence with Hadrian too, promising to return for it when the time came for the link from Falleaf to Spellshadow to be restored.

Trying not to let the sadness overwhelm him, he and Aamir made their way out of the pagoda, still dressed in their scarlet uniforms. They passed a long exodus of weary-looking staff on the stairs, making their way out of the building and back to the classrooms and dormitories of the school within the forest, but Alex didn't see the bespectacled boy again, the one who had thrown the uniform at him. There were other students, but they didn't pay Alex and Aamir much mind as the two boys darted past in their hurry to return to Kingstone. It didn't even seem to occur to them that Alex and Aamir didn't belong to the student body from which they had been dragged.

You'll be free soon enough, Alex promised them as he and Aamir hurried down the hallway, past the kitchens, down the stone steps to the unused cellar, and out into the crisp forest air.

They darted through the trees, old hands at figuring out traps and barriers now, with Alex taking the lead as they ran toward the spot where he had left Storm. As they neared, Alex had an inexplicable sinking feeling that the bird had been taken. She didn't come out, as she had done before, and Alex couldn't see her anywhere about.

"Storm!" he called.

"Who's Storm?" Aamir whispered.

"You'll see… hopefully," Alex replied, frowning.

A chirp erupted close by Alex's ear, startling him, and the Thunderbird burst upward from an enormous pile of twigs and mown grass. She had camouflaged herself beneath it, smothering her highly suspect shape with whatever was handy. Aamir staggered backwards, away from her, a terrified expression on his face. She ran after him, tapping at his shoulder with her beak.

Alex chuckled. "Stay still, she's friendly!"

"She doesn't seem very friendly!" Aamir remarked, trying to shield his face with his hands.

"She's our mode of transport. This is the Thunderbird I was telling you about."

Aamir looked at Alex in disbelief. "You can ride this thing?"

Storm chirped loudly, the tone showing how affronted she was.

"She's not a thing, Aamir, she's a Thunderbird," Alex said. "And she understands more than you'd think, so you'd best be polite."

Aamir turned toward Storm. "There, there, good bird."

"Hold your palm out flat," Alex suggested.

Aamir did so, and Storm placed her beak gently into the center.

"What does that mean?"

Alex grinned. "That means we're good to go—she's given

her permission," he said, performing the same gesture. With a ruffle of feathers, Storm rested on her haunches, making it easier for the two boys to climb aboard.

Aamir went first, under the supervision of Alex, who hopped on after. Once they were safely on board, with the essence stowed away securely, they set off. Knowing what it would feel like this time, rising up from a ground-level take off, Alex could enjoy the experience a little more, though it was clear that Aamir wasn't exactly thrilled by the prospect as the Thunderbird sped along the ground and took sudden, alarming flight.

"What the—!" Aamir yelped.

"You haven't seen anything yet," Alex shouted as Storm sped up to her full capacity, the world bending and stretching all around them.

Aamir still hadn't recovered by the time they reached the turret of the keep, which seemed to be Storm's preferred roosting spot. Clambering down, he swayed unsteadily for a moment, as if he had just stepped off a particularly turbulent boat. Alex struggled not to laugh.

"Don't you dare say a word," Aamir grumbled.

Alex lifted his hands. "Hey—flying isn't for everyone."

Making their way down the turret steps, into the body of the keep, Alex could tell instantly that his gut feeling had been right. Where before there had been silence and creepy eyes staring from between the bars of the central peepholes, now there was chaos. The prison was in utter disarray, with voices clamoring along the hallways, and the sound of people running amok bouncing from the rafters. At the bottom of the stairs, Alex grabbed Aamir and pressed him back against the wall, just as a group of particularly nasty-looking individuals sprinted past, whooping loudly, clutching homemade shivs in their hands.

Once the coast was clear of weapon-wielding criminals, the two young men broke into a run, weaving their respective energies as they did so, in order to knock aside the various miscreants who charged toward them, with menace on their minds. They encountered several on the route toward the courtyard, where Alex hoped the portal still stood. One woman, dressed in tattered rags, came howling toward the duo, spinning her arms wildly, like windmills. Alex dispensed with her, sending a blockade of ice and snow down the corridor, to knock out anyone who might try to run up.

As Alex turned around a corner, a pair of hands grabbed him, dragging him into one of the cells. He felt the cold bite of something sharp and metallic against his neck, and prayed it didn't get the chance to slice his flesh open. It took everything he had to remain calm as he lifted his hands to the sides of his attacker's head and pressed the strands of his anti-magic through, into the villain's skull. Whoever the man was, he wasn't expecting Alex's sneak attack, and Alex made quick work of his assailant's mind, sifting through a series of vile memories in search of just one he could put into the forefront of the man's mind to ease the dark, violent thoughts that were prevalent there. Eventually, he did, and the attacker calmed instantly, dropping his hands to his sides before creeping away to the corner of the room to play with invisible toys on the dank floor.

Alex burst out of the cell to find Aamir also being dragged away. He hurried to catch up, and dispatched Aamir's assailant easily, with a stealthy attack from behind. None of the criminals he had met so far had particularly nice memories to search through, and the horrifying thoughts kept returning to him, like flashbacks in a horror movie, as he made his way toward the courtyard.

Running down one of the hallways, not far from the corridor that connected the courtyard to the rest of the keep, Alex saw Vincent slumped in front of a cell door at the far end of the passageway. The necromancer looked to be in a bad state, though his hands were raised, and there were twisting whorls of black magic weaving between his fingers. Agatha was there too, though she was on her feet, fending off any intruders that sought to reach them. She was ferocious, her eyes wild, a banshee-like scream erupting from the back of her throat. It was a sound Alex had heard once before, and it chilled him to the bone. He approached with caution.

"Alex?" Ellabell's voice distracted him. She was standing in the cell behind Vincent, peering out through the small, barred opening in the middle of the door.

Vincent smiled wearily. "Just protecting your dear love, Alex," he said, firing off a bolt of jet-black energy that hit a sprinting attacker square in the chest, freezing him instantly. "Things have taken something of a turn."

Alex jogged toward them, one eye cautiously assessing Agatha in case she decided to suddenly launch an attack at him instead. Fortunately, she didn't seem to remember any former animosity toward Alex. "What happened here?" he asked.

In between shots that kept dropping assailing criminals to their knees, Vincent began to shed some light on what had been going on in Alex's absence.

"Alypia, I'm sad to say, has managed to escape," the necromancer said. "I went to attend to her one day, and before I could stop her, she had woven her mind control into my brain, and I was helpless to do anything but obey. I was already under her grasp when you were last here, but there was a little spark in these old bones. I had a second wind when she threatened Ellabell—I fought like a demon. Of course, by then, it was much too late—she was gone."

Alex frowned, trying to let it all sink in. It had been his greatest fear, and it had come true. Alypia was free again, and there was no telling what devastation she could cause if they didn't catch up with her soon and put her away again, for good.

"Do you know where she is?" Alex asked.

Vincent shook his head. "I'm afraid not, dear boy. She ran from me, and she has continued to evade me in my search. I have scoured high and low for a sign of her, but she has not been very forthcoming. Once she saw I had returned to my ordinary self, she took off. I didn't see where."

"Do you think she's still in the keep?" Aamir chimed in, casting a sharp spear of golden light toward a knife-wielding individual who had been making a beeline for Alex.

Vincent shrugged. "I cannot be sure. She let all of these prisoners out as she went, and we have been dealing with them ever since. She weakened the barrier as well, so that the red fog was not released. It seems she knew exactly where the worst of the prisoners were being held."

It wasn't what Alex wanted to hear.

"So she could be anywhere," he muttered. Everything seemed to be falling apart in front of his eyes, crashing down like dominoes.

Worse than that, if Alypia was on the loose, that meant

they were all in very real trouble. Not from the onslaught of marauding criminals, but from the potential of what Alypia could do. If she was out and free, all she had to do was sound the alarm, and Julius would be hurtling down upon them before they could make a move to escape.

He could only hope that the continuation of the assailants, and the ongoing haze of the keep's barrier, meant that Julius wasn't imminently on his way. Alex had seen how quickly the king could be summoned, and it appeared that no such message had reached him—not yet, anyway.

With a sudden jolt of realization, Alex understood how he might better pinpoint Alypia's position. There was only one place the Headmistress would go in order to restore the power that had been taken away from her.

"We have to get to the portal," Alex said, taking off down the hallway.

"Wait for us!" Ellabell yelled, as Vincent let her loose from the cell, but he had already gone. He didn't have time to wait for them; he just hoped that the sound of footsteps he could hear on the flagstones behind him were those of his friends.

With a look of abject horror, Alex skidded to a halt at the end of the corridor that connected the courtyard to the rest of the keep. The others jogged up behind him—Ellabell, Aamir, Vincent, and Agatha. The shock registered on their faces, too, as they all looked ahead. Where there should have been a bright portal of glowing light leading to Stillwater House, there was nothing but a solid, impenetrable wall.

Alypia had gone home, and she had closed the route behind her.

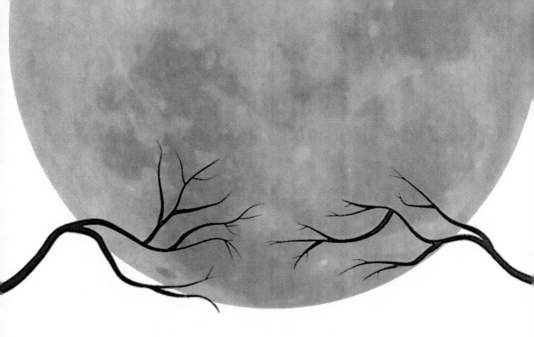

CHAPTER 23

"She's gone back to Stillwater," Alex muttered.

"She might be trying to get a message to Julius," Vincent suggested. The necromancer was being held up by Agatha's surprisingly strong arms.

Ellabell frowned. "Couldn't she do that here?"

"Not if she wanted to send something specific. The royals have a means of communicating with one another, but it seems to be personal to each haven curator—I have never witnessed Caius do it, but I am aware that there is a way," Vincent explained.

Whatever it was Alypia needed in order to summon her father to Stillwater, Alex knew that was precisely what she would be headed for.

"We need to get there as quickly as possible," Alex stated.

"We could fly?" Ellabell gestured in the direction of the turret, where the Thunderbird roosted.

"Storm can only handle three people at most," Alex replied. He was determined to drag Alypia back here and see her locked away for good, but that meant the gateway would have to be rebuilt. He unfastened the sack of essence from his shoulders, and opened the drawstrings, taking a look inside.

"Aamir, do you remember how to build a portal, from the way Lintz did it?" he asked.

Aamir nodded. "I should be able to figure it out."

"Good. I'm going to need you to reopen the portal to Stillwater, while Ellabell and I go on ahead. We'll meet you there," Alex said, leaving no room for negotiation.

"With pleasure." Aamir took the bag of essence from Alex.

"We'll keep these rapscallions at bay!" Agatha whooped, though Vincent didn't seem quite as enthusiastic.

"We shall certainly do our best not to let any miscreants sneak through after you," Vincent said with a dry smile.

The trio looked like a paltry defense squad, but Alex

245

knew there was more power between them than met the eye.

"If you need to use the essence to defend yourselves and the portal, you do it, okay?" Alex insisted.

Aamir smiled. "Always the worrier. You needn't be—the three of us have got this. Go on, there's no time to lose."

Patting his friend hard on the back, Alex took off down the hallway, with Ellabell sprinting close beside him. They ducked and weaved away from the remaining attackers, though their numbers seemed to be dwindling. They passed small piles of sleeping individuals, who had evidently been on the receiving end of Agatha and Vincent's wrath. Alex's thought of the shiv-wielding ruffians sparked into his mind—there would be more prisoners to contend with. Hopefully, the necromancer and the wild-eyed hippie would see to them, in due course.

Heading back up to the turret, Alex and Ellabell took the steps three at a time, bursting out onto the open platform, their cheeks red with exertion. Storm chirped and rested on her haunches without seeking their permission first. There was a glimmer of understanding in her eyes, as if she knew there was only one reason they would be sprinting so fast.

"We need to go to Stillwater," Alex said, pausing in front of her.

Storm chirruped, dipping her head in acknowledgement.

"Thank you," Alex whispered, stroking the smooth

feathers of her face before jumping up onto her back in one smooth, expert movement. He was getting good at this flying business. Ellabell seemed to be too, as she took hold of the protrusions by Storm's shoulders and pulled her knees up like a jockey.

A moment later, they were diving from the turret, then rising on a hot current of air. The next minute, they were speeding along, Alex recognizing the familiar feeling that came just before they slipped through a barrier between realms. It was like spinning too fast on an amusement park ride, a great pressure rising through the body, pushed outwards by the centrifugal force. Everything felt heavy and light, all at once, as if he were about to be flung away at any second, like a ragdoll.

With the stretch and strain of the landscape, Storm emerged into a world that set Alex's nerves on edge. It seemed like forever ago that they had made their escape from this place, from the cruel beauty of Stillwater House. Below, the vast lake sparkled, shrouding the sight of the skulls beneath the water. It didn't make them any less visible to Alex's mind as they swooped low, passing across it, the steady beat of Storm's wings rippling the surface.

The bright walls of Stillwater rushed ever closer, the white stone adorned with vibrant flowers. Their perfume clung to Alex's senses, reviving his memories of the school.

It hadn't changed at all—it was still one of the most stunning buildings he had ever seen, resting close to the shore of the sparkling lake. It was only the inside that was ugly.

Storm curved upward, landing on the outer battlements of the villa, her talons crumbling the stone edge. She had landed just above the training courtyard, where Alex and Jari had caught sight of Helena for the first time, and it was a bittersweet return. For a short while, they had found safety for the first time since setting foot through the gate of Spellshadow Manor, but Alex knew it could never have lasted. Careful not to put a foot wrong, he got down from Storm's back, reaching out to steady Ellabell as she teetered on the ledge.

"We should get to Helena—she'll know where her mother might go," he whispered, glancing at the courtyard below. There didn't seem to be any movement in the cloisters that framed the square, nor did any voices float up from the hallways beyond. It made Alex nervous, not knowing what state the school was in; he couldn't gauge a thing from the walls.

"Hopefully, we got here ahead of her," Ellabell said.

Alex sighed. "I really hope so."

They scrambled down the side of the wall and hurried through the semi-familiar hallways of Stillwater House, in search of Helena. They came across nobody they could ask as they ran through the labyrinth, heading for the refectory.

In any school, be it ordinary or magical, Alex assumed it was almost a guarantee that there would be people in the cafeteria. On the surface, nothing seemed amiss. There was no clash of energies, or shouts of warring students—just a disconcerting peace that drifted throughout the place.

Alex and Ellabell burst through the doors of the refectory. A series of surprised faces turned in their direction. If Alypia was here, it didn't appear the Headmistress had created too much chaos. Nobody seemed to be jumping into action, which gave Alex hope that they were not too late. The most surprised faces were those of Natalie and Jari, their expressions quickly turning to ones of delight as they saw their dear friends. Helena was there too, though she was in deep conversation with a red-haired girl who looked extremely familiar. It was only when Natalie nudged her in the arm that Helena turned her attention to the new arrivals.

"Alex? Ellabell? How did you get here?" the silver-haired girl asked, charging over to them. "Not that I'm not pleased to see you, it's just that we didn't receive a message of your arrival."

Alex grimaced. "No, you wouldn't have. We got here another way—I'll explain later. Right now, we need to search this place from top to bottom. Your mother is here. She escaped from Kingstone and closed the portal behind her. Aamir is building another one, but we need to get to Alypia before she summons her father," he explained in rapid fire.

Helena's face fell. "She's here?"

"That's our guess. There's nowhere else she could have gone," said Ellabell. "Do you know where she might go, to call her father?"

Helena nodded. "Follow me. There's only one place she could go to contact Julius."

As Helena strode toward the doors of the refectory, Alex glanced back at the room, and marveled at the numbers within. It seemed that most of the student body was gathered in one place, and all appeared to be rallying to the cause. And, although they were still striking in their appearance, Alex felt as if they'd lost some of the otherworldly sheen that had been placed upon them, shrouding the real beauty beneath. All except Helena herself, who was just as beautiful as she had been when they had parted ways, though he knew better than to vocalize that particular thought.

"You managed to rally them all?" Alex asked as they sped along.

Helena nodded. "Those who wouldn't comply are in the school dungeons." The comment took Alex aback for a moment; this wasn't the same sweet-natured girl they had left behind, and Alex wondered what newfound darkness lay beneath her pretty surface.

"You locked them up?" said Ellabell, dumbfounded.

The silver-haired girl looked bashful for a second. "Only if they were being truly disruptive," she replied, her voice softening. "Most came around to the idea pretty easily, once my mother's magic began to wear off, but there were a few who flat-out refused to join the cause. Rather than have them running off, telling someone who might try to stop us, I felt it best to put them away. They are safe, and are being well taken care of, I assure you. I have not turned into my mother." She smiled, and Alex could see that it was the truth. Nothing in her was twisted up, the way it was on her mother's face.

"You had me worried for a moment there," Alex said.

"I'm still me," Helena assured him.

Jari bounded in front of Alex, evidently trying to distract him from his lady love. "How are things at Falleaf, anyway? Don't keep us in suspense, dude!"

Alex smiled tightly. "It's been… weird. Hadrian has been helping us out, but things have gotten tense. We found the book, but the spell requires the blood of a royal. I tried to get Venus to come down to see Hadrian, but Julius came with her. Needless to say, it all got messed up, and we are still shy several drops of royal blood."

"But you have the book?" Natalie asked.

Alex nodded. "There were challenges to complete, but we made it through, and we got it. It's at Falleaf now—we thought it'd be better off there for now, until we're ready. There are too many places it could go missing."

"Would Helena's blood not work?" she wondered.

Alex glanced between Natalie and Helena. "What do you mean?"

"Well, she has royal blood running in her veins, right? Could you not simply use her blood instead?" Natalie elaborated.

Alex shook his head. "It's not just any royal blood, actually. The book said it had to be from the king or queen."

"That's a shame. I'd have been happy to donate whatever you needed," Helena said remorsefully.

She wasn't the only one feeling regret. Surely, the blood running in the king and queen's veins was the same blood that ran in Helena's, or at least similar enough. Alex kept the idea in his mind, just in case it became the only option they had.

"Lintz didn't make it out of the place where we got the book, by the way," Alex murmured, knowing it had to be said. A gasp went up from the others. "He gave his life so we could have it."

"No! No, not the professor!" Jari yelped.

"Lintz is dead?" Natalie whispered, her eyes glittering with new-sprung tears. "How can he be dead? Did someone kill him? You tell me who did this and I will—"

Alex cut her off gently. "It was voluntary. He did it because there was no other option... I still can't believe he's really gone. I keep expecting to turn around and find him there, tinkering away with some bit of clockwork."

"Lintz was a good guy... a true hero. One of the best," Jari added solemnly, wiping his eyes.

Alex nodded. "He was, and it's because of what he did, because of the book, that we were coming here in the first place, Helena—to see if you knew of any way to infiltrate the royal circle, so we might get our hands on some of the queen's blood," Alex explained. "We figured Julius would be too tricky, so we thought Venus might be our best target. If we hadn't run into the carnage that's still going on at Kingstone, that's what we'd have been doing." He sighed reluctantly.

"Wait, what carnage?" Helena asked, another troubled expression darkening her face.

Alex nodded. "We have people taking care of it, but there are a lot of prisoners on the loose. I kind of hoped we could all help clear up the mess, once we get your mother back into custody. If Aamir manages to get the portal back open, it shouldn't be too difficult to take back control."

"Do you think she killed my messengers?" Helena whispered, her voice laced in sadness.

"In order to conceal her arrival at Stillwater House,

I wouldn't put it past her," Ellabell murmured, resting a friendly hand on Helena's shoulder.

Helena's pale eyes flashed with sudden steeliness. "They were just kids. This can't be allowed to go unpunished— none of this can."

The silver-haired girl quickened her pace, with Alex and the others hurrying to keep up. Glancing around, Alex realized where they were headed, and knew it would have been his first port of call too. It was the route he had taken a few times before, after being booted out of Alypia's glass office.

A shiver ran up his spine as he pictured Alypia with her torn face, creeping her way through the old hallways she undoubtedly knew like the back of her hand. While they had been discussing tactics and maneuvers, Alypia had been slithering from shadow to shadow through Stillwater, in search of vengeance, wanting to bring down the royal rage upon the unruly havens.

Alex just hoped their time hadn't run out.

CHAPTER 24

ELENA STORMED UP THE STEPS TOWARD THE VAST double doors that led onto the office. She didn't bother to knock, just pushed them wide open. Alex and the others followed her.

Alex had forgotten how beautiful Alypia's office was, with the early evening glow of fading sunlight pouring in through the endless windows. Exotic trees and coiling vines still grew in abundance, showing off the plump fruit that had swollen to ripeness in the heat, though it was clear they had been somewhat neglected of late. Where ordinarily they would have been trimmed and primped, the plants were overgrowing, the creepers and roots stretching toward the huge marble desk that stood in front of the lake-view window. On one tree, Alex saw a lemon that looked about the size of a baby's head. Evidently, nobody was keeping up with the caretaker duties, not even Siren Mave.

I refuse to think about her, he told himself as he edged farther into the room.

He froze.

There was something moving among the trees. It was hard to make out at first, but a shard of sunlight revealed the unmistakable sheen of impossibly white hair.

Alypia lunged toward the desk, where the top drawer lay open, revealing a large red orb within. Not knowing who had been coming, Alypia had clearly thought she could hide until they left again, but upon seeing that it was Alex and his friends, she must have realized she had been backed into a corner, and she had left her treasure out in the open. The object she seemed intent on reaching looked like the biggest ruby Alex had ever seen, attached to a frame of metalwork that had been shaped to look like a queen bee, with golden wings emerging from the multifaceted surface.

Before Alypia could reach the gem, however, Helena had darted forward and snatched it away.

"Give me that!" Alypia snarled.

"You will not ruin everything, not this time," Helena

replied fiercely.

"You think these idiots are your friends? They would betray you in a heartbeat, if it meant they could get what they wanted," Alypia spat. "You have always been naïve, Helena, but I never thought you would end up being such a disappointment. You are every bit your father's daughter—he was weak, just like you."

"At every turn, you meet the world with cruelty and violence," Helena hissed, her voice trembling. "Where you should show compassion, you show disdain. Where you should have taught me empathy, you taught me to manipulate. Perhaps I am more like my father, and I am glad to be so!"

"That is precisely what he would have said!" Alypia snapped. "He made you soft, spoiling you, coddling you. It was hardly a surprise that he got himself killed for his kindness. I made you tough. You think you could stand here now, trying to face off against me, if I had not taught you to be fearless?"

Helena glowered. "You have had nothing to do with making me the woman I am today. Maybe that's why you hated my father so much—because he loved me and treasured me in a way yours never could! You're both as heartless as each other."

Alex watched as angry tears sprang to Helena's eyes,

but it didn't look like she was backing down anytime soon. Leadership suited her, and had clearly given her a taste for strength. Mother and daughter circled one another, stepping out of the way of the tangled roots that snaked across the floor.

"Give me that orb!" Alypia boomed.

Helena backed away, clutching the ruby queen bee even tighter. "I won't let you run to him, just to bring destruction down on everything we are trying to build. You have all been on this earth too long, and you have forgotten that it belongs to the young. It isn't yours anymore—you had your chance, and you all chose to go to war. Now, it's our turn. Just imagine what might have happened if you'd asked us, if you'd bothered to wonder whether we'd be willing to give up some part of ourselves for the cause of saving everyone. I imagine you'd have been surprised by the response," she said softly.

Whatever effect Alypia's magic had had on the students of Stillwater, Alex could see that it was long gone. In its place, stronger, brighter, bolder students had emerged, if Helena was anything to go by.

"I am your mother," Alypia said, her voice low. "You will hand that over to me, or you will suffer the consequences."

Helena shook her head. "I will not let you summon him."

Without warning, Alypia rose to her full height, twisting

her hands rapidly in the air. Golden light shot from her palms, surging toward Helena, who ducked out of the way just in time. Scorch marks appeared on the wall behind her, where the explosion impacted. Undeterred, Alypia tried again, feeding swift-moving strands of golden energy toward her daughter. This time, they did not miss their mark—they took hold, binding Helena, squeezing her like a boa constrictor.

No matter how tightly the glittering strands were pulled, Helena would not release her hold on the queen bee. Alex stepped up to try to help defend Helena, while Jari crept around one side, approaching the fight from a different direction. Natalie and Ellabell skirted around the opposite edge of the room, trying to form a circle around mother and daughter.

"Stop!" Helena shouted over her shoulder. "This isn't your fight!"

The group stepped back, keeping to the walls, though it wasn't a sight any of them felt comfortable watching. Alypia was, quite literally, squeezing the life out of Helena, her twist of golden magic digging into her daughter's skin.

A violent explosion rippled through the office, sending Alex and the others flying backwards, as the glass overhead shattered into a million pieces, collapsing like shimmering rainfall onto the floor and the people standing beneath.

Ellabell sent up a barrier, covering Natalie, though it didn't manage to reach Jari, who hadn't thought fast enough and had to make do with his arms for protection.

Alex staggered to his feet, not quite able to make out what it was that Helena had done to create the blast, but it had served its purpose. Alypia was on the ground, and the golden threads were no longer binding Helena.

Helena jumped back into action, taking Alypia's brief moment of confusion to strike. Weaving a ball of bristling bronze magic between her hands, she launched a series of missiles at her mother. With each one that hit, Alypia let out a yelp, her hands rising quickly to her face.

Using a gap in Helena's onslaught, Alypia rolled out of the way, tucking herself behind the big marble desk, which was now covered in glass shards.

It was then that Alex noticed something moving beneath the floor, in a slithering motion that made it almost undetectable. He rushed toward Helena and pushed her out of the way. A monstrous creature, forged from magic, erupted from the ground and snapped its jaws at the empty air. As the creature lunged again, a rumble vibrated through the earth, cracking the floor.

This time, Helena was ready for it. She swiped it away, forcing her own magic into the very innards of the being, until it disintegrated in a glittering mass that blew away on the breeze now rushing in from the broken windows. The queen bee device had fallen from Helena's hands as she had hit the ground, but Natalie swooped in and scooped it into her palms. Seeing that the orb was in good hands, the others retreated from the central battle, which was gathering heat— Alex didn't want to get caught in the crossfire.

It appeared mother and daughter were so deep in their fight with one another that the cause had almost been forgotten. Golden shards of light pierced the air as magical artillery sailed from one side of the room to the other, occasionally hitting home, eliciting a cry of pain from mother or daughter whenever it did. But still they struggled on against each other. The whole room thrummed with the spent energy of the two fierce females, a gauzy mist appearing in the air.

Sweat trickled down Helena's face, her forehead slick with the exertion of continuous battle. Alypia wasn't faring much better, damp strands of white hair plastered to her textured cheeks. Alex knew these two would fight it out to the bitter end, their skills evenly matched, despite it seeming as if Alypia had the upper hand. Perhaps all those years of hard training and tough love had finally paid off, at a time when Alypia least desired it. Alex frowned, watching the to and fro of the magic being hurled this way and that; he had a feeling the loser would be the one who slipped up first.

"You would be nothing without me!" Alypia roared as she sent a particularly savage spear of energy toward Helena's shoulder. It glanced off, causing the girl to wince.

"Neither would you!" Helena retorted, taking a brief second to recover from the blow before sending a surging blockade of gleaming electricity in her mother's direction.

Most of it hit the desk harmlessly, but a few sparks fell upon Alypia's skin, causing a sharp intake of breath, as if she had touched something hot. In retaliation, she sent one back, the blockade consuming Helena whole. From within the glittering light that froze her to the spot, Alex saw Helena's body convulse. It was violent and difficult to watch. Even Alypia seemed to show regret as she peered over the lip of the desk, flicking her hand to one side, taking the blockade with it.

The blockade smacked dully into the far wall, narrowly missing Jari, and Helena fell to the ground, collapsing in a heap. If it hadn't been for the tiny rise and fall of her shoulders, Alex would have thought she was dead.

Cautiously, the Headmistress emerged from her hiding spot. Ellabell moved as if to strike, but Alypia raised her hand in warning, keeping the curly-haired girl back. She raised her other hand as Jari mirrored Ellabell's movement, his body freezing like a statue. The warning was enough. Taking her time, Alypia approached the barely moving figure of her daughter. As it was, nobody dared to make any move toward her. There was an eerie impropriety in the idea of attacking the mother as she was coming to the slow aid of her daughter. It didn't matter that Alypia was responsible for Helena's current state—her concerned, pained expression of remorse said everything. When all was said and done, she was still a mother who loved her daughter, despite what the daughter might think.

Had it been in any other circumstance, Alex thought it might have been a touching moment, but he could not quite remove the image of the pair of them sending vicious bolts of magic at one another in a genuine attempt to inflict grievous bodily harm. Neither of them had been pulling any punches.

Slowly, Alypia knelt beside her daughter.

"Helena?" she whispered. "Helena, can you hear me?"

The girl was silent, her eyes closed.

"Helena, my sweet girl—please, wake up," Alypia urged, still ignoring the group of individuals who were watching the scene play out, their minds filled with the worst-case scenario. "Let's not fight anymore. If you wake up, I promise we won't fight anymore."

Helena mumbled something, but Alex couldn't make out the words.

"What did you say, my dearest?" Alypia asked, bending

closer to her daughter, enveloping the girl in her arms.

"I said, I am not done fighting," Helena whispered, her head snapping up. With sudden force, she reached up to her mother's temples and forced her magic through the skull beneath. Her intent was clear, and Alex just hoped she knew what she was doing, messing around in the minds of others. Alypia began to spasm in her daughter's arms, and then she crumpled, her knees buckling and her pale eyes going blank. She fell to the floor, her head landing on the ground with a dull thud.

Alypia lay there, completely still, devoid of feeling or movement. It was akin to the catatonic state that Alex had seen Caius in, when he had raced from the clutches of the keep. Whether or not she would wake up from this sleep, he had no idea. Caius hadn't, so why should Alypia?

"It had to be done," Helena whispered, her voice tinged with heartbreak. A vacant look appeared in her eyes too, though it had not been brought on by any blow to the head.

And, though Alex knew she was right, he worried that the price for her capture was too high for the daughter who had paid it.

CHAPTER 25

NOBODY SAID A WORD FOR A LONG TIME AS Helena knelt on the floor, a mirror image of the position her mother had been in moments before. With shaking hands, the girl pulled Alypia to her, but no amount of nudging or whispering could make the still form move.

"I had to… I had to do this," Helena said, rocking back and forth. She looked up at Alex and the others, her eyes panicked and desperate. Jari dropped to her side, grabbing her hand, and she clutched his fingers as if she were drowning.

Natalie knelt down beside her. "Yes. You did what you had to."

Ellabell and Alex stood apart. Alex's fists clenched at the sight of Helena so broken. He remembered when they had first met her and she had sung her mother's praises—a result of the mind-altering magic, no doubt, but there might have been some honesty to it, once upon a time.

"We should take Alypia back to Kingstone," Alex said softly.

Helena looked up, tears in her eyes. "No, I won't leave her there."

"It's the only place we'll be able to keep her safe," Alex said, though he wasn't entirely sure of that anymore. There was no telling what state the prison would be in when they returned.

She shook her head. "There are cells here at Stillwater where she will be just as safe. There are people I trust here, who can watch over her—I do not know these people you know, at Kingstone Keep. I cannot trust them as you do. You said so yourself—that criminals are running riot. To take her back there would be to put her in harm's way."

"As long as you trust she won't be able to escape again, at least until all of this is over," Alex murmured.

She flashed him a look of hurt. "I doubt she will be going anywhere anytime soon."

"No, I suppose not," said Alex reluctantly.

With a visible shiver, she shook the sad expression from her face, replacing it with a mask of bravery. "I shall see to it that my mother is kept secure for the duration of the battles that will lie ahead, but there is more we must do—you said something about calling my grandmother down?"

Alex nodded, knowing it was a bad time to make such requests. "We need to get Venus to come to us, alone, unless you know where the king and queen live?"

"If I go to them, they will suspect something," Helena replied. "I go once a year, when summoned. It would not be taken well if I were to simply show up."

Natalie glanced at her friend thoughtfully. "So, we will have to use *that* to get her to come to us?" she asked, pointing toward the ruby bee that Ellabell still clutched in her hands.

Helena nodded. "In theory, but I won't lie—it will be difficult to get my grandmother on her own. Julius doesn't like to let her out of his sight, given their history. I think he lives in fear of her being snatched up by a wandering Romeo," Helena said wryly.

Alex realized this was precisely the reason calling Venus to Falleaf had failed so spectacularly; he hadn't taken into account the strength of Julius's neuroses. Of course the king wouldn't let his queen go off on her own, not after what had presumably happened the last time he did. Virgil was no doubt a constant reminder of that.

"How does it work?" Jari asked, peering curiously at the scarlet orb.

"It works like a coded messenger, I suppose," Helena explained. "You feed your magic into it, tell it what you want to say, and it encrypts the message before sending it to the recipient. I think Julius has four at his end, but the havens must only have one each, though I've only seen my mother's."

Alex nodded. "Would you be able to get a message to Venus, pretending to be your mother, or would Julius still come along for the ride?"

"It's hard to say," said Helena. "Ordinarily, the only people whose call Venus would answer alone would be my mother's or Virgil's, what with them being her kids, but I can't make any promises."

"They're not bad odds—better than the Falleaf ones," Alex said, hoping to raise the optimism of the others in the room. "So we could get her to come to Stillwater, and get everyone into battle positions while we're waiting."

Ellabell spoke up, loosening her white-knuckle grip on the ruby bee. "Wouldn't it be better if we called her to Spellshadow? I imagine, knowing what we know about Julius, he would be far less likely to join his wife there, given his hatred for Virgil," she said. "I don't think he'd want to spend any time around the dirty royal secret."

Helena nodded. "You could be onto something there."

"I hadn't thought of that," said Alex, knowing it was probably the best chance they had. It was true—of all the havens, Spellshadow was the one the king was most likely to avoid. Plus, it would mean they'd have the Head and the royal blood in one place, making the preparation for the counter-spell much easier. "You think Virgil will have one of these things in his office somewhere?" Alex asked, gesturing toward the device.

"I think it's a very strong possibility," Helena replied.

Alex smiled. "Then that's what we're going to have to go with," he said. "If you send for your grandmother, pretending to be Virgil, using the device that will hopefully be in Virgil's office, we can infiltrate the manor and do a clean sweep. When she arrives, we can attack and take both Virgil and Venus into custody at once. It'll give us enough time to get prepared, and to try to rally some of the Spellshadow students to the cause."

"Sounds like a good plan to me!" Jari whooped. The others nodded in agreement.

"Although, we may have to meet the rest of you at Spellshadow by coming through from Falleaf, instead of coming through from Stillwater," Ellabell said.

Alex frowned. "How so?"

"We need to make sure Kingstone is secure again—failing that, we need to at least make sure that we get Aamir, Vincent, and Agatha out, and see if Hadrian can offer the latter two a bit of sanctuary after their long incarceration. Hadrian will want to know what's going on too. He might be able to offer some assistance," she explained.

Alex nodded. In his excitement, he had almost forgotten that they were still waiting on Aamir and the Kingstone duo.

"You might want to pick Demeter up on the way," said Natalie with a concerned expression.

Alex had simply presumed the auburn-haired teacher was otherwise occupied with training students, or imparting his Spellbreaker knowledge on unwilling ears, but it appeared there was more to the man's absence than met the eye.

"Where is he?" Alex asked.

"Demeter went through to Spellshadow several days ago. He was intending to meet up with you at Falleaf, but I am guessing he hadn't managed it by the time you left?" Natalie said, her brow furrowed.

Alex shook his head. "He wasn't there when we traveled to Kingstone, though he might have arrived while we've been gone. I'm sure he's fine, wherever he is."

"I really hope so," murmured Natalie.

"I'm sure he made it through just as we left, and this is

nothing more than a case of really bad timing," he assured her. "We'll head back through to Falleaf, via Kingstone, picking up our various strays as we go, and update Hadrian on what is going on."

"Do you think we should send troops through to Kingstone, to help clear it?" Helena asked, a look of determination appearing on her face.

Alex shook his head. "I think we should scope out the state of it first. If it's a lost cause, I'll remove the portal between it and here, and leave it to destroy itself. There are too many strong mages running free in there; I wouldn't want to waste our resources on a fight we can't win."

"But what if someone gets word to Julius?" Ellabell said, her voice worried.

"If I know anything about Caius, he will have kept his messenger device in the gatehouse, way beyond the walls of the keep," Alex replied. "The only way they will be able to call Julius is by triggering the barrier, the way we did, which may not be a bad thing. If we can distract the king, we might be able to buy ourselves more time."

It was an idea he had been toying with. If they couldn't fight the newly escaped criminals and restore order to Kingstone Keep themselves, perhaps a visit from the king would be just what the doctor ordered. As crazed as many of them were, nobody dared defy the strength of Julius. He would have everyone back in their cells and toeing the line far quicker than Alex and his friends could, and, as long as he didn't suspect anything unusual in the other havens, Alex had a feeling they might just get away with it.

"How will we know when to meet, if the portal gets closed?" Helena asked, glancing down at the vacant face of her mother.

"Let's say we meet at Spellshadow in two days' time, in the walled gardens at the back of the manor. Natalie and Jari know where it is," Alex suggested. "In two days, we can rally more troops, if possible, giving us a bigger force to take the two royals down."

"And if you can't, we'll have to be enough!" Jari grinned.

Alex had missed the effervescent nature of his friend, and realized they had barely even said hello to one another. In the fracas of Alypia's stealthy escape, their reunion had been forgotten. Even now, it didn't seem as if there would be time to properly catch up with one another.

"We can take them on, right?" Natalie smiled.

Alex nodded. "If anyone can, it's us."

"We should get my mother into one of the cells. Hopefully, Aamir will have opened the portal from Kingstone by the time we are done," Helena said, breaking the moment of levity as she cradled her mother to her.

"Of course," promised Alex. He bent to help the girl

lift Alypia up. It was strange to see the formerly powerful Headmistress dangling limply, no sign of consciousness visible in her eyes. As much as Alex was glad of it, knowing they could stop worrying about Alypia hounding them in their future tasks, he couldn't help feeling sorry for Helena, who was clearly struggling.

Silent tears trickled down Helena's face as she forged a cushion of golden light beneath her mother, taking the strain away from Alex's shoulders as the woman's body lifted up horizontally, the way she had done with Aamir upon their first meeting. Alex let go. The strength of the magic carried Alypia with ease, and Helena floated her toward the double doors of the shattered office. Barely a shard of glass remained in the roof, the raw breeze rushing in, shaking the leaves of the overgrown plants and trees. Alex cast a glance back at the scene as they departed. For some reason, he had a feeling he would never return to this place, one way or another.

Turning his back on the vision of the lake, the glittering graveyard that held his ancestors beneath the surface, Alex followed Helena, the others falling into line with the solemnity of a funeral procession.

They remained that way, following the royal princess down into the belly of Stillwater House, to the underground cells where they had themselves been kept, what seemed like forever ago. Young, pale faces appeared at the grates in the doors, quiet voices pleading to be set free. It was unsettling, but Alex understood why Helena had placed them in here.

"Helena, I take it all back. I'll follow your lead! I'll fight the system. Just let me out!" a girl with raven hair begged, but there was little sincerity in her expression.

"Me too! I was an idiot. I should have listened—of course we are being oppressed. I will fight. I'm ready to fight!" a young man with a strong jaw added, pushing his face between the bars. There was a wildness to him that Alex didn't trust one bit.

No matter what they said, or how they pleaded, Helena ignored them all. Her mind was elsewhere. It was evident in the palpable reluctance in her movements as she opened one of the cells at the far end of the dimly lit corridor and ushered the floating figure of Alypia inside.

With great care, she set her mother down on the floor and removed the cushion of light from beneath her, snapping it back into her palms. Tenderly, she picked up a moth-eaten blanket and wrapped it around Alypia's floppy form, tucking it around her motionless chin. Alex watched, feeling strange about sharing such an intimate moment, as Helena leaned in to kiss her mother gently on the forehead. A moment later, he saw her mouth move as she whispered something nobody else was meant to hear.

With that, she stood, brushing the dust from her legs.

"We should go. We can't waste any more time on senti-ment—there will be a moment for that when we have freed everyone from the clutches of the Great Evil," Helena said boldly, keeping the tremor from her voice.

Alex nodded. "Ellabell and I will set off for Kingstone. Let's just hope we can stop Aamir before he opens the portal. For once, we have to hope he's not as efficient as usual."

With that, they set off toward the abandoned quarter of the villa. They were almost at the point of no return, and one thing was for certain: nothing was ever going to be the same again.

CHAPTER 26

STORM LED THE DUO SAFELY BACK TO THE TURRET OF Kingstone Keep, though it became apparent that nothing had changed within the prison. The roar of incensed prisoners could be heard even before they set foot into the main body of the keep, and they had to be cautious as they crept through the hallways. The piles of sleeping bodies that Alex had passed on his way out of the keep had disappeared, but he was fairly certain it wasn't because they had been returned to their cells. There were too many people running wild for that to be the case.

Speeding up, they reached the hallway that led down

to the open courtyard, dodging an artillery of magic that surged from the hands of Vincent and Agatha.

"Hey! It's us!" Alex shouted, ducking out of the way of a golden spear.

"Alex? Ellabell?" Vincent shouted, peering through the glimmering mist of spent magic that had filled the corridor between them.

"Yes, ceasefire!"

"Goodness, I am sorry," Vincent said. "We have simply been shooting at anything that moves. As you can see, things have continued to get out of hand." He frowned, his black eyes showing his displeasure at the state of affairs.

"It looks like it," Ellabell remarked, as Agatha shot a bolt of magic over her shoulder, striking a one-eyed man square in the forehead and sending him scarpering away.

Alex hurried toward Aamir, who was halfway through the portal build. It was impressive to behold, the shimmering strands crisscrossing, the oval of the portal taking shape. Alex almost felt bad that he had to stop the process, midway through.

He tapped Aamir on the shoulder. "You can stop now," he said.

Aamir turned, his eyes wide with surprise. "You're back?"

"Don't sound too enthusiastic." Alex grinned.

"No, not at all, I was just expecting you to be coming this way," he said, nodding toward the half-finished portal.

"There was a change of plans," said Alex apologetically. "We should probably save whatever you haven't used," he added, looking down at the open bag of essence that lay on the floor.

"Were you too late?" Aamir asked anxiously.

Alex shook his head. "No, we got to her in time. I don't think she'll be bothering us again for a while," he said solemnly, trying to push the image of Alypia's blank, ghoulish face from his head. "We were hoping we could get back to you before you finished."

Aamir smiled. "I was a long way off, I think, though I haven't done too badly. Are we leaving it closed?"

"For now," Alex said. "I don't think we can fix this place. It's probably best we leave it to somebody who can."

"Who did you have in mind?"

"Julius," Alex admitted. "If I can break a barrier module on the way out, it'll hopefully bring him to fix this mess. If he doesn't come, then this place will just go to the dogs."

"*Lord of the Flies.*" Aamir smiled.

"Something like that."

"So we definitely don't need this portal anymore?" Aamir asked.

"Definitely not—we're meeting the others at

Spellshadow, but we're going to go around the other way," Alex explained.

With a smile on his face, Aamir pressed his palms into the center of the woven structure, allowing his magic to flow through the strands. Had it been complete, Alex knew the energy would have melded together and imploded to reveal the landscape of Stillwater beyond. In its half-complete state, the energy didn't meld as it should, but disintegrated instead, the strands falling to the stone floor like confetti. They broke apart as they hit the ground, spreading out in an almost liquid trickle before being absorbed into the earth.

"Are we heading back to Falleaf?" Aamir asked.

Alex nodded. "Yeah—we'd better take that bag with us. We're going to need it."

Aamir rolled his eyes. "*More* portal-building?"

"You got it," Alex chuckled, scooping up the sack of essence.

Joining with Ellabell, Vincent, and Agatha, Alex quickly brought the two Kingstone denizens up to date with what was going on, and what the plan of action was where they were concerned. It was clear they needed to get out of Kingstone, if they were to survive, and Alex was more than happy to provide the escape route. Once the pair of them were fully briefed, the group began to make their way through the keep, toward the spot where Lintz had constructed the portal to Falleaf. Alex remembered what the professor had said about it being easier to open up an already existing gateway, and he was determined to get the others back to Falleaf as quickly as possible.

"Where are we off to? Are we having an adventure, cherubs?" Agatha asked, her eyes glancing around as if in a daze.

"We're going somewhere safe," Ellabell said, her tone soothing.

The aging hippie clapped her hands together in delight. "Well, how very exciting! Did you hear that, Vincent? We're going on an adventure!"

"Indeed we are, dear heart." The necromancer smiled.

"I'm not even sure I remember what the outside world looks like, cherubs. If I see a tree, I am fairly sure I shall explode with joy!" Agatha said enthusiastically, while firing shots at anyone who tried to catch them off guard. She seemed to have a sixth sense about it, able to fire off a bolt of defensive magic before anyone else was even aware that there was an enemy in their midst.

They moved in formation, the five of them walking along in a pentagonal shape, ensuring all bases were covered and nobody could sneak up on them or catch them unawares. At every turn and every opened door, Alex braced himself for the impact of wild-eyed prisoners. Down one narrow corridor, a swarm of individuals, their teeth sharpened to jagged points, rushed at the quintet. Alex and his friends pooled their resources, binding their energies together into one fearsome blockade of energy. The core was silver and black, surrounded by the golden swell of the others' magic, and it exploded with an ear-splitting blast as it hit the charging assailants, sending them sprawling back. To Alex's relief, they stayed down, utterly disoriented. All they were missing were little birds spinning around their heads.

Heading down another hallway, which appeared silent and safe, a shrieking woman shrouded in a black cloak jumped down from the rafters, knocking Aamir flat on his back. She pummeled his chest, howling close to his face, her eyes spooked.

"You traitor! You betrayed me, you coward!" she screamed, clawing at Aamir's neck. The older boy fought to defend himself against her, but her strength was borderline supernatural.

The others jumped into action, trying to haul the screaming woman off their friend. Alex reached forwards and touched the side of her head, feeding his anti-magic into her skull, but the images that came back to him were too upsetting and too alarming to stay there for long. He saw the betrayal of which she spoke. A lover had persuaded her to perform a heist, and she had done as he had asked, only for him to run away when the authorities came, leaving her to shoulder the full weight of the law. Her grief was overwhelming, and Alex could feel it melting through into his own veins as he struggled to find a happy image to distract her with.

Vincent stepped in just as Alex was losing his grip on her mind. It was impossible to sift through the tangle of misery, and try as he might, Alex couldn't find anything happy within the woman's head. It was all tainted with heartbreak. With a flicker of white light, the necromancer twisted his energy into the screaming woman's mind, replacing the tendrils of Alex's. With a final howl, she fell limp in Agatha and Ellabell's arms.

With no time to waste, they dragged her off Aamir and placed her gently down in one of the nearby cells. It would be a long while before she awoke, and Alex just hoped that Vincent had given the poor girl something good to dream about.

That was the thing that constantly surprised him about the keep and its inhabitants. Around every corner, he found himself faced with another dark recess of the human condition, and the struggles people had experienced. It showed him how people continued to endure, even in the hardest circumstances imaginable, when everything else had been taken away. The world either broke a person or made them unbreakable. Alex wondered which side of that he'd be standing on, when all of this came to an end.

Aamir got up, brushing himself off. "I know I have a certain magnetism, but that was too close for comfort," he murmured, though there was a tremor of fear in his voice.

Alex and the others moved onward, their eyes and ears more alert than before. It seemed like a never-ending barrage of attackers and retaliation, Alex's palms growing strangely itchy from persistent use. Each time his anti-magic rippled from his hands, it felt like pins and needles, and yet he forced himself to continue.

Finally, they reached the doorway that led to the spot where Lintz had built the portal to Falleaf. Quickly, they darted inside and closed the door behind them. The whole room held bad memories for Alex, and they came rushing back into his mind. Gulping, he pushed down a rising nausea as his eyes rested on the place where Caius had lain with specters circling around him. Vincent flashed Alex a look of understanding.

"Where did you put Caius?" Alex asked.

"He is in what was formerly my cell," Vincent replied. "The door is locked, on the off chance he rises from his ailment."

"Then we should get on with this," said Alex, opening the bag of essence. Everyone took a bottle, and they began to weave and shape the gateway that would lead them through to Falleaf House, and the veritable sanctuary that lay there. Anywhere was better than here.

They made swift work of building the new portal, made easier by the fact they were opening up an existing connection once more, but Alex's head kept snapping over his shoulder at the smallest sound coming from the corridor beyond the door. He kept expecting someone to burst in, wielding a blade or something worse.

Alex and the others stepped backwards as the portal expanded outwards with a burst of light, revealing the familiar scene of the bronzed forest canopy, the leaves falling softly to the ground. Agatha shrieked in delight as she saw it.

"Is this where we're going?" she asked.

Alex nodded. "This is where you'll be safe."

"Can you believe this, Vincent? We are leaving, at long last!" she cried, tears shining in her eyes.

Alex smiled, not quite realizing until that moment what freedom might mean to Agatha and Vincent. The necromancer wasn't nearly as open with his emotions, but Alex could tell there was a sense of happiness brimming beneath the serene surface of Vincent's face.

"Indeed we are, dear heart. Did you ever think you'd see the day?" Vincent asked, his voice calm.

"I thought I'd die in this hellhole," Agatha cackled. "Even now, I've managed to defy them all!"

"You should hurry through," Alex insisted. "Ellabell and I will follow, just make your way to that willow tree there. Aamir, you know the way, right?" he said, pointing to the draped fronds of the willow where Storm had camouflaged herself. Aamir nodded.

"Why, where are you going?" Vincent wondered.

Alex smiled. "You'll see."

He waited until Agatha, Aamir, and Vincent were safely through the glowing gateway before pressing his palms into the center, drawing the fabric of the threads apart. They crumbled, floating to the stone floor. It was too bitter a memory for Alex, as he envisioned the way Caius must have done exactly what he had just done, blocking his exit.

It's in the past. Caius paid for his betrayal, Alex thought to himself grimly, wishing it hadn't had to be that way. He had longed for the old warden to be as true as he'd seemed, and perhaps he might have been, had he not been so twisted up by grief and loss.

Ellabell took Alex's hand, bringing him back to reality.

"Let's go," she said encouragingly. They crept back out into the hallway, careful to avoid the sound of footsteps coming in their direction.

It seemed the prisoners were elsewhere for the time being, though it didn't prevent Alex from peering around every single corner, convinced something was going to jump out at him. They were almost at the stairs leading to the turret where Storm was waiting when Alex paused beside one of the golden cylinders that controlled the flow of the barrier shrouding Kingstone. The metal casing had been bashed in, to the point where it was dangling from its screws, but whoever had inflicted the damage had been held back by the defensive magic within. Alex wasn't deterred by such things.

"As soon as I do this, we're going to have to run, okay?" he warned.

Ellabell nodded. "I'm ready."

Yanking the rest of the casing off, Alex forged a small blade of anti-magic, and cut the band at the top of the clockwork within, severing the shield. A snapping creature, shaped like a savage hound, pounced from the glittering energy, but Alex and Ellabell were ready for it. While Ellabell distracted it by running around the space, Alex fed his anti-magic toward it in shimmering silver-and-black ribbons, constricting the translucent body. The hound yelped as the energy began to disintegrate its form, until there was nothing left of the shimmering creature.

With the defenses down, Alex turned to the actual clockwork, resting his hands on the mechanisms as he forced a volatile pulse of his energy through the cogs and connectors. There was a loud crack as it broke. Still, Alex knew they were going to need something else to stop the small section of barrier from functioning. Thinking fast, he picked up the dented metal casing and shoved it with all his might into the clockwork, blocking the system. It wasn't quite as elegant as Lintz's beautiful crab-shaped jammers, but Alex hoped it would do the job and bring the king down upon the prison to restore peace.

Not wanting to wait around to see if it had worked, Alex and Ellabell left Kingstone Keep to wrack and ruin, hurrying up the steps of the turret and hopping onto Storm's back. As she flew, Alex made the mistake of looking back, just in time to see a swarm of criminals appear at the lip of one of the other turrets. They were lifting a figure above their heads, and Alex squinted to see who it was.

With a sinking feeling in his stomach, Alex realized Vincent must not have locked the door as well as he'd thought. The limp figure being lifted above the heads of the prisoners was Caius, weakened by the specters and unable to fight back. Alex wished he could turn Storm around, to save the warden from the revenge of the inmates, but it was already too late. With an unceremonious shove, the prisoners threw Caius from the turret.

His limp body plummeted to the ground like a sack of potatoes, hitting the water with an almighty smack that ricocheted toward Alex's ears, even at such a distance. A split second later, an enormous mouth surged upward, enveloping Caius, dragging him below the surface. The moat monster never resurfaced, and nor did the warden. It didn't seem like a fitting end for a man who had been, for the most part, a good soul.

You weren't a bad guy, Alex thought solemnly. *You were consumed by grief. Rest in peace now, Caius—may you be reunited with your true love.*

For the second time that day, Alex had a feeling he would never return to this place, though he was certain the memories would always haunt him.

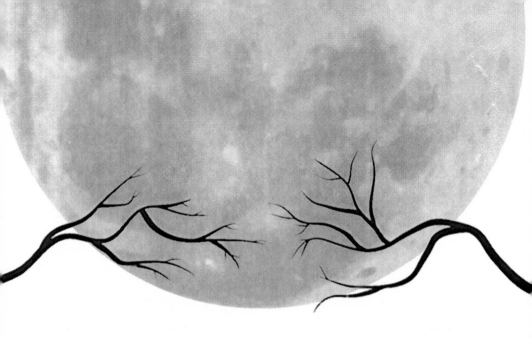

CHAPTER 27

MEETING UP WITH AGATHA, AAMIR, AND
Vincent on the way, Alex led the newly rostered
quintet through the forest, toward the pagoda. It
was second nature now to listen for the buzz and thrum of
the traps that would seek to ensnare them, but Agatha was
something of a liability in this new, fresh setting. She kept
wandering off, bending to pick up a seemingly innocuous
flower or mushroom, only to be stopped just in time by
Alex.

"You mustn't go near anything," he warned. "There are
traps all over this place."

Agatha frowned. "I am sorry, my cherub, you must pardon my enthusiasm. It has been so long since I've felt fresh air on my face, and seen the beauty of a tree, or a flower. I shall attempt to restrain myself, using only my eyes to drink it all in," she promised.

Despite her assurances, Alex and the others had to stop her on several more occasions on their way to the pagoda. She was childlike in her inability to pass something pretty without reaching out to touch it, or squatting down nearby to get a closer look. There was endearing quality to it that prevented Alex from losing his patience. Trying to put himself in her shoes, he wondered how he'd feel if he hadn't seen nature in decades—he imagined it would be more magical than anything he had encountered so far. Real magic would pale in comparison.

He tried to picture himself returning to Middledale after all of this. What had once seemed ordinary and everyday would undoubtedly feel rare and special, but it worried him too—what if he didn't fit in anymore? Would he still belong among ordinary humans, or would he be irrevocably altered by the challenges he'd endured?

Alex shook off his fears, knowing he first had to get out of the magical realm before he could even begin to think about his re-entry into normality. They arrived at the edge of the forest, the pagoda rising up regally from the center of the clearing ahead. Agatha's eyes went wide with amazement, and even Vincent seemed impressed.

"This place is ancient. You can feel the vibrations of its rich history in the air," the necromancer whispered, twirling his long fingers around as if touching the imagined ripples of time. "I imagine it stood long before the mages came along, and shall stand long after they are gone."

"This isn't mage-built?" Aamir asked, frowning thoughtfully.

Vincent smiled a knowing smile. "Few things are, even in these realms. The mages were renowned cherry-pickers, commandeering what they liked the look of, and molding it to their own purpose. I imagine this place belonged to a race far older than mage-kind, though you will likely find no trace they ever existed, save for their architecture and a few stolen treasures."

Alex found himself looking at the pagoda in a different light, wondering what the people who had been here before might have looked like, and what had brought them to this part of the world. Had they been a peaceful race? Had that been their downfall, when the mages came to take their land? He guessed nobody would ever know, unless there was a forgotten history book, tucked away in the library beneath the ground, that spoke of the lost race.

But who would bother to look? he reasoned, his thoughts

turning sad. It made him wonder how many other places the mages had stolen. None of the architecture he'd seen so far seemed to belong to the same style, but that was the truth across the globe.

Seeing a gap in the change of the guard, Alex and the others darted across to the pagoda and emerged beside the kitchen, though there was no comforting clash of crockery or sizzle of something delicious frying in a pan. It was silent. In fact, as they made their way through the pagoda's floors, cautiously peering around every corner, Alex realized the whole place was silent. Where there should have been posted guards, there were none.

It made the climb up to the top floor much easier, but it did nothing to settle Alex's nerves. Reaching the solitary doorway that led into Hadrian's private chambers, Alex pushed on it tentatively, half expecting it to be locked. It wasn't, giving easily.

"Hadrian?" Alex called as they stepped into the open space.

The remnants of a meal lay on the low table in the center of the room, but everything had congealed, looking about as unappetizing as it was possible to be. Whoever had eaten the food had been gone a while.

"Hadrian, are you here?" Alex called again, but there was no reply.

With time running short, and a lot to do in two days, Alex found himself growing frustrated by Hadrian's absence. He needed the royal's help, and he wasn't willing to simply wait around for the man to come back.

Wracking his brain, he thought about where Hadrian might be. He wondered if the man had gone to teach a class, perhaps, in the treehouses that branched off from the central pagoda? If so, Alex knew he wouldn't be able to disturb Hadrian; there weren't any guards in the pagoda, for the time being, but there were plenty out beyond the sanctuary of it. Peering from the window, he could count at least thirty, and they would spot him before he even had the chance to explore the mysterious buildings that nestled in the treetops.

"Where is he?" Ellabell asked, opening all the doors that led off from the central space.

The only other place Alex could think of was the cave in the middle of the forest. "He might have gone to see his sister," Alex replied.

Aamir nodded. "Then let us go. It would be better than waiting around for him to return."

"You took the words right out of my mouth," said Alex, moving back toward the entrance. Time was of the essence, and they needed to figure out what resources they had at their disposal, before that time ran out.

Just then, Alex heard footsteps coming from the back of the room, where the silver fox statue stood proud.

"Hide!" Alex whispered. The group scattered.

CHAPTER 28

AS THE SECRET DOOR AT THE BACK OF THE ROOM slid open, Alex realized he had no reason to fear. They were not soldiers, coming to take Alex and his friends away. The first person to emerge was Hadrian, his head turned over his shoulder as he spoke to someone behind him. That person, stepping into the glowing light of the fifth floor gallery, was Demeter.

They were laughing over a shared joke Alex hadn't heard, and seemed surprisingly friendly with one another. It didn't look like they were strangers, as they moved farther into the room, an easy familiarity flowing between them.

Alex stepped out from his hiding place behind a bulbous vase, and Hadrian jumped out of his skin when he saw him.

"Alex! You m-mustn't creep up on p-people like that!" Hadrian cried, clutching his chest.

Alex smiled. "Sorry, I thought it would be weirder if I stayed hidden."

As if granted permission, the others emerged from their hiding places. Ellabell had been sandwiched between two bookcases. Aamir had ducked down behind a lamp. Agatha had merely stood behind one of the curtains, and Vincent had somehow stayed precisely where he was, yet Alex hadn't noticed him until he stepped forward. The necromancer, it appeared, was something of a chameleon.

"I suppose it's true what they say—absence does make the heart grow bigger!" Demeter grinned, rushing to greet the trio. "And you two—I must say, it's a touch peculiar seeing you both outside the prison walls! Fugitives from the law, very cool. Hadrian was telling me you'd gone to Kingstone, and here I was thinking it'd be quicker for me to get you up to speed if I came the short way round. I should have stayed where I was!" He pulled an eager Agatha and a less-than-willing Vincent into a tight bear hug.

"You came through from Spellshadow?" Alex pressed.

Demeter nodded. "Well, that was the plan, but I got myself into a spot of trouble and it took me longer than expected to get here. I suppose I'm here now, and that's what matters, right?" He smiled brightly. It was a cheerfulness Alex realized he had missed.

Hadrian frowned. "Wait, did you just say f-fugitives?"

Vincent stepped forward, offering his hand. "We are acquaintances of Alex and his friends—we know Demeter extremely well, given the time he spent with us, festering inside the walls of Kingstone Keep. I assure you, we come in peace."

Hadrian visibly relaxed. "Well, any friend of Demeter's is a friend of mine," he said, his expression softening.

"Do you two know each other?" Aamir asked, gesturing at the royal and redhead.

They smiled warmly at one another, clapping each other on the back.

"We certainly do," said Hadrian, grinning. "And it seems my old pal hasn't changed one bit—you're as clumsy as ever. I found him in a trap, struggling to find a way out. Gave me quite a shock on my afternoon stroll. I'm glad I found you first." He chuckled.

Demeter nodded. "Always helping me out of scrapes, this one. We go way back. The two of us were part of a peacekeeping unit during the war, though we were younger then. You're looking a little gray these days," he joked, ruffling Hadrian's white hair.

"I've always been this color." Hadrian grinned. "But yes, we transported refugees out of the magical realms and into the real world. We worked for a unit that tried to protect Spellbreakers too, smuggling them to safer territories, but it didn't do much good in the end. I think we just stretched out their suffering," he said, his voice tinged with remorse.

"Didn't you get caught?" Aamir asked.

Demeter shook his head. "I evaded capture, and the organization I worked for arranged for me to be installed at Stillwater as a teacher, until everything had blown over. When I started telling my stories, I think they began to suspect," he said, shrugging. "Hadrian flew straight under the microscope—nobody thought he had the guts to defy Julius, and so he got away with it. Sly dog!"

"They tried to break Demeter, once they began to suspect what he was. They thought that if they tortured him, they might get some names out of him, but he's always been tight-lipped. He didn't say a word," said Hadrian proudly, though there was sorrow in his eyes too.

Alex wondered if that was why Demeter's head was so muddled, because of the torture he had been put under. It would make sense. After all, Demeter was a smart guy, with a proven track record of intellect, and yet he couldn't for the life of him remember how to piece an idiom together.

"I think they forgot what I was capable of, though."

Demeter laughed. "When they sent me to Kingstone, I used my powers to make everyone believe I was a guard instead of a prisoner. A neat trick, and one of the only things I've ever prided myself on, where my talents are concerned."

"So, why *did* you come through the other way?" Ellabell wondered, changing the subject.

"I wanted to scope out Spellshadow, make sure it was safe to strike," the auburn-haired man explained. "If I hadn't gotten myself trapped, I'd probably have made it here before you left."

"Did anyone see you?" Aamir pressed.

Demeter shook his head. "I promise I didn't raise any checkered flags coming through Spellshadow," he promised, raising his hands solemnly. "I was the stealthiest I have ever been, I swear."

"You think it looks ripe for the picking?" Vincent asked, a hint of curiosity in his strange voice. It was the first time Alex had seen the necromancer show more than a fleeting interest in the realm of Spellshadow Manor.

"I'd say we have as good a chance as we've ever had." Demeter shrugged. "I couldn't see Virgil while I was there, but it doesn't mean he's not around."

"That's precisely why we were looking for you, Hadrian," Alex said, turning his attention to the royal. "We've agreed with Helena and her team to meet at Spellshadow in two days' time, which gives us enough leeway to rally some more troops to the cause. Right now, it's just us and one and a half bags of essence. We could probably do with more hands. Do you think Ceres would help? Maybe we could ask some of the recovered students if they'd like to join us?"

Hadrian shook his head. "I don't think that is such a good idea."

"Why not?" Alex pressed, noticing that Demeter had gone strangely silent.

"I don't want to get them involved, Alex," Hadrian replied, with uncharacteristic strength in his voice. "They have been through enough, and though they would undoubtedly jump at the chance to help, they would not be able to take the strain. They aren't as strong as they once were, but they think they are—a fragile mind is more easily broken than one that is whole."

"Don't you think we should give them the choice?" Ellabell asked.

Agatha nodded. "The girl is right—you should give them the option. It isn't right to take choice away from a person, just because they are weaker than before."

"I won't put them through it," Hadrian insisted, his eyes narrowing. This wasn't like the nervous royal they knew at all; there was a defiant streak emerging. "If they come with you, they will have suffered for so long, only to die anyway.

As the guardian here at Falleaf, they are under my care, and I will do what is best for them." There was no hint of a stutter in his voice, nor were his hands wringing in alarm. Perhaps, Alex thought, this strength had been there all along, it was simply reserved for what the royal deemed a righteous cause.

Alex smiled. "But they aren't at Falleaf, are they?"

Hadrian looked worried for a moment. "They are," he insisted.

"No, they aren't," Alex repeated. "They're hidden away somewhere safe—somewhere Julius and his cronies can't get to them. If they were at Falleaf, Julius would have found them. No... you have found somewhere else to put them, I'm sure of it, somewhere far away from here."

"Even if I had, I would not take you there. I won't let them fight." Hadrian would not budge on the matter; that much was clear.

"Then you are taking away any hope they have left," Aamir said quietly, though his words were barbed.

Alex glanced at Demeter to see what the auburn-haired man might have to say on the matter, but a wistful, dreamy look had washed over his face. Whatever the ex-teacher was thinking about, Alex knew it wasn't how they might go about recruiting more troops.

"Demeter?" he said, nudging the man in the arm.

Demeter snapped back to reality. "Sorry... I was miles

away. Did you say something about Ceres?" he asked, a hopeful gleam in his eyes.

Alex nodded. "Yeah, we met her a few days ago. She's hiding out with Hadrian's secret squadron of broken children," he said sourly, catching a flicker of glee that sparked across Demeter's face.

"Ceres? Ceres is here?" Demeter asked excitedly.

Hadrian sighed. "Yes, she is here."

"I have to go and see her," Demeter insisted, but Hadrian did not look like he could be swayed.

"I have said it too many times already: I will not take any of you to where those students are. It is for the greater good that nobody knows the whereabouts of the sanctuary. I will not put their safety at risk," he muttered, his resolve unwavering. "I know what you are doing is for a truly magnificent cause, but there is simply too much at stake. If the odds weren't so uncertain, I might consider it, but there can be no guarantee of anyone's survival in this act of yours. The only people I can truly swear to protect are those I already have, and I won't go back on that."

"You have to take me to her!" Demeter demanded.

"I am sorry, dear friend, but I can't… Please understand the position you are putting me in," Hadrian said softly, leveling his gaze at Demeter.

Demeter looked crestfallen. "You really won't?"

"I can't… but I will pass on a message to her that you are alive and well, and eager to be reunited with her. If she wants to see you, she will come to you," Hadrian replied, evidently trying to give the broken-hearted man a sliver of positivity to cling to.

"Hadrian, we're running out of time. We need those extra people," Alex insisted, hoping he didn't sound too cold toward Demeter's plight. He didn't know the full story of what had happened between Ceres and Demeter, but it was obvious that there had been a romance, once upon a time. No man carried that expression in his eyes unless he clung to the bittersweet memories of lost love.

Hadrian shrugged, his features sagging with exhaustion. "You will have to come up with something else. It is too risky to begin a rebellion here, with so many eyes on us. I'm not taking you."

"It's in the cave, isn't it? There's something in the cave that leads to this secret place?" Alex asked, making a last-ditch effort to get Hadrian to take them there, or at least spill the beans.

Hadrian flashed an angry look in Alex's direction. "I ask, politely, that you shelve this idea of yours and use what little time you have left to perfect the counter-spell. That will be where it counts. You can have all the numbers in the world, but if you do not know that spell, it will all be moot," he said, his voice tense. "Ensure there is nothing you have missed."

"I already know what we're missing," Alex muttered.

Hadrian exhaled deeply. "I shall be in the kitchens, ordering a fine meal for you all. When you are done trying to persuade yourselves that I will change my mind, I will be waiting for you with a hot supper. Until you can push those thoughts from your mind, I suggest you remain absent. Shut yourselves in your rooms if you must." With that, the wearied royal left the room.

"As much as I hate to admit it, I don't think you should have said those things," said Demeter quietly. "Hadrian has sacrificed a lot to be where he is, and to have achieved what he has with the essence. He does every extraction himself, you know? He told me, as we were returning. The man has a good heart, and if he says we shouldn't involve the victims he is trying to keep safe, then we shouldn't."

Alex frowned, thinking about what that entailed. It was no wonder the royal looked so tired. He could only imagine what kind of strain that sort of exertion would put a man under—to pull the living pulse of a person out of them, listening to their agonized screams, all the while trying to soothe and fix whatever remained.

"We need the numbers," Alex insisted, despite the unease he felt at Demeter's chiding. "No matter what he says, we will struggle with what we have."

Aamir placed a hand on his friend's shoulder. "It will have to be enough."

It wasn't what Alex wanted to hear, but he knew he was fighting a losing battle. If he wanted to seek out the assistance of the recovering students, he was going to have to get it himself.

"We'll talk more tomorrow, figure out our next move," Alex said, though he already had a plan formulating in his mind. He didn't dare look at Ellabell, but he could feel the heat of a knowing look coming from her direction.

"And you'll come sit with us now?" she asked pointedly.

He nodded. "Of course. We'll just have to pray there are enough at Stillwater to take on the task. Two royals and a school full of undoubtedly brainwashed students—how hard can it be?" he said, his voice dripping sarcasm.

Obediently, he followed everyone else toward the low table, where they sat in readiness for the meal Hadrian had promised. When it arrived, they ate in uncomfortable silence. The food was delicious, but everything left a bitter taste in Alex's mouth. After eating his fill, he retired to his chamber, plucking the Book of Jupiter off the shelf as he went. Perhaps Hadrian was right; maybe it would be best to have a thorough read-through, just to make sure he hadn't missed anything important, although he would never admit that to his friends.

In re-reading the spell, nothing new jumped out at him. He already knew he needed more than five drops of royal blood, and that the spell had to be performed at the Mouth of Evil. Alex presumed that to be one of the cavernous pits into which the essence was poured. Soon, he would have the blood too, if everything ran smoothly. It was all coming together, so long as there were no nasty surprises that would weaken their forces. He couldn't get that notion out of his mind, hard as he tried.

We need more, he told himself, moving over to the small window that beckoned from the far wall of the chamber. The others had all gone to bed not long after he had, and he found himself hoping they were all asleep as he clambered out of the window and dropped down onto the ledge below him, barely making a sound with his bare feet.

A sharp, white-hot flash to the brain stopped him in his tracks.

CHAPTER 29

"AND JUST WHERE DO YOU THINK YOU'RE sneaking off to?" Elias purred, dropping from the head of a carved green dragon.

Alex sighed loudly. "You disappear for ages, without a word, and yet you show up again at the most inopportune moments. I don't know how you do it—you're like the world's most irritating ninja."

Elias cackled. "I'm far stealthier than any ninja, trust me. And I come and go as I please; I am beholden to no one."

"Well, I wish you'd be one or the other—here or not. That is all I ask," Alex remarked, sitting down on the wooden ledge, knowing he was going to be there for the long haul. Walking below, in their crisp uniforms, was a band of soldiers who had chosen that exact spot, directly underneath Alex, to stop and have a lewd discussion. He could make out a few words, and they made him blush—far too rude for his ears.

Elias, however, had coiled downward to get a better eavesdropping position. His teeth flashed in a wolfish grin.

"Elias!" Alex hissed.

The shadow-man slunk back upward. "Spoilsport," he teased.

"I presume you came to bother me for a reason?" Alex whispered, careful not to alert the bawdy men below to his presence.

"It's more that I came to stop you for a reason," said the shadow-man, shrugging his vaporous shoulders.

Alex frowned. "Stop me from doing what?"

"Now, you know I'm the last person on this planet who would seek to prevent you from delving into dark and delicious secrets, but on this occasion, I must clamber to the moral high ground. An unfamiliar spot for me, I'm sure you'll agree, but nevertheless I find myself standing here." Elias sighed. "You must heed the words of Hadrian on this occasion. It will do you no good to go sniffing out these… half-people, shall we call them?"

"I'm not sure that's a polite term for them," Alex remarked, raising a stern eyebrow.

Elias flashed a butter-wouldn't-melt smile. "I says it how I sees it."

"Why shouldn't I go looking?" Alex asked, moving the subject away from Elias's lack of political correctness.

"They won't do anyone any good," the shadow-man said simply. "It's worse than you've imagined. I should know—that's where I've been all this time. You think I'd just run off and leave poor baby Alex alone, if I didn't have a good reason? Perhaps you don't know me at all." He scoffed, feigning hurt.

"How is it worse than I imagined? You don't know what I'm thinking," Alex retorted, only to pause as Elias began to laugh. Did Elias know what he was thinking, or could he only make visual suggestions? Either way, Alex wasn't happy about the shadow-man messing about in his mind. "Which reminds me, stay out of my head! That last one hurt—plus, I could have fallen."

Elias grinned. "And I would have caught you!"

"Oh, yeah, I forget you're not as incapable as you let on." Alex glared, his mind flitting back to the half-formed vision of Elias carrying Ellabell toward the mountain, with the intent of leaving her to the wolves.

Elias had the decency to look ashamed. "Water under

the bridge?" he asked, his voice comically high.

"Jury is still out," Alex muttered, stifling a laugh. "Anyway, what's wrong with the... victims?"

Elias visibly shuddered. "What *isn't* wrong with them? To look at them, you'd think they were fine, but there's a creepy blank stare that a lot of them have. I kept to the shadows, as I am prone to doing, but I swear most of them could sense me. A couple even tried to start up a conversation, but I was having none of it," he said, inspecting the shadows where his fingernails should have been. "They're broken... That's the only way I can put it. They are damaged inside, wandering around like zombies." Holding out his wispy arms, Elias began to do a humorous rendition of "Thriller," stalking this way and that, getting himself distracted as per usual.

"Are none of them healthy?"

Elias let out a bored sigh. "Depends what you mean by 'healthy.' They can walk and talk, but they're like ghosts inside. Sad little spirits trying to find something that has been taken away."

It reminded Alex of the spirits he'd encountered in the vault, with their sad voices and fractured memories. Perhaps that's what happened to a person if the extraction process went too far, taking them across the line between alive and dead.

"Aren't you technically one of them?" Alex asked.

Elias made a rude sound. "How dare you! I am fully functioning, thank you very much. I might not be solid, but I have all my faculties about me still. There are no missing pieces here... except for the little bit you stole, but I can do without it for a while, just as long as you are near," he said, batting eyelashes that didn't exist.

"How come you're not a zombie?"

"Because I didn't have the same thing done to me," Elias explained. "The spell used on me was a dark, vicious, nasty little thing, intended to create a supernatural being that could..." He trailed off, wincing, a look of sudden panic appearing on his face. For a moment, he went very still, as if expecting something bad to happen. Even Alex felt tense, watching the shadow-man frozen to the spot, awaiting a zap of light or a snap of electricity that would drag him away from the mortal world for good.

"Did you say too much?" Alex asked quietly.

Elias raised a vaporous finger to his lips, and the minutes ticked by in complete silence. Neither Alex nor the shadow-man dared break the tension, listening instead to the rustle of the treetops and the guttural laughter of the soldiers, way below.

After enough time had passed, Elias swept his hand across his starry forehead. "Phew! That was a close call! I have *got* to learn to keep this trap shut!" he said, chastising himself with a slap to the wrist.

"Maybe you can't get punished while I'm carrying a pesky bit of your soul?" Alex suggested. It was a thought that had been bothering him for a while, especially once he had seen Elias moving so easily in the daylight, which he hadn't been able to do before. Something had changed, and it had all started with the tearing off of the shadow-man's soul. Somehow, Alex had made Elias hardier, less vulnerable to the vengeance of whatever otherworldly overlords he served.

The shadow-man seemed intrigued by this idea. "Could be... Hmm... Very interesting," he remarked, tapping his chin silently. "Anyway, the long and short of it is, it was a different spell. I'm not saying where that spell might be, but if you really wanted to find it, I'm sure it would be easy," the shadow-man said, making a point of opening his impossibly black eyes wide, to ensure Alex understood what he was saying without actually having to say it.

"Is it in the Book of Jupiter?" Alex prompted.

"Perhaps it is, perhaps it isn't," Elias replied.

Alex frowned. "But I asked a direct question."

"Not strictly related to what you need to know, though," Elias whispered.

"Are you going to be hanging around from now on?" Alex asked, secretly hoping the answer might be yes. If they were going to enter the fray, they would need somebody like Elias on their side, who could do things none of them could do, and could taunt the Head better than anyone else.

Elias grinned. "Perhaps I may, perhaps I may not."

"Well, whatever you do, I think we might need you. If we don't have any hope of greater numbers, we'll need power, and you seem to have it in abundance, as long as you're not saying something you shouldn't," Alex joked, deciding to be truthful.

The shadow-man looked taken aback for a moment, his gaze settling on Alex in the most perturbing manner. Elias almost seemed moved by what Alex had said, and Alex fought the urge to take back his compliments.

Alex grinned awkwardly. "What's the matter, cat got your tongue?"

"Very well then," said Elias, with no hint of sarcasm in his voice. "If you think you will need me, I will be there. You forget… and sometimes I forget too, but my job is to protect you as best I can, and I will uphold that task until the moment you no longer require my help," he added, with uncharacteristic solemnity.

Alex smiled. "Thank you, Elias."

"Now, if you don't mind, I'd like to catch the end of this conversation." He flashed his teeth in a comical grin before slithering down the wall of the pagoda toward the congregated soldiers standing below, their laughter drifting upward.

With Elias's attention diverted, Alex clambered back up through the window of the chamber. It was a tight squeeze, but he managed it, collapsing in a heap on the low divan that had been laid out for him. The room was pitch black, the torches blown out.

"Where have you been?" Ellabell's voice pierced the darkness.

Alex grimaced. "If I said nowhere, would you believe me?"

Lighting a match that illuminated her face for a brief instant, the curly-haired girl lit one of the lamps that hung from the walls. A dangerous place to put a naked flame, so close to a structure built from wood, but so far nothing had gone up in flames, aside from Alex's hopes.

"That would depend how you felt about lying to me," she countered, fully illuminated now, as the lamp bathed the room in a soft glow.

"Awful," Alex admitted.

Ellabell smiled. "Good. I'm glad. I know it's none of my business, but I knocked and you didn't answer. I shouldn't have pried, but I opened the door and saw you weren't here. You can't just go running off without telling anyone. For all I knew, you could have been snatched by someone, or worse.

It's happened before," she murmured, dropping her gaze to the floor. It wasn't fast enough—Alex caught a glimpse of pain flashing across her eyes. Before he could offer any words of comfort, she continued. "There's a price on your head, Alex, whether you like it or not, and you have to be conscious of that when you make these decisions. It's like everyone keeps saying—the stakes are so high now, and if one of us goes missing, there's no guarantee they'll return safely."

Alex walked toward Ellabell, holding out his hands for hers. With a shy smile, she reached out, interlacing her fingers with his.

"I didn't go to the cave," he assured her, knowing what she was thinking.

"I didn't say you did," she murmured as he pulled her to him in a tight embrace.

It had been a long while since they had been able to snatch a moment alone together, and it felt wonderful to have her so close. After the events at Kingstone, and the trepidation he'd felt leaving her there, not even knowing she'd have to deal with the chaos that had ensued, he was just glad to hold her again. At every turn, he was reminded how treacherous the magical world could be. And she was right, the stakes were improbably high now, and the moment for action would soon be upon them. Two days would go by in an instant, and then... who knew if any of them would come back in one piece? There had never been a guarantee. As much as Alex pined to see home and his mother again, he knew there was a decent chance he might never set foot in the ordinary world again, let alone see his mother's face once more. He had chosen this path—the only thing left to do was walk it.

He kissed her hair gently, a freshly washed, jasmine-like scent filling his nose. "I saw Elias—he stopped me," he explained.

She pulled back to look at him. "Elias *stopped* you?"

Alex nodded. "He said the survivors of Falleaf won't be of any use to us. They're... broken, to use his word. I think Hadrian might've been right; they aren't strong enough to join our ranks, and I don't think I'd feel right asking. Not now."

"Those poor things," Ellabell whispered, kissing Alex's shoulder.

"We'll free them soon enough," Alex murmured, unwilling to listen to the niggling voice in the back of his head that said otherwise. There was still ample time for them to fail.

Ellabell smiled against his shirt. "Well, I'm off to bed. We've got a big day of planning ahead of us tomorrow," she said, pulling away from Alex's arms.

"Could I be cheeky and ask for a goodnight kiss?" he

asked, locking eyes with her. She smiled gleefully, and Alex wasn't sure he'd ever seen a more beautiful sight than her standing there, smiling at him in the romantic glow of the lamplight.

"I thought you'd never ask," she whispered, and their lips met in a tender kiss.

Just for that one moment, that joyful bubble of frozen time, everything seemed right with the world. With Ellabell in his arms, his mind consumed by her, he had no room to think of vengeful royals, or cannibalistic silver mist, or the intricacies of a spell in which one false move signaled failure. It was just him and her, feeling the heartwarming glow of first love.

CHAPTER 30

AS THE END OF THE FIRST DAY CAME TO A CLOSE, Alex wished he'd told Helena to meet earlier. They had gone over the plan of action, with Hadrian promising to fetch another bagful of essence to replace the bottles that had been used in portal-building. After that, there hadn't been much else to do, and the mood quickly became fractious. Adding to it was the fact that Agatha had taken ill again, which set Alex on edge. He kept expecting her to burst from the flimsy doors of her chamber and chase him down. Vincent was patiently seeing to her, with the assistance of Hadrian, who was feeding her a potent concoction the color of violets at regular intervals.

All Alex could do was pace and worry, and pace some more, and wait for the next day to be over. Keeping to his room for the most part, he went over and over the counter-spell until he couldn't bear to look at it anymore. Even then, he kept going, forcing his eyes to move across the page, absorbing the text. No matter how many times he read it, he knew he could never prepare himself for the enormity of what was to come. At this point, there were still a lot of "ifs" flying around, and until they were cemented in reality, they were still at the starting line.

Finally, the next day dawned.

With two bulging sacks of essence, one refreshed, one being the spare that had never quite reached Helena and the others, they made their way down to the forest. Alex had the Book of Jupiter stowed safely away in a satchel, but he could not let go of it as they walked, his hands insistently clamped on the straps. Nerves were running high, nobody speaking much as Hadrian led the way, though he wasn't coming with them. Nor was Agatha, who was being left in the capable hands of the nervous royal. Alex had been surprised that Vincent hadn't attempted to stay too, but the necromancer had insisted he join the main group.

Vincent and Agatha had shared their farewells sitting off to the side, by one of the windows of the pagoda, where Alex had heard the woeful snuffle of Agatha's tears. Regardless of the old woman's hatred for Spellbreakers, she was a good person, and it was hard to hear the sound of her heart breaking as her best friend left her behind, potentially forever.

"I have lived a good old time, Agatha dearest, and if it is finally my moment to go, then I shall embrace the grim reaper with open arms," Vincent had murmured to her, trying to soothe her.

"I will die a second later, if you're to leave me," she had wailed.

"Then, let it be so, and I shall see you on the other side, dear heart," Vincent had promised. "You have been beside me for more years than I care to count, and death shall not change that. The universe guides everything, and it shall liberate the both of us."

Vincent had put on his calmest face as he had emerged from Agatha's sick room. The stoic expression was still on his face when he joined the others on their journey to the spot where they would open up the portal to Spellshadow Manor.

"Let's agree to meet on the perimeter of the school, where the trees meet the smoking field. Aamir, you remember where that is, right?" Alex asked. Having come down through the pagoda and run to the safety of the trees, they had reached the point where they had to part ways, with Aamir, Demeter, Vincent, and Hadrian going one way, while

Alex and Ellabell went the other. Hadrian had explained before they left that the old gateway to Spellshadow stood at the other side of the forest, in the section Alex and his friends had never ventured into before, which meant it was on the opposite side of the forest from the place Alex had left Storm, giving them no choice but to split up temporarily. Just as Alex and Ellabell turned to leave, however, Hadrian handed one of the bags of essence to Alex, who took it gratefully.

"Better chance of one of them making it through this way," the royal joked.

Alex smiled tensely. "I'll keep it safe," he promised.

It felt strange to watch the others walk off in the opposite direction, with nothing but a gut instinct to say that they would see one another again. He tried not to dwell on it too much while they made their way toward the spot where Alex had left Storm. It was always a delight to see that she was still there, and hadn't flown off in frustration. With a chirp, she rushed out to meet the duo, though she paused just short, tilting her head to one side. Alex could see that she was looking at something behind him, and when he turned to see what it was, he caught a glimpse of something flitting furtively in the shadows.

"He's...he's not exactly an enemy," Alex whispered, stroking the soft feathers of Storm's face.

She chirruped again, the tone a dubious one.

Alex smiled, amused by the Thunderbird's keen perceptions. "I promise you, he means no harm."

They jumped onto her back, and Storm began to sprint along the ground, before lifting into the air with ease, speeding up with every beat of her enormous wings. It had almost become second nature to Alex. Where once he had felt riddled with anxiety, now he simply sat back and enjoyed the ride, though he couldn't help but marvel at her skill. That, he guessed, would never lose its novelty.

As the swooped over the woods, Alex caught sight of the treehouses again, just visible beneath the dense canopy. Several figures moved slowly across the walkways between the boughs, their faces ordinary and pleasant, each of them dressed in a dark green uniform. There were soldiers too, stationed at every platform. Alex's blood boiled as he watched one familiar-looking soldier shove a boy to the ground, pressing a heavy boot to the back of the young man's neck as he pushed him perilously close to the edge of the walkway. The cruel cackle that emerged from the soldier's throat rose up to meet Alex. He wanted to dive-bomb the cold-hearted man, but knew he couldn't. After a moment, the soldier let the boy get up.

What will you do when you have nothing left to guard? Alex thought, hoping the soldier could feel his anger. *What will your life be, when I strip it of purpose? I hope it is as sad and lonely as you are.*

As hard as it was to watch such banal cruelty, it spurred Alex on, making him want more than ever to succeed in the task that lay ahead. Turning over his shoulder to check the horizon, he saw a familiar glint of something golden in the distance. It looked very much like the spires he had seen when they had crossed from Kingstone, and he wondered if that was exactly what it was. Another section of the same noble city, perhaps, or maybe it was an entirely new one? It bothered him slightly that he would never get to visit one of the glittering cities of the elite mages.

Who knows? Maybe if I get this spell done, they will parade me through the streets like a hero, he mused to himself.

The world around them began to stretch, and soon they were no longer in the autumnal realm of Falleaf. Ahead of them, beyond the edge of the forest where they had appeared, Spellshadow Manor stood in all its bleakness. Storm let out a chirp that sounded like a yelp as the manor's overarching barrier met with her feathers, forcing her to fly lower in the sky than she usually liked, to avoid the edges of it.

With an awkward landing, she set them down on the very edge of the sickly-looking woods that ringed the smoking field before them. Ruffling her feathers, Alex could sense she didn't like the feel of the place, and he couldn't blame her—it was more than a little eerie to be back, at the beginning of all their grievances.

The others hadn't arrived yet, which was to be expected, considering they had a portal to build. With the four powerful mages working on it, however, he knew it wouldn't take too much longer. Gazing out upon the smoking field, the looming structure of Spellshadow in the distance, Alex felt a wave of discomfort crash over him. It was weird to be back, and with the strangeness came a flood of memories that seemed to belong to another life. Another Alex.

He remembered the terror of Derhin's battle with Aamir, the way the professor had fallen, only to be carried away screaming by a reluctant Lintz. The excitement of discovering the wine cellar, and the good and bad times they had spent in that musty cavern beneath the earth. It had shaped him, in many ways, but how grateful he felt for that, he wasn't sure. To be back in the place where it all began made everything seem twice as real. His friendships had flourished here. Without it, he'd never have met Aamir, or Jari, or Ellabell, or anyone who had joined them on their journey, for that matter.

Silver linings, he thought.

Back then, they'd had no idea what lay before them. Spellbreakers, mages, essence, Great Evils, they had been unknown to him then—the stuff of dreams and fiction. Now, they were almost ordinary. He thought about what might have happened if they hadn't made the choices they'd made. If they hadn't sought to destroy Finder, down in the tombs, where would they be now? Would they be wandering the halls still, going to lessons, learning what they could, stealing private moments in the wine cellar? Would they be as strong as they were now, if all they'd done was wait for the day when they would be called up to graduation? If Aamir hadn't striven to defeat Derhin, would he be dead?

Spellshadow Manor still held a plethora of unanswered questions. The truth was, they had taken the path they had taken, and there was no going back. He just had to continue to convince himself that it was all for a reason, that they had done all of this for a greater good. Even if he didn't make it out alive, he knew he had to remember the reasons they had gone down this road in the first place. Where there was injustice, there had to be a leveling. It just so happened that he was the leveler.

"Do you ever wonder what life we might be leading, if we hadn't escaped?" he asked, turning to Ellabell, who had come to stand beside him.

She smiled wistfully. "Sometimes."

"Do you think we'd be better off?"

"I think we did the right thing… We took the action nobody else would," she replied quietly.

"Being back here, it's weird," Alex murmured.

She nodded. "It is. It's like coming back to the scene of a crime."

"I just hope this is all worth it." He sighed.

"It will be," she assured him, squeezing his hand tightly.

A rustle behind him broke his reverie. For a moment, he felt a flutter of panic, which was swiftly squashed as Aamir, Demeter, and Vincent appeared between the crumbling trunks of the trees, seemingly unhurt.

"You got through okay?" Alex asked, turning to greet them.

Aamir shrugged. "We had a bit of a close call with some guards, while we were building, but Hadrian managed to steer them away. We had to close it as soon as we came through," he explained, his dark eyes turning toward the gloomy façade of Spellshadow. Alex smiled, imagining his friend's expression mirrored his own—a mixture of dread and anticipation.

"Weird, right?" Alex chuckled.

"Very weird," Aamir agreed. "I never thought we would end up back here."

"I don't think any of us did," Alex muttered. "But, we're here now—we should probably head for the gardens," he suggested, thinking of Helena and the others, who should have been through by then.

"What is that?" Demeter asked, pointing at the gigantic bird hidden in the trees.

Alex smiled. "This is Storm. She's a Thunderbird—perhaps the last."

"May I?" Demeter asked, walking up to the feathered creature.

"By all means," Alex replied.

With tentative steps, Demeter approached Storm, laying his palm flat. Alex glanced at the ex-teacher in bemusement, not knowing how it was that the auburn-haired man knew more about these creatures than he did. Perhaps, somewhere in the annals of Spellbreaker literature that Demeter had read, there had been a passage on taming these magnificent beasts.

"She's a beauty," Demeter marveled, as Storm placed her beak in the palm of his hand.

Alex nodded. "She certainly is."

"So, this is the fabled Spellshadow Manor?" Vincent asked, staring out at the barren landscape, toward the school.

"Welcome," said Alex wryly, turning his attention back to what lay before them.

With nothing more to say, the quintet began to move across the field, with Storm flying low overhead. However, as soon as they set foot on the dried earth, something felt wrong. This place was unearthly, and the eeriness didn't fade as they took a few more steps. It became clear, seconds later, why it felt so utterly unpleasant. With a gathering groan, the ground began to rumble, the cracked earth splitting in places, puffs of searing-hot steam erupting from within.

"Run!" Alex yelled, as the smoky streams began to turn into long, snake-like creatures.

The quick-moving apparitions followed Alex and his friends as they sprinted toward the rise of the hill in the near distance. Snapping at their heels, the snakes were persistent, moving fast, but the quintet was faster, reaching the edge of the smoking field before the summoned beings could do any real harm. At the grassy lip between hill and field, the snakes retreated, slithering back down into the scorched earth.

Even so, Alex and the others did not slow down, scrambling up the hill until they reached the summit. Only then did they dare to turn and look back, just in time to see the snakes sucked back into the ground, lying in wait for the next trespassers. Catching his breath, Alex wondered what the creatures were, given that he had never seen them before. He wondered if it was simply because he had never ventured across the wasteland before, or if it was a new addition, put in place by the Head to ensure added security, after the debacle of their failed uprising. It would certainly be an escape deterrent, he thought, recalling the serpents in the moat at Kingstone.

No longer fearful of snapping snakes of fiery steam following them, the anxious group walked toward the walled garden, which lay just up ahead. Alex went first, climbing through a broken section in the wall, trying to sense any traps that might ensnare them. Fortunately, there didn't seem to be any, and he squeezed through to the other side.

As the others clambered through after him, Alex took the time to look around. The sickening feeling of déjà vu was even stronger here. The gardens were exactly as they had left them, though the barrier around the place felt infinitely stronger. He didn't even need to touch the wall to know that; his body was already attempting to retaliate. Forcing the impulse down, he wandered toward a lichen-covered water fountain, and found himself picturing it in its heyday, when everything was bright and beautiful. It was a hard image to conjure, but he managed it, and wondered if one day it might return to that, or if this place would be left to rot, as it ought to have been long ago.

The increased potency of the barrier surrounding the school seemed to be another example of Virgil's heightened security levels, but it didn't release anything foul, which provided some comfort to Alex's shattered nerves. Either that, or the Head knew they were coming, and this was his way of letting them know. He hoped not.

Knowing she would be noticed if she came with them

any farther, Alex decided to leave Storm in the relative safety of the gardens, tucking her away in a spot where she blended seamlessly into the masonry, her silver feathers barely visible against the pale stone. It didn't feel right, leaving her there, but he knew he had no other choice. She wasn't exactly discreet.

They moved farther into the grounds, Alex keeping his eyes and ears open for any sign of Helena and her team.

Wherever they went, everything felt strange, like the worst kind of nightmare. Glancing around, Alex could see that his feelings were shared—everyone looked uneasy, with the exception of Demeter, who seemed to be his usual cheerful self, despite everything. It was a disposition Alex envied, though considering his theory as to how the teacher had ended up like that, he didn't think it was something he'd like to share. However, he did wish the auburn-haired man would use a little of his empathic ability to reduce the tension in the ranks.

Coming to an abrupt halt behind one of the low walls, Alex caught his first glimpse of the Spellshadow students walking around the grounds. They were strolling in pairs, speaking in low voices, their faces miserable. Alex recognized one of them as Billy Foer, the boy who had never seemed to have much luck, and he wondered whether or not to call out to his old acquaintance. He stopped short, realizing he didn't know who could be trusted in this place anymore. After what had happened last time, he knew they might not be so willing to help out, given that he and his friends had all but abandoned them to their fate. He couldn't blame them for any distrust they might feel toward him. The only person who had stood up for them and protected them was Gaze, and she was gone.

Keeping silent, they waited for the students to pass by, pressing back tightly against the wall so as not to be seen. As soon as the students had moved on, Alex peered back over the wall, only to be met with another familiar sight. Stalking the stairwell that led up to the school were two of the old final-year students, Aamir's peers, now dressed in the unmistakable robes of professors. One of them was Jun Asano, but the young woman beside him wasn't quite as familiar.

"Do you know her?" Alex asked Aamir, keeping his voice to a whisper.

Aamir nodded. "Her name is Catherine de Marchmont. She was one of the best in our class," he murmured. "A force to be reckoned with."

Alex could well believe it. There was something about the robes they wore that made them both look imposing, and more than a little menacing. He couldn't recall whether he'd felt that way about the other professors, but there was definitely something about these two that spelled danger.

Scrutinizing them more closely for a moment, he saw the unmistakable glow of golden bands visible on their wrists. Even if he had wanted to recruit them to the cause, he knew he couldn't—the Head already had control over them. It was a shame, but there was no time to break the bands and hope the two former students returned to their normal selves, the ones who might have been eager to fight the hierarchy before.

As he watched the two new professors go back inside, Alex was glad he and his friends had decided to approach the school with stealth, instead of going in all guns blazing. If there were more like Jun Asano and Catherine de Marchmont inside, he knew they were going to have a tough time of infiltrating the building.

The Head, however, was nowhere to be seen, which was to be entirely expected. If he was at home, he would surely be awaiting them inside.

CHAPTER 31

"SHOULD WE KEEP WAITING?" ELLABELL ASKED.

The group had been standing outside, hiding behind the wall for half an hour, and there was still no sign of Helena anywhere. The only explanation Alex could think of that didn't fill him with dread that something bad had happened to them, was that she had gotten her wires crossed, and they were waiting inside, in the Head's office, though they had clearly agreed to meet in the walled gardens. It made sense, considering that was where the portal from Stillwater went, and Helena's main objective had been to find the messenger device to send word to Venus.

However, Alex wasn't sure he wanted to press on, in case they suddenly appeared. Perhaps they had just been held up a little and would be along at any moment.

"Let's wait a little bit longer," he replied, though it irked him to say so.

Ten minutes later, he'd had enough of waiting. Whether something bad had happened or Helena had gotten her wires crossed, it was pointless to stay out in the gardens. With the teachers and students back inside the building, they had a free window of opportunity to enter the school unnoticed. It would be foolish to waste it. Any option was better than wasting time cowering behind a wall.

With the decision made, Alex led the way, hurrying across the front lawn where Derhin had fallen to reach the steps where they had had their last battle with Virgil. Alex could still remember the bristle of magic in the air, and the adrenaline pulsing in his veins as they took on the Head. The remembrance of Lintz and Gaze made him smile too, with bittersweet sentiment, as he conjured up the memory of them hurling bombs and shooting powerful bolts across the grass. He knew they would never have made it this far, if it hadn't been for the two benevolent professors.

They paused by the entrance to the school, Alex glancing down to see that a golden line had been fitted across the doorway. Bending quickly, he let his anti-magic weave into the solid form of a knife, and cut the glowing ribbon of energy. It retaliated instantly, and tendrils of golden light snaked toward Alex, rising up to grasp at his throat. He felt the first cold tingles of it clawing at his neck, but the others jumped in, dispensing with the strangling threads, turning them into nothing more than golden dust. It made a difference from the old days, when the sight of such entities would have sent a shiver of fear through him. Now, they were simply par for the course, and he was ready for any more that might await them.

Leaving the shattered ends of the golden line, Alex and his friends stepped through into the echoing foyer of the manor, their footsteps seeming much too loud for Alex's liking. Once he was sure nobody was coming to discover them, he beckoned for the others to press on.

He couldn't shake the strange sensation of being back as they took to the hallways. The gray ivy littered the flagstones, draping the walls until there was barely any wall left to see. It had overtaken the place, more so than it ever had before. The group were careful not to get too close to the energy-sapping plants, picking their way across sparser sections.

Moving into one of the wider corridors, where Alex knew they might be vulnerable, they came across their first adversary. At the end of the hall stood another robed professor, though it was not Jun or Catherine, but his back was turned, and he appeared distracted by something farther up.

"With me," Alex whispered, gesturing toward Demeter.

The ex-teacher nodded, following Alex quietly up the corridor toward the robed figure. In a preemptive strike, Alex lunged at the young man, smothering his mouth tightly with his hand and bringing him down to the ground. Demeter moved in, pressing his palms to the sides of the young man's head, weaving strands of white magic into the professor's skull until his eyes went blank, and Alex could hear the soft sound of snoring coming from the boy's throat.

"Nice job," Alex said, smiling anxiously.

"I try," replied Demeter, resting the young man's head gently down on the stone.

Moving on, it seemed the auburn-haired man was on something of a roll, as he worked his mind control on person after person. Occasionally, Vincent would get involved, if there was too much of a struggle, and Alex realized he and Demeter made quite the team as they dealt with the students they came across, quickly losing count of the number of individuals they had left sleeping in the hallways. It wasn't ideal to leave them there, in case their slumbering bodies were discovered, but Alex knew they would waste too much time if they dragged each and every one into one of the side rooms that branched off from the corridors.

As they entered the focal point of the school, where the

classrooms were, stealth grew trickier. Here, the students moved in pairs, though Aamir and Ellabell had formed quite the tag-team too, binding the passing students in a silencing shield, which kept them both quiet and immobile.

Creeping around a corner, Alex didn't see the figure running toward them until it was too late. It seemed the sprinting boy hadn't seen them either, and they collided. It was Billy Foer again, his eyes going wide as he saw the group before him. Alex realized they probably did look like quite the motley crew, but there was no time for a reunion. Alex reached for Billy. The boy struggled, opening his mouth to shout, but Ellabell quickly formed a gag around his mouth, silencing him. Alex felt almost guilty as he let tendrils of energy flow into the boy's brain.

There were flashbacks of an idyllic home life, in which Billy was running with his dog across a sun-drenched beach. A family sat nearby, lounging on a picnic blanket, and one of them, an older boy, had just told a joke that had everyone in stitches. Alex settled on this image, feeding it to the forefront of Billy's mind. However, it seemed the memory was slightly too jovial, leaving the boy a giggling wreck on the floor. It was a good thing that Ellabell had gagged him; otherwise, his laughter would have brought the whole school running.

"Sorry, Billy," whispered Alex. "You always seem to end up on the wrong side of people's spells."

After dealing with another handful of students, this time hiding the evidence in the rooms that led off from the hallways, they reached the entrance to a familiar corridor. A golden line still buzzed across it, keeping the Head's personal quarters private.

"Keep watch for anyone coming," said Alex, bracing himself. Vincent and Demeter took a corridor each. Alex knelt beside the golden line. He conjured another glowing knife of raw anti-magic and pressed it firmly against the buzzing barrier. It was an act he had performed many times before, and he couldn't help the rush of memories that came hurtling back. In his mind's eye, he saw Aamir, telling them the Head knew about Finder, before his face contorted with pain. It wasn't a pleasant memory, and Alex could see that Aamir shared some of his distress.

"Never thought we'd be doing this again, either," Aamir said, as if answering Alex's thoughts.

Alex smiled. "You're telling me."

With a loud fizz, the golden line broke apart, followed by the thunderous roar of something rushing toward them from the darkness of the corridor. It was a blockade of pure energy, bristling with strength as it picked up speed. Alex jumped up, the others joining him in a line as they wove their respective magics and pushed it toward the blockade. White and gold mixed with black and silver, with hints of gray and the coiling ribbons of necromantic magic. With an earth-shuddering slam, the two walls of energy collided, shards flying everywhere. Alex and his friends ducked to avoid the worst of it, Ellabell sending up a shield around them all, in an attempt to protect them from the fallout.

It seemed to work, and, as the haze cleared, Alex saw that the blockade had been evaporated. The path to the Head's office was clear. Alex just hoped that Virgil was home.

As they were about to enter the corridor, Demeter paused.

"I think my services will be of better use here, ensuring nobody follows," he said.

Alex frowned, glancing back at the empty crossroads. Although he was loathe to lose Demeter's skillset, he knew that the ex-teacher was right. Somebody would have to stay to guard the entrance, in the event of any professors or students giving in to curiosity.

"Are you sure?" asked Ellabell, looking equally concerned.

Demeter nodded. "I can stop anyone who might try to raise an alarm."

"We'll come back for you once Helena has sent the message," Alex assured him.

Leaving Demeter camouflaged in the shadows at the entrance to the hallway, the foursome moved along, picking up the pace. The torches flickered as they crept through the corridors, though they saw nobody. It was deathly silent in the inner sanctum of the manor, and it troubled Alex. He couldn't sense the Head at all, but it didn't stop the anxiety spreading through him, that Virgil might suddenly appear and take them by surprise. The Head was crafty like that.

They still had the book and two bags of essence, now strapped awkwardly across his back and Aamir's, but he didn't know if it would be enough when the time came.

Walking past familiar rooms, Alex knew they were drawing close to the antechamber with the dangling manacles. He could smell it, even before he saw it. The metallic tang of blood and fear was unmistakable, more potent than any scent he'd ever encountered. He paused by the imposing door, shrouded in shadow, and wondered whether to stop now and pick up as many bottles of essence as they could carry, in the hopes of bolstering their ammunition. Envisioning the racks of black vials, he knew the energy within them was far stronger than the half-life essence they carried already, but he couldn't quite bring himself to enter the vile room.

Promising to come back for it once they had sent the message, Alex headed on up the hallway, toward the door to the Head's office. It was still splintered from the last time they had been there, when Virgil was battering it down.

Evidently, he had seen no need to repair it. Perhaps the Head had never expected Alex and his friends to return either.

Steeling himself, Alex pushed open the door, and was pleasantly surprised by the sight that met him. Jari and Helena were already standing within the room, fixated on the sprawling tree that grew against the wall.

As nice as it was to see them, Alex's initial feeling of joy quickly turned to dread. Virgil wasn't anywhere to be seen. If Virgil wasn't here, and had gone on some royal jaunt somewhere, Alex wasn't sure how he was supposed to find the Head and execute his plan of action. Sure, he had the book, and would hopefully have the blood soon enough, but it was all pointless if he didn't have Virgil.

If it comes down to it, are you ready to do the spell? he asked himself, but he already knew the answer. His feelings hadn't changed, despite the bigger picture. Yes, the survival of an entire race was greater than the sum of his one life, but that didn't mean he was prepared to give it up. Not yet, not when there was still a flicker of hope.

"I thought we said we'd meet at the gardens?" Alex said, startling the duo.

Helena whirled around. "Alex! Don't creep up on people like that!" she protested, her face softening. "Did we say the gardens? I thought we said here. Jari, you swore you remembered Alex saying to meet in the office!"

Jari blushed. "Garden, office, it all sounds the same, right? Anyway, you're here now, and that's what matters," he murmured sheepishly.

"Honestly! What if they'd been waiting out there all day?" Helena scolded.

"It was an honest mistake!"

Aamir grinned. "You already sound like an old married couple."

Jari flashed his friend a warning look, which only served to make Aamir's smile wider. It appeared the blond-haired boy had yet to drum up the courage to tell Helena about his feelings.

"What are you looking at?" asked Vincent, saving Jari from further embarrassment.

Helena frowned. "Sorry to sound rude, but who are you?" she asked.

"I am Vincent—an acquaintance of Alex's. I realize my face is somewhat surprising, so I take no offence," he replied, smiling.

"Oh, well, in that case… We're looking for the messenger device. I think it's in the hollow of this tree, but I can't reach it," she explained, pointing at the gnarled trunk.

"May I?" Vincent asked, stepping over the tangled roots, moving toward the spot where Helena was pointing.

"Of course," said Helena, stepping aside.

With his long, slender fingers, oddly similar to those of Virgil, Vincent slid his hand into the hollow of the trunk and reached upward, contorting his arm at such a strange angle that Alex was convinced he'd dislocated something. A moment later, he drew his arm back out again, clutching something red and shiny in his hand.

"Is this what you were looking for?" Vincent said, holding the object out with a dramatic flourish.

In his palm he held another scarlet orb, very similar to the one in Alypia's office, only this one was shaped like a ripe, red apple, with a golden stalk, complete with carved golden leaf, curving out of the top. It was beautiful, the bright color sharply contrasting the pale skin of Vincent's hand.

"Just the thing!" Helena beamed, taking the proffered apple. "Now, to send the message."

"Where's everyone else?" Alex asked, causing the silver-haired girl to pause in her task. He had been expecting an army of people, but there were only the two of them.

"Natalie stayed behind with a small group to protect the school should anything happen. It'll be our only escape route if we can't take the heat," Jari cried, doing an army roll toward the window. "Oh, and the others are down there," he added, gesturing over the sill.

Alex approached the open window, trying to keep his gaze from wandering toward the lake in the distance. It wasn't a sight he was ever happy to see, but the one waiting below was far more pleasant. Standing on the grass, awaiting instruction, was a small army of at least fifty students. They looked up as Alex poked his head out.

"Is it time?" one called.

Alex shook his head. "Not quite yet—soon!" he shouted back, feeling a tremor of nervous excitement as the words left his lips. It was true. Soon, the message would be sent, and Venus would be coming. Soon, they would be able to perform the counter-spell. Soon, all of this would be over, one way or another.

Turning back to the office, Alex watched as Helena fiddled with the ruby-red apple, weaving her magic into the very core. He couldn't tell if she knew what she was doing, but the display was convincing enough for him. After a short while, the orb began to glow.

"Message delivered!" Helena said, clearly thrilled.

Just then, the door to the office burst open, and Demeter came hurtling through.

"You have to come! Something is happening!" he shouted, breathless.

Alex looked from the orb to Demeter and back again. There was no way it could be Venus, not yet—surely, there hadn't been enough time? He remembered the way Julius had arrived after the breaking of the modules, and knew he could be wrong.

"We need to go now!" Demeter insisted, his voice dripping with panic.

As Alex and the others set off after the ex-teacher, Helena darted to the window, calling for the soldiers to start coming through. All Alex could hear as his feet pounded against the flagstones was the rush of his own blood in his ears, and the thunder of his heartbeat.

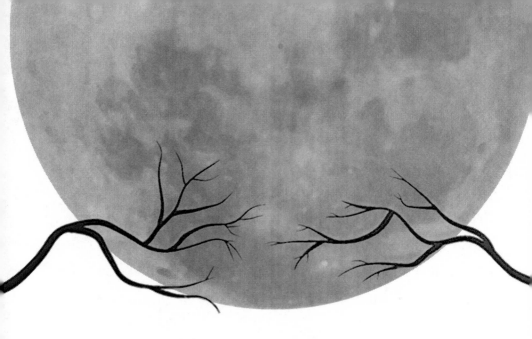

CHAPTER 32

THEY SPRINTED THROUGH THE HALLS AT BREAKNECK speed, jumping over the sleeping forms of the hypnotized students as if it were a steeplechase. Demeter was way ahead, but he skidded to a sudden halt as he reached the foyer. Alex and the others stopped as the auburn-haired man raised his hand and lifted a finger to his lips, demanding silence.

Alex crept forward, wanting to see what it was that had Demeter so spooked. Peering out at the front lawn, it became horrifyingly apparent what the problem was. Virgil was standing on the grass, his hood raised to block the sunlight from his face. How he had gotten there without anyone seeing, Alex didn't know, but there was no mistaking the skeletal man with his pale features and bony fingers.

Following the Head's line of sight, Alex noticed that a peculiar electrical storm was brewing in the sky above, turning it a dark, bruised gray where moments before it had been a tranquil azure. It wasn't a natural occurrence; that much was clear. Bolts of lightning flew across the swollen clouds, but there was no trace of thunder or rain.

Looking closer, he saw that a figure was emerging from the center of the strange tempest, the clouds parting to make way for her. Virgil, waiting on the lawn, stretched his arms out wide toward the appearing figure. With a horrible jolt of realization, Alex understood that the Head was welcoming his mother, though not because of anything Helena had done. Virgil must have already sent word to Venus, and here she was, responding to the call. Why he had called her down remained a mystery, though Alex was pretty certain it had something to do with him and his friends. He didn't appreciate the irony.

Venus was just as beautiful as Alex remembered, now dressed in a bronze gown that flowed around her like liquid, and watching her float downward from the heavens made her all the more angelic. Shaking off his mesmerized state, he saw the opportunity that lay directly before him. There would never be another like it.

"Why have you called me?" Venus's silky voice rippled through the air, though she was still a fair way off.

"Mother!" called Virgil. "I am so glad to see you! I know it's a hindrance, but I haven't been able to get in touch with my sister, and I thought you could help!"

Alex didn't wait around to hear the rest. He grasped Demeter sharply by the arm. "Follow my lead!" he instructed, bounding across the threshold of the manor's entrance. "Storm!" he yelled.

For a brief second, everything seemed to freeze. Venus maintained the speed of her descent, evidently oblivious of the danger she was in. To her, Alex knew they must just look like any other students. She was too far away to see that they were people she had already met, at Falleaf. Virgil turned around in slow motion, but he was too late.

Overhead, the heavy beat of wings vibrated. Storm had answered the call. The magnificent Thunderbird swooped low, Alex grasping the handles on her shoulders as he swung up onto her back. Demeter followed suit.

As they soared into the air, Alex looked back to see that the others were rushing out into the open space of the front lawn to take on Virgil, who was clearly still trying to process what was happening. Aamir tore the sack full of essence from his back and started throwing bottles to the others, who caught them deftly and ripped the stoppers from the vials. Weaving in and out of the fighters, Alex spied the shadowy figure of Elias joining the fray. With the shadow-man on their side, and the essence at their disposal, Alex hoped it would put them on a more even ground.

Facing forward once more, Alex reached out to grasp Venus as they hit her head-on. She was completely taken aback, her shriek piercing the air as Alex plucked her from the sky.

"Now!" Alex yelled, trying not to lose his grip on Storm as he held Venus tightly.

Demeter pressed his palms against the side of the queen's head and wove the glistening threads that would put her to sleep, moving her to a place of happiness. For good measure, Alex conjured the black-and-silver wisps of his own energy, wrapping her in a shield of anti-magic.

Once he was confident that she couldn't escape, Alex awkwardly moved over her, passing her backwards to Demeter, who clamped his arms around her protectively, ensuring she didn't fall from Storm's back and plummet to her death. Alex wasn't quite sure how Demeter was staying on with such apparent ease, but he seemed to be clamping his thighs against the Thunderbird's body, riding on her back in a jockey-like style.

Now, where do we take her? Alex thought, though he

knew there was only one place they could go.

"Take us to where Ceres is," he told Storm. She chirped in understanding, her wings beating faster as they stretched the fabric of time and space in pursuit of the secret sanctuary.

Rushing over the walled gardens and sparse, dried-up woods of Spellshadow Manor, they shot through the barrier toward the unknown territory, though not before Alex had the chance to look back at the others. He had forgotten how strong Virgil was, and although they were many, and they were better prepared than the last time, it seemed as if the Head was putting up a good fight. It pained Alex, knowing he wouldn't hear of the outcome until he returned. Still, it pressed him onward, giving him the drive he needed to get this over and done with as quickly as possible.

What added to his worries, however, was the turbulence they were experiencing. The world had stretched around them, as per usual when Storm was crossing between realms, but there was something different about this journey. It was rough and jarring, nothing like the smooth transitions he'd experienced so far. Storm's despairing squawks did little to quell his fears as she soldiered on.

"Is it supposed to be like this?" Demeter yelled, his voice barely audible above the rush of wind.

Alex shook his head, his cheeks pushed back by the

force of the journey. "No!"

"Didn't think so!" shouted Demeter, though the ex-teacher still seemed relatively unruffled.

Alex clung on for dear life, whispering soothing words to the struggling Thunderbird, as she forced her way through the barrier between worlds. As she beat her wings ever faster, Alex wondered if this was the end for him. He had a sinking feeling he was about to get lost in the ether, never to be discovered again.

A moment later, the world snapped back into place, making Alex feel slightly foolish for having had such gloomy thoughts.

"You okay back there?" Alex asked, looking over his shoulder.

Demeter grinned. "A-Okay!"

"Cargo intact?"

"Aye, aye, Captain," he confirmed, pulling a face that Alex guessed was supposed to resemble a pirate's.

Turning back around, Alex gaped in awe, taking in his surroundings. He had been expecting somewhere like Kingstone or Stillwater, just farther away from the main structures, but this place wasn't familiar at all. Alex realized it was a haven, but not one of the four. It had to be one of the nine that was thought to have fallen, though it didn't look very desolate. It made him wonder whether there was a central building somewhere here too, like the pagoda at Falleaf, or the keep at Kingstone.

The air was warm and the sky clear, not a cloud to be seen, but there was no magical barrier at work here. It was simply nature showing off. Lush fields filled with golden corn and brightly colored wildflowers kissed the shores of sparkling lakes, eventually giving way to a vast settlement that ran up to the edge of a deep, inviting river. On the banks stood many wooden, homemade-looking structures, clustered in a vaguely uniform pattern. From the looks of it, the place was thriving.

The population appeared to be fairly young, though there were a couple of older faces too. It made Alex wonder if supernaturally long life was reserved solely for the noble and extraordinarily powerful, and not meant for the likes of ordinary magical folk. It was the only explanation he had for the number of older faces staring up at him as he made his entrance.

Open-mouthed, they all rushed to get closer to the majestic Thunderbird as she landed elegantly in a patch of open space. Once they were at a standstill, Alex and Demeter dismounted, the ex-teacher still holding the sleeping Venus to him.

Though Alex was a stranger to these parts, the inhabitants of the mystery haven seemed more preoccupied with the majesty of Storm, who was playing up to their adoration, chirping and cooing, though she snapped at a couple of hands that drew too close.

"Who are you?" asked one of them. The speaker was an older woman, her hair just beginning to gray, who eyed the newcomers with open suspicion. In truth, it was the reaction Alex had expected from most of the people who had gathered around.

"We're looking for Ceres. We're friends of her brother, and we need her help," Alex said, hoping Ceres wasn't too far. He was antsy to get back to the fight and capture Virgil, not wanting to leave his friends alone for too long. They were more than capable, but he knew he needed to return as soon as possible, if only for the fact he still had one of the bags of essence in his possession. If previous encounters were anything to go by, they would need it.

"Why should we take you to her?" the older woman replied, her tone less than friendly.

"We need her help," Alex repeated.

He didn't have to wait long, however, as the very woman he wanted to meet pushed her way through the throng, arriving to see what the commotion was. She looked horrified when her eyes fell on Alex, her shock only intensifying as she glanced from him to the quarry clutched in Demeter's arms. Then there was Demeter himself. Alex only saw it for a moment, but he glimpsed a flutter of sadness passing over her face.

Alex braced himself for a tirade that never came.

"Come with me," she muttered, though it was clear she was holding back her rage. Without another word, she whirled around and stalked back through the crowd. Alex and Demeter hurried after her, feeling the burn of a thousand eyes on them as they did so.

"Wouldn't want to be in his shoes," Alex heard someone mutter.

It didn't exactly fill him with warm, fuzzy feelings as they followed Ceres toward a large tent that had been set up at the far edge of the shantytown. The heavy scarlet material flapped in the breeze, the yellow flag perched at the top rippling wildly. Inside, the tent was sparsely decorated, with patterned cushions and plush rugs scattered about the place. Alex didn't have much time to take in his surroundings, because as soon as they were inside, Ceres turned to glare at them.

"What are you doing here?" she snapped. "And what possessed you to bring *her* here?" she added, running an anxious hand through her brightly streaked hair.

"We need you to keep Venus here for us," said Alex.

Ceres shook her head vehemently. "No, no way, not a chance. I warned you. How *dare* you bring her here! Do you understand what you've done?" she asked, glowering in Alex's direction. "And you! You should have known better," she growled, turning her attention fully to Demeter for the first time.

"It's good to see you," said Demeter quietly, garnering a savage eye-roll from the bright-haired woman.

"So not the time!" she remarked. "I can't believe you've done this, after everything I've said—after everything Hadrian said. Did you choose not to listen, or are you just that dense? You brought the damned queen here! Of every single person in the entire world, *she* is the worst possible person you could have brought here. You realize Julius will come for her, right? And then everyone will die, or worse, beneath his wrath. He doesn't forgive, ever, and you have just sealed everyone's fate!" she yelled, through teeth gritted in pure fury.

"Not if you help us—we're running out of time." Alex explained as quickly as he could. "My friends are in the middle of a battle with Virgil, and this might be our only chance to get some blood that we need to do a spell that could signal the end of all of this—no more needless death, no more essence collection, no more running. If I can get it done before Julius hears any whisper of this, we'll all be free. You won't have to hide anymore. Nobody will."

She softened a fraction, her expression thoughtful. "This

is a stupid risk."

"I know you want to see an end to this, Ceres; it is all you've ever wanted, and it's finally within our reach," Demeter said, utterly impassioned. "Think of all the lives that could be saved, all the young people who will never have to suffer what those kids out there have suffered."

Alex was surprised to see this side of Demeter, but evidently it worked on Ceres, whose expression softened another fraction.

"How did you even get here?" she asked, scrutinizing the pair. "There's only one way in and out of Starcross Pond, and none of my security alarms went off."

"Starcross Pond?" Alex asked, running the name across his tongue. It had a nice ring to it.

"Formerly Starcross Castle, but the castle is long gone," Ceres replied. "But that doesn't answer my question—*how* can you be here?"

Demeter smiled. "That giant bird you saw out there is a Thunderbird. She flies between realms," he said matter-of-factly.

A wistful look flashed in Ceres's eyes. "One of these?" she asked, pulling up the sleeve of her shirt to reveal a colorful tattoo. It was in the shape of a Thunderbird, though more brightly colored than Storm. Where she had silver-and-blue feathers, the ones in the image were a ferocious red, tinged with black and orange.

Demeter nodded. "The very same, only this one is real."

"You drew this, remember?" she said softly.

"How could I forget?" he replied, and the two stared at each other with an intensity that made Alex uncomfortable.

"Did anyone follow you?" Ceres asked, her tone anxious.

The auburn-haired man shook his head. "Not unless someone is hiding a secret Thunderbird somewhere."

This seemed to calm Ceres a smidgen, though not as much as Alex would have liked.

"We're desperate, Ceres," said Alex, trying to hold onto his frustration. "I need you to hold Venus here, so there's no chance of her running off to the one man we both hate. Nobody will find her here, because nobody knows this place exists."

"I can't just—" Ceres began, but Alex cut her off.

"I care just as much about the way this is going to end as you do—I want my people to live. I want my friends, and all those stolen kids, and all those people out there who are yet to be taken, to be safe from these people who see them as nothing more than a commodity. I want what you want, but I have to do this first." He let all his pent-up emotions rattle out of his mouth, until there was only one question left. "So, Ceres, will you help me?"

A moment of silence passed between the tense figures

gathered in the tent.

Ceres sighed. "I will hold you personally responsible if anything does happen, and I will make you pay. Is that understood?" she said slowly. "Even if I am the only person left standing, I will find you and I will make you suffer."

"That sounds fair," Alex replied. He had expected no less from Ceres and knew she would be sure to carry out every threat. "So, you'll keep Venus here, until we have either failed or won?"

She raised an eyebrow. "You had better not lose."

"I'm just covering all our bases," Alex admitted. "If it comes to it, and we do lose, it might be wise to use Venus as a bargaining chip. It might be your last chance for freedom."

"You're not as dim as you appear, are you?" Ceres flashed a half smile.

Alex shrugged. "That's yet to be seen."

"Will you stop staring at me?" she sighed, turning toward Demeter, who hadn't been able to take his eyes off her the whole time they had been talking. Though he was still weaving strands of energy into Venus's mind, the majority of his attention was on Ceres.

Demeter smiled. "I can't, not after so long. I didn't even know you were alive until a few days ago, and to see you again is like having all my lost hopes and broken dreams restored to me in one piece. You can't know the joy I feel, seeing you again," he breathed, overcome with emotion.

"I think I have some idea," Ceres murmured, breaking eye contact.

Demeter did something that knocked Venus into a whole other level of slumber, though she still looked well enough as he lay her down on a nearby rug. For added security, he fashioned some cuffs around her wrists and left her to sleep.

Alex saw his opportunity.

"Do you have a knife?" he asked, aware that he was shattering a potentially romantic moment between them.

Ceres nodded, picking one up off a table and passing it to Alex, who took it gratefully. Moving over to the sleeping woman, he knelt down beside her and lifted her arm up. Just as he was about to press the blade to her pale skin, he paused, realizing he didn't have anything to carry the blood in. An idea came to him suddenly. He pulled the sack of essence from his back and took one solitary vial from within. Taking out the stopper, he poured the glowing red essence carefully into the ground, watching as it sank back into the earth.

Breathing deeply, he pressed the sharp edge of the blade as delicately as he could into the queen's skin, just above the dip of her elbow. Scarlet blood blossomed to the surface. Alex pushed the lip of the vial up to the viscous liquid, and it trickled into the bottle. Drop after drop fell into the black glass bottle, but he did not stop until he had a full spoonful sloshing at the bottom.

Better to be safe than sorry, he told himself. He tore a strip of fabric from his shirt and bound it around the wound.

Pocketing the singular vial, he strapped the bag of essence to his back once more, and stood. Turning to look at Ceres and Demeter, he saw that they were in the middle of a tearful reunion—one that made Alex feel slightly like a third wheel, and more than a touch reluctant to interrupt.

"After so many years apart, I will never leave your side again," Demeter said defiantly.

Alex had to speak up. "You're staying? You can't—you need to come back with me."

Demeter turned to Alex, shaking his head. "I won't be coming with you, Alex... I can't."

"What if we need you?" Alex pressed, eager to be on his way back to Spellshadow.

"I am needed here," Demeter replied. "I will keep an eye on Venus. If you want her to remain asleep, she is going to require constant attention from me, and so I must stay. You have proven yourself at every turn, and you will not fail now. I know it... I can feel it in my heart." He clapped Alex on the back.

Alex had a feeling that convincing Demeter to leave

Ceres was one battle he definitely couldn't win. Glancing between the two lovebirds, he could see the happiness written all over their faces.

"It won't be the same without you, and your powers will be sorely missed… not to mention you, yourself," Alex said sorrowfully. "When this is all over, we'll come back. Until then, I suppose the pair of you have a lot of catching up to do," he added, grinning.

"We'll meet again soon, Spellbreaker," Demeter promised. "Now, go, before it's too late."

Ceres nodded. "Give them hell!"

Alex didn't need telling twice. He tore from the tent and sprinted back across the field, weaving in and out of the crowd that still stood around Storm. They parted as Alex approached, and he jumped up onto her back.

"To Spellshadow," he told her, but she was already running along the riverbank, building up to a take-off.

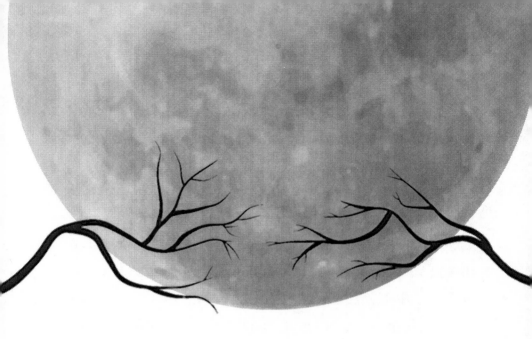

CHAPTER 33

HURTLING BACK THROUGH INTO THE REALM OF Spellshadow Manor, the flight as violently turbulent the second time around, Storm didn't slow as she swooped across the sickly woods, before thundering over the smoking field and soaring up and over the crumbling ruins of the walled garden. As they neared the front lawn, Alex could see that the fight was still raging below, though more people had come to swell the ranks on either side.

Alex's friends and the Stillwater volunteers stood on one side of the grass, while others had joined Virgil's side.

Along with the professors, who were to be expected, Alex was surprised to see that a handful of Spellshadow students stood on the opposing side of the lawn. It seemed they were hedging their bets, going for the side that looked to have a better chance of winning, and the sight made Alex's heart ache. As silly as it seemed, he felt a pang of betrayal to see so many standing with the Head. Jun Asano and Catherine de Marchmont, their golden bands forcing their loyalty, stood on either side of Virgil, with another standing behind, protecting him.

Golden creatures bounded through the melee, savage and snapping, but they didn't appear to have much understanding of whose side they were on, striking whoever came near. The roars and screams of the fighters echoed in Alex's ears as Storm swooped low over the chaos.

He saw that his friends were holding their own, sending wave after wave of rippling magic through the air, toward their aggressors, but Alex knew it was a fragile balance. At this point, there was no telling who would emerge triumphant. There would be many injured, or worse, by the time this was done.

Grabbing the sack of essence from his back, Alex rested it on the neck of the Thunderbird, hooking the drawstring ends around the bony protrusions of Storm's shoulders. With it securely in place, he grasped for the closest bottles.

Circling the scene below, he felt a wave of panic as he saw the cloaked figure of Jun Asano approaching with lightning speed, moving so fast he wasn't even sure Natalie saw him coming. Jun's hands were raised to strike, a glint of sinister magic, tinged slightly crimson, surging from his palms, clearly intended to inflict real harm upon Natalie, if not something worse. The new professor's eyes were wild, and Alex could see the influence of the Head, twisting Jun's mind into darkness.

Glancing at the closing gap between Natalie and Jun, Alex knew he had to step in—the new professor was barely more than a blur, gaining fast, his crimson-tinged magic building before his palms. Alex gulped. There was nothing else he could do but yank out the stoppers, feeding the pulsing light onto his hands. Focusing on the energy, he sent streams of his own into the glow. They morphed into the same golden creatures who were striding below. His golden beasts plummeted to the ground, landing directly on top of the unsuspecting enemy.

One bore a wolf's shape, and it lunged for the throat of Jun Asano, tearing at it with gnashing jaws. Light glowed from within the former student as the essence-forged beast clawed the very life force from the young man. Alex wished he could un-see it. Jun screamed, the sound silenced in mid-flow by the wolf snatching the soul away from the new professor. Jun crumpled, lying still on the grass, his eyes blank and unseeing. It wasn't what Alex had wanted to do, but his quick thinking had saved Natalie's life, the French girl still oblivious to how close she'd come to harm at the hands of Jun Asano.

Catherine ran to what had presumably been her friend, but it was too late to do anything. As hard as she shook him, and as loud as she howled his name, he could not be woken. There was no life left inside him, his essence now trailing from the jaws of the golden beast.

Both sides looked up to see where the deadly creatures had come from, their mouths opening in shock as they saw Alex astride the great Thunderbird. The only ones who seemed less fearful were his friends, a wave of relief passing across their faces. Alex knew it might be a little bit too early for relief—this fight wasn't nearly over yet.

A second later, it was Alex who felt surprise as Storm swept across a small band of Spellshadow students, who had joined the Head. Opening her beak wide, Alex felt a rumble beneath him, from deep inside the lungs of the bird. Directing her head toward the enemies, she let out a blood-chilling roar, followed by a blast of ice that rocketed toward the suddenly terrified group. It hit them with full force, smothering them in a wave of ice. As the mist of it cleared, Alex saw that the front line had turned into a series of ice-sculptures, their bodies frozen to the spot. Those who were left ran, but there was nowhere to hide.

Storm wheeled around, and Alex hoped the band of Spellshadow students would not permanently remain frozen. He didn't feel right hurting anyone, the act leaving him unsettled, but Storm was, by her very nature, a warbird, and so the fate of those poor souls remained to be seen.

With one professor down, Alex circled Storm back toward the place where Catherine stood. She had managed to dispense with the wolf and the second creature, shaped like a lion, but she was not paying attention to the enormous bird above her. There was too much going on, and it was clear she was no longer looking at the sky.

Seeing his opportunity, Alex pulled the stoppers from another two vials, feeding his energy into them, before dropping them on top of Catherine. These took the shape of a bear and a wolverine, but the bear took off toward a different band of Spellshadow students, who stood to the other side of the Head. Alex didn't dare see what mess it was making, his eyes drawn instead to the smaller shape of the wolverine, which had its sights set firmly on Catherine. Running fast, it sank its golden jaws into her leg, dragging it out from under her. She fell, sending out panicked flurries of magic, as the wolverine pounced on top of her, clawing at her with blade-like nails.

Alex didn't see what happened to her as Storm did a loop-the-loop, turning them back around. But when he looked back down, Catherine was lying still on the ground beside Jun Asano, the wolverine nowhere to be seen.

A rapid bolt of energy flew past Alex's ear. The Head had focused his attention on Storm. Ducking and diving out of the way, Storm managed to evade every wave, until a stray shot caught her in the wing. With a pained squawk, she flew toward the ground, close enough that Alex could jump off, though he pulled closed the bag before he did so. She would protect the bottles, until he needed them again. Landing squarely on the ground, he patted the Thunderbird's side.

"Go to safety!" he told her.

She chirped, brushing her beak across his hand, before rising back up into the air.

Alex was close to where Catherine had been standing, but it seemed the wolverine hadn't quite gotten the better of Catherine de Marchmont. She was slowly rising, though the Head had moved a fair way from her, presumably to avoid the same fate at the jaws of a golden wolverine. Alex ran over to her before she could fully get up, and pressed his hands to the sides of her head, manipulating her thoughts into believing the Head was evil. Seeing the golden band still gleaming on her wrist, he reached down to break it, forcing his anti-magic into the circlet and shattering it from the inside out. Almost as soon as he had done it, he regretted it, re-membering the consequences of the released curse. She con-vulsed for a moment, before lying still once more. As much as he wished he'd waited, he knew she'd have a better chance of survival if he could get Helena to deal with the inner tur-moil of the curse later.

A shadow passed across him. Glancing up, he saw that Storm hadn't quite heeded his warning, as the vast Thunderbird crashed down upon the figure of the Head, grasping at him with her fierce talons. Virgil tried to fight back, but she was aggressive, battering him with her sharp claws, kicking out at him with a vengeful fury, and pecking at him viciously with her spiked beak. No matter how hard the Head tried to retaliate, Storm was everywhere at once, snapping and biting at him, keeping him distracted.

Looking around, Alex did a quick count. With Jun and Catherine down, the right-hand band of Spellshadow defec-tors mostly frozen or hiding, and the left-hand band still try-ing to fend off the attacks of a wolverine and a bear, Alex saw that an advantage was slowly appearing. The essence-crea-tures wouldn't last forever, but they were doing a good job of keeping the opposition at bay.

Alex beckoned to his friends. They came running, with the Stillwater students and the supporting Spellshadow stu-dents following suit. All of them formed an arc around the place where Virgil and the third new professor stood. She was not somebody Alex recognized, but she already looked battle hardened, with curly red hair and a stern face. Nor was she willing to go down without a vicious fight, as she immediately set to work, firing blockades at the oncoming group.

Alex sent a blockade of his own toward her, knocking her backwards into a huge cluster of ivy that clung to the wall of Spellshadow. She sat there for a moment, apparently stunned, unable to get up, as the plant sapped the energy from her. There was so much of it, and it was all around her—there was no escaping so much. It was something of a relief, however, knowing that she would be okay once she was removed from the ivy. At least they could save her, Alex thought, trying very hard not to look at the lifeless form of Jun Asano.

Finally, it had come down to just the Head. Storm was still doing an exceptional job of keeping him distracted, blasting him every so often with a fierce bolt of ice, but he wasn't backing down.

"Don't kill him!" Alex warned. The fighters around him nodded. He knew that was the worst thing that could happen, right now, if someone were to get a little over-eager and end the Head's life, just before the spell could be done.

Pushing the worries from his mind, Alex stepped up,

weaving threads of black and silver in the air. He forged them into a whirling ball of raw energy and sent it hurtling toward Virgil, only for it to smack into the Head with relatively little effect. It seemed like it caused more of a nuisance than an injury. With a twist of frustration, Alex remembered why. He had almost forgotten that his anti-magical powers were not nearly as effective on Virgil as they were on others.

Ellabell and Helena took the lead. Combining their forces, they created a huge orb of power, the bronze crackle of Helena's exceptional force bristling in the center. With a formidable push, they sent the orb toward the Head. It him it square on, and though the Head wasn't very susceptible to the power of mages either, it had some of the desired effect. The skeletal man sagged, clutching his stomach, as a flurry of snowflakes fell around him. Aamir and Jari did the same. Pair after pair approached, sending an orb of fierce light toward the struggling Head, but still he did not fall.

Alex clenched his fists, wondering what he could do to shift the balance in their favor. A flash of shadow cut across the scene, and Elias hit the Head square in the jaw, only aggravating the skeletal man further. It gave Alex an idea. Closing his eyes, he searched deep inside himself, looking for the piece of torn-off soul he had unwittingly taken from Elias. Eventually he found the strange pulse of something that did not belong to him. Drawing the power of it into his hands, he allowed it to flow into the swirling fabric of his own energy. Opening his eyes, he saw that a vast black mass was twisting and turning in front of him. It looked almost liquid and seemed to have a life of its own, but Alex could sense the throb of power emanating from within.

Steeling himself, he let it flow toward Virgil. It swamped the Head, smothering him like oil, slithering beneath his skin, turning the blue veins black. The Head doubled over in pain, letting out a blood-curdling cry as he crumpled into a heap on the ground, already half frozen to death by the impact of Storm's relentless ice beams. Pain seared through Alex too, and he struggled to ignore it—there was too much at stake.

Alex raced toward the slumped, skeletal figure and hauled him up. Aamir ran up to help, each boy taking an arm across their shoulders as they dragged the weakened Virgil across the lawn, up the steps, and into the school. The hallways were empty, save for the few figures who were still recovering from the effects of Demeter's influence, giving them an easy route. Passing Billy Foer, Alex saw that the boy was still giggling uncontrollably on the floor. He hoped he hadn't done any irreversible damage, but there would be time to see about those things later.

"We need to take him to the room with the manacles," Alex explained.

Aamir nodded. "I thought as much," he said, with a hint of remorse. It wasn't somewhere that held particularly good memories for the older boy.

With Virgil still somewhere between asleep and awake, they reached the door to the chamber. The metallic scent of fear and blood seemed all the more potent. Pushing the door open, they hauled Virgil inside, and quickly clamped the manacles around his skeletal wrists. The Head offered no resistance, still suffering the effects of whatever Alex had done to him, but it was strange to see the thin, bony man dangling from the chains, looking so vulnerable.

Alex stepped back. It was a fitting tribute, he thought, considering all the others that Virgil had strung up here, with the sole purpose of stealing their lives.

"Could you leave us alone?" Alex asked, turning to Aamir.

Aamir frowned, looking dubious. "I'm not sure that is such a good idea, Alex. You don't know how useful these chains will be against him when he wakes up."

"Please… I need to do this alone," Alex insisted.

"Alex—"

"Aamir, please do this. Please, leave us be," Alex repeated, more determined than ever. "Tend to the wounded, fix those who have been brainwashed. Your help is needed out there, not here."

For a moment, it looked like Aamir was going to stay, regardless of what Alex said, but, eventually, he relented, moving toward the door of the chamber.

"You must come and get us the moment you even think about doing the counter-spell. If you do not swear that to me, I will not leave," Aamir said firmly.

Alex smiled. "I promise."

With a reluctant sigh, Aamir departed, leaving Alex alone with the man who had caused so much suffering.

CHAPTER 34

"**T**HIS HAS BEEN A LONG TIME COMING," A VOICE whispered, the shadows by the entrance to the chamber shifting as Elias emerged.

The Head hung limply from the dangling manacles, still knocked out by the blast that had weakened him. Alex watched him closely, paying little attention to the shadow-man as he sauntered up to the skeletal figure. The Head's hood had fallen away, revealing the pale skin and sunken cheeks Alex recognized. It was strange to see him so vulnerable, but there was a triumph in their achievement. They had done what they had intended to do, and now redemption wasn't far off. Alex inhaled deeply, feeling the weight of the Book of Jupiter in the satchel slung across his body.

"He doesn't look so powerful now, does he?" Elias mused, lifting a wispy finger to the Head's face.

The contact, however gentle, made Virgil stir.

"He's just a man," Alex replied, more to himself than anyone else. It was true—Virgil was just a mortal person, with a history that had formed him into the being that dangled before them. In a different life, the Head might have been different. Had he been cherished, the way a son ought to have been, perhaps he would have taken an alternate path.

Elias touched the Head's face again, causing him to stir once more. A low groan emitted from Virgil's mouth, his strange eyes blinking slowly open, as if he had just woken from a nightmare. His head snapped up, those same eyes going wide as Virgil took in his surroundings, looking up to see the restraints that held him firmly in place. There was panic on the ghoulish man's face, but Alex felt little remorse. No amount of sympathy for Virgil's past could wipe the slate clean of the things he had done, and it was time for him to pay for those gross misdemeanors.

"Release me," the Head croaked.

It was Elias who spoke first. "You will never be free again," he hissed.

Alex glanced at the shadow-man, feeling the hatred

radiating from the wispy creature. The ferocity of his loathing was frightening to behold, especially as Alex could now feel it coursing through his own body—an unexpected byproduct of their shared energy.

"Release me this instant!" Virgil demanded, pulling against his restraints. The chains rattled, but there was no escape for the pale figure. It was the Head's own security measures that now held him in place. Nobody, Spellbreaker, mage or hybrid, could break free of the sapping energy of the manacles.

"I want you to beg for your life," Elias purred. "I want you to plead for it, the way I once pleaded for mine. I shall show you the same mercy you showed me."

The Head sneered. "You will never see me beg, Elias. You flaunted your power, and you suffered for your pride. I will admit... I made an error in judgment, listening to Derhin, but you would not cooperate. I asked you to volunteer and you wouldn't. When I told you of my own suffering, you laughed in my face—or have you forgotten?"

"I have forgotten nothing, Virgil," Elias replied. "I wasn't responsible for what Julius made you do, but you only sought to weasel your way out of it. You saw me, saw what I could do, and thought you'd take it for yourself. You were jealous and idiotic, but you'll find it's me who gets the last laugh."

Virgil gave a low, menacing chuckle. "You are mistaken.

I will not beg, and you will not succeed in taking whatever it is you think you can draw from me. You are weak, both of you."

Alex frowned. There was a defiance in the skeletal creature that Alex hadn't quite expected. Having seen him cowed in front of Alypia, Alex had forgotten that the Head could actually be quite intimidating when he wanted to be, especially at such close quarters. There was resentment in him too, as if Virgil blamed Elias and Alex for his own state of affairs, and the suffering he had undergone.

"Even now, you're blaming someone else for your failings," Elias taunted, flashing his teeth in a wry smile.

"We're not here to take your essence," Alex said, keeping his voice strong. "An apology wouldn't save you now, even if you wanted to make amends for all the horrible things you've done."

"I did what I had to," Virgil remarked, showing no hint of remorse for the acts that had brought him here. "You think you have some sort of power over me, but no matter what you do to me, you will get your comeuppance. The chaos you have caused will not go unpunished. Once Julius hears of this, he will kill you in the most horrible manner you can imagine," he spat, glowering in Alex's direction.

Alex smiled. "With your help, whether you like it or not, we are going to put a stop to the Great Evil," he said quietly, letting the words sink in.

To his surprise, the Head showed little fear. "You're bluffing, Alex Webber," he sneered. "The king of this nation could not make me do the act that would stop the Great Evil—what makes you think you can?"

"I know things Julius didn't," said Alex simply. "I am exactly the person who can make you do it. Let's not forget, you and I share a common ancestor," he added, gauging the Head's reaction.

Virgil looked puzzled. "You and I share only our cursed power."

Alex shook his head. "Not just that," he said, and it felt so good to gloat. It didn't seem the Head knew about his ancestry at all. Perhaps Julius and Venus had kept it from him all these years, in fear of how he might react, or how others might react to such a revelation, if the secret was more widely known. It wouldn't be right to have a descendant of Leander Wyvern in such close association with the royal elite. "Have you heard of Leander Wyvern?" he asked.

"Rebel scum," Virgil spat.

"Not a very nice thing to say about your father," Alex remarked. "Your mother loved him, and their love created something impossible... *you*. My ancestor was also his child. You and I are blood, and no amount of defiance can change that."

A look of pure rage flashed across Virgil's face. "LIAR!"

"Afraid not, Virgil," Elias purred. "The boy speaks the truth. You were the product of a love so rare, it defied the laws of nature."

"I'm going to need you to tell me where the Spellshadow pit room is," Alex said, relishing in the look of confusion that played across the Head's ghoulish features.

A menacing smile stretched Virgil's lips. "'Pit room?' I don't know what you're talking about."

"Don't play dumb, Virgil. You know precisely where it is," Elias said.

"Even if I did, I would never tell you," Virgil hissed. "You are liars… I will never help you. You think a shared 'bond' will change my mind? After all this time, you think I care where I came from? Even if you were telling the truth, it wouldn't matter. I know where my loyalties lie, and no tainted blood can alter that. I will never breathe a word of what you want to know," he added, his voice dripping with hatred.

Alex smiled. "You don't have to."

Slowly, Alex approached the dangling figure, and though the Head fought against his restraints, there was nowhere to run. He could not stop what Alex was about to do, and for the first time, Alex saw a glimpse of something close to fear in the Head's eyes. Reaching out his hands, Alex pressed his palms tightly against the struggling figure's skull, keeping his head still as Virgil thrashed. Focusing intently, Alex weaved strands of white light into the Head's mind. All the while, the skeletal man fought back, but there was nothing he could do to prevent the seeking strands of Alex's powers.

Memories flooded Alex's mind as he sifted through Virgil's thoughts. He saw the Head standing in the sunshine with Finder, discussing the events that had brought them to that point. It was strange for Alex to see the discussion from a different perspective, looking at things through Virgil's eyes, and their current symbiosis was the most unsettled Alex had felt in using his skillset. As their conversation came to a close, Alex knew Virgil had only been trying to do what was best, and what Julius expected of him, but it made no difference. Like anyone else in the world, he'd had a choice, and he'd followed the path of evil.

There were images of Virgil as a younger man, before the peculiar living decay had set in, giving him his current skeletal appearance. Flashes of Alypia's cruelty peppered the scenes. She had been a cold-hearted sibling, taunting and hurting him at every opportunity, forever getting him into trouble with a step-father who loathed him. Seeing the familiar face of Julius screaming in the face of the younger Virgil, a hand raised to strike, Alex almost recoiled, feeling the ripple of intense fear that Virgil had felt now coursing through his veins.

Moving quickly on, he came to the vision he was looking for. Virgil was walking through the hallways of Spellshadow, carrying a large bag of clinking bottles with him, though there wasn't quite so much gray ivy littering the place. He seemed to be heading for the secret corridors of his private quarters. Reaching the library where Ellabell had been left screaming after Elias's attack, Virgil stopped, opening the door. Casting a glance back over his shoulder, he stepped into the room and closed the door firmly behind him.

It looked exactly the same as it had the last time Alex had entered the library, but Virgil didn't seem interested in the rare and antique books. He moved on past the stacks, heading for a structure at the back of the room. It was a vast statue, tucked away behind a large bookshelf. When he pulled down on a splayed-out book carved from marble, a doorway appeared in the base of the statue. It was narrow, the Head having to turn sideways to slip through, but his thin frame made it easy.

Beyond, there was a staircase, leading down into the underground depths of the school. Alex watched through Virgil's eyes as he descended hurriedly, his feet barely making a sound on the stone steps. At the bottom of the staircase was a hallway, hewn from the rock, much like the one Alex had witnessed at Kingstone, and at the end of the hallway stood a very familiar door. It was tall and sturdy-looking, with two great iron rings on either side.

Virgil approached it, opening up one of the doors. Alex already knew what he was going to see when he followed the vision through, but the sight was no less impressive for his anticipation. A huge pit yawned at the center of the cavernous room, a golden bird perched above it, flapping its wings wildly, its screeches piercing the stale air. It seemed Virgil had arrived just in time with his bottles of essence—the Great Evil was ravenous.

Now knowing where he needed to go, Alex began to recoil from the mind of Virgil. However, just before he removed the last of his strands from the Head's mind, he paused, realizing he was going to have to do something to keep the Head malleable. The pit wasn't too far, but Virgil wasn't likely to come willingly.

Remembering what he had done to Virgil out on the lawn, Alex reached down into himself, seeking out the dim pulse of the piece of Elias's soul. Drawing on it, he brought the magic into his hands and let the dark energy flow into Virgil's mind, hopefully dazing him enough to get him to the pit without too much trouble.

Recoiling fully, Alex stepped back to review his handiwork. The Head had gone limp again, his whole body swaying lifelessly from the chains.

"You better not have killed him," said Elias.

Alex grasped the Head's wrist, checking for a pulse. To his relief, there was still a light thud beneath the skin.

"Don't worry me like that!" Alex snapped, ignoring the grin Elias flashed back.

Unlocking the manacles, Alex released Virgil from his restraints, only to realize their next problem. With Aamir no longer around, it would be up to Alex to carry the Head to the library by himself. Stooping, Alex hauled the Head's arm around his neck and began to drag him toward the door of the chamber. Elias cackled, evidently delighted at the comical sight.

"You could always help," Alex said, losing patience.

Elias gave a casual shrug of his wispy shoulders. "I suppose I could," he replied, swooping to help with Virgil's other arm. It was a pleasant surprise, to have the shadow-man assist in the dirty work for once, and as much as Alex wanted to say as much, he held his tongue. The last thing he needed was for Elias to take offense and disappear into the darkness.

Sharing the weight, though the Head didn't weigh all that much, given his skeletal frame, Alex and Elias hurried out of the chamber and headed toward the library. Turning the handle, Alex pushed open the door and pulled Virgil inside, leaving the door standing wide open as he carried the Head over to the statue he had seen in the memory. The splayed-out book was there, just as Alex had seen it. The anticipation was overwhelming as Alex pulled down on the book and watched the secret entrance slide open. They were impossibly close to success now.

With every awkward step they took down into the earth, Alex's heart pounded harder and harder, until he thought it might burst from his chest. Eventually, they reached the bottom, where the hallway with the huge double doors stood at the far end. Alex paused for a second in front of the iron rungs, gripping the right-hand knocker until his knuckles whitened. It was getting a little too real, and part of Alex wanted to savor the moment as he pulled the doors wide.

The pit lay before him, but the golden bird perched above was barely moving.

You will never be fed again, Alex promised.

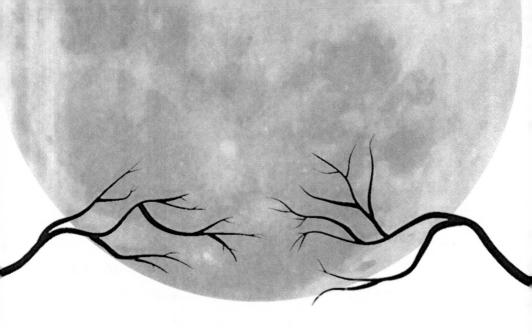

CHAPTER 35

L AYING VIRGIL DOWN AT THE SIDE OF THE PIT, ALEX
retrieved the Book of Jupiter from his bag and flipped
to the correct page. Holding out a thin square of
energy, he watched the glyphs morph into words, revealing
the content of the counter-spell. Remembering a trick he'd
seen Helena use, he fed more anti-magic into the edges
of the square, causing it to remain, even when he took his
hands away.

It was time, and yet something held him back.

"What are you waiting for?" asked Elias impatiently.

"I should get the others," said Alex, having completely

forgotten the promise he'd made to Aamir, in all the excitement of getting Virgil to the pit room. "I swore I'd go back to get them before I did the spell."

Elias rolled his eyes. "You don't have time to fetch them, Alex, not to mention the fact it's not a good idea to have them around this kind of spell. I haven't seen it done before, but I have seen spells like it, and I know there can sometimes be collateral. If a bystander is unworthy, or just happens to get in the way, they're toast. You wouldn't want something awful happening to your itty-bitty chums now, would you?" the shadow-man asked.

Alex glanced at Elias uncertainly. There was a lot of sense in what he said, but it didn't feel quite right not to go back and tell the others. This conclusion was as much a part of their journey as it was his.

"I should go and get them," Alex insisted.

Elias slithered toward the door, blocking the way. "You will put their lives at risk, Alex. I am not saying this because I am me, though I know that is likely what you are thinking—for once, I am saying this because I would hate to see them die so close to the end."

"You really think it's that dangerous?" Alex asked, realizing how stupid the question sounded. Of course it was dangerous. If it weren't, he wouldn't have had to run a gauntlet of challenges to attain the book that would allow him to do it.

"Is that a serious question?" Elias countered, raising a starry brow.

Alex shook his head. "No, I suppose not. I guess they won't mind, if it all goes well," he reasoned.

Turning his focus away from his friends, Alex knelt beside the slumped figure of Virgil, and began to feed the strands of his mind control into the Head's brain. Alex made the skeletal figure get to his feet, like a macabre marionette, and move toward the edge of the pit. Holding him there with one hand, Alex reached into his pocket and pulled out the vial full of blood, resting it on the open page. That part came later.

Noting all the stages in order, Alex moved on to the incantation. First, he placed Virgil's hand on the page, as instructed. For a moment, nothing happened, but then the book began to glow subtly, then burst into a fierce luminescence. The writing on the pages lifted up, swirling like a tornado before settling in the air before them, hovering just above the pit. The words were laid out in large, glowing lettering, making the incantation easier to read. Alex hoped this meant things were going well, if the book was responding as it should.

Taking a deep breath, he delved back into the depths of Virgil's mind, making suggestions that forced strands of anti-magic to rise up from the Head's palms. It was a strange, out-of-body experience for Alex, controlling somebody else's energy, but he felt the strength of Virgil's power.

Alex pulled the strings that made Virgil's voice ring out across the cavern. The incantation had begun, the words moving through Alex's mind and into Virgil's mouth.

I come to thee with honesty and purity in my heart. My intentions are good and my motives are true. I stand at the precipice of destruction, knowing the price that must be paid. I come to thee with no hand forcing my path, and I seek redemption on behalf of those who seek to destroy. Where wounds have been cut, I shall repair. Where evil has traveled, I shall make amends. Where there has been death, I shall bring life. Where there has been war, I bring peace.

Alex paused at the end of the first paragraph, letting the words sink in. A slight rumble shook the earth, but he couldn't be sure if it was the spell that had caused it. Overcome with nervous excitement, he pressed on, moving from second stanza, to third, to fourth, to fifth, to sixth, to seventh, to eighth, to ninth, to tenth, to eleventh, and, finally, to twelfth. Not once did he stutter, ensuring he took his time to feed the words carefully into the Head's mind, so he could recite them precisely as they ought to be spoken. All the while, Alex was conscious of what he had been told about not making a single error. It was a terrifying prospect, to know that one false move could ruin everything, and it took everything he had not to focus on that fear.

Slowly, he came to the end of the twelfth and final stanza. Never had a finish line seemed so close and yet so far away. He could see the final line, but he was careful not to jump ahead and miss anything as he moved slowly through the final paragraph, Virgil's voice speaking the words with a confident fluidity that Alex didn't quite feel himself.

His heart was thundering in his chest as he reached the last line.

"With the blood of my enemies, I close the circle of pain," said Virgil, speaking the words as Alex fed them into his mind. The Head had performed perfectly, but it wasn't yet over. There was one step left.

As the final word echoed across the cavern, Alex leaned over to read the next step of the spell, looking over the section that said the spell's performer must drink the blood at the very end of the incantation. Alex grasped the bottle from the page, removing the stopper and lifting the vial to his lips. A yelp from Elias halted him just before the liquid touched his mouth.

"You're not the performer!" the shadow-man cried.

Alex faltered, his hands shaking, as he realized what a catastrophic move he had been about to make. Gathering his thoughts, pushing down his panic, he moved the vial toward

Virgil's lips instead. Tilting the Head's neck back, he trickled the scarlet liquid into his mouth, watching as the gulp reflex took care of business.

With the blood swallowed, Alex knew it was just a waiting game. The spell was complete. There was nothing more he could do.

Stepping back, Alex watched the pit closely for any change, but nothing seemed to be different. He glanced at Elias, wanting reassurance from the shadow-man, but the wispy figure just shrugged. A few minutes passed, and still nothing happened.

"Did I do something wrong?" Alex whispered.

"Just wait," said Elias.

Suddenly, the rumble beneath the earth grew louder, the ground shaking so hard it knocked Alex and Virgil backward. They sprawled to the floor, Alex getting up quickly to see what was happening. He gasped in horror as he looked back toward the edge of the pit. A blood-red swell had filled the room, undulating across the surface of the gaping crevasse. It didn't look right, and Alex felt his whole body go rigid with dread. The blood-red waves bobbed there, in the center of the room, for what seemed like forever. Nobody moved. Alex hoped irrationally that if he stayed perfectly still, the swell would simply stay there, and everything would be fine.

Instead, the swell surged downward like a scarlet water-fall. A bone-shaking boom thundered below ground, as the last of the red waves disappeared into the pit.

In its place, a mist appeared, creeping slowly over the edges of the chasm. Alex felt the temperature of the room drop as the mist rolled over the lip of the pit, like clawing tendrils intent on reaching its prey. Alex saw, with a sinking feeling, that the mist was silver, and though he had never ac-tually seen the fabled mist before, he knew what it meant.

Terror ripped through his body.

"You did it wrong!" shouted Elias, above the roar of the quake.

"I did everything it said!" Alex yelled back, his heart gripped in a vise as he snatched up the Book of Jupiter and shoved it back into his satchel.

"We have to get out of here!" Elias insisted.

"Yes—help me!" Alex said, grasping Virgil under the armpits. Glancing around, he saw that the mist was almost at the threshold of the exit. He didn't know what to do, or how to reverse what he had done, but one thing was for sure—they couldn't stay here to try to figure it out.

Just then, a figure burst in, rushing right toward the deadly hands of the silver mist. Alex's eyes went wide with a horror so intense he couldn't bear the sensation of it.

"AAMIR! NO!" he roared.

Aamir skidded to a halt as a wave of silver mist surged in his direction, drawn by his essence. Alex dropped Virgil and barreled toward his friend, desperate to put himself between the deadly fog and Aamir. They had to escape this place before the mist consumed them, before it reached everyone on the battlefield.

They had unleashed the Great Evil.

EPILOGUE

ELIAS COULD SENSE ALEX'S PURE SHOCK PULSING through his own shadowy chest, and the sensation spurred him on, giving him strength as he pulled Virgil along the ground, toward the door. They had to get out, before the mist truly began to wreak havoc.

Something had gone wrong. Terribly, terribly wrong.

The shadow-man had a feeling he knew what might have been responsible, but he didn't dare voice it. Alex would undoubtedly blame him if he began to explain where he thought the problem lay. Spells were a tricky thing, but they were the same as any good work of literature—there were nuances in the text.

The blood of the king or queen, Elias mused, realizing that Alex may well have jumped upon the wrong interpretation. Yes, Venus was the queen, but she did not share the royal blood that Julius possessed, as the rightful ruler of the nation. His blood was different from hers. It was obvious, now that Elias thought about it. The spell meant the blood had to come from the current ruler, be they a king or a queen, but not from a spouse, whose blood was clearly inferior.

Perhaps we should have read the small print a touch closer.

There was no instruction manual for this. The spell book did not say what to do if it didn't work out the first time, and Elias presumed it didn't for a reason. The spell had to be performed to perfection, and they had all been found wanting.

The shadow-man realized what had to happen next.

Virgil had performed the spell as he was supposed to, and everything had run as smoothly as a well-oiled machine, up until the tiny hiccup with the blood.

They had been so close, but they had another chance.

Elias knew what needed to be done… and, as he threw a glance back at the deadly mist surging higher and higher out of the chasm, he knew it needed to be done fast.

Ready for the FINAL book in Alex's story?

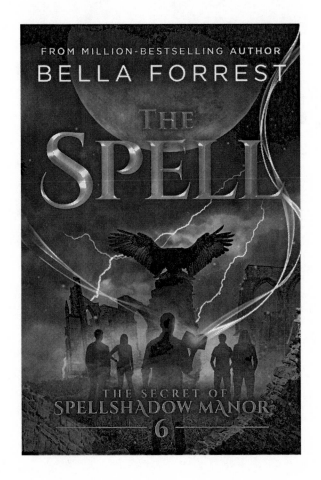

Dear Reader,

Thank you for reading The Test.

The next book is called The Spell, and it is the grand finale of the series!

The Spell releases September 30th, 2017.

Visit: www.bellaforrest.net for details.

I'll see you there!

Love,

Bella x

P.S. Sign up to my VIP email list and I'll send you a personal heads up when my next book releases:

www.morebellaforrest.com

(Your email will be kept 100% private and you can unsubscribe at any time.)

ALSO BY BELLA FORREST

THE SECRET OF SPELLSHADOW MANOR
The Secret of Spellshadow Manor (Book 1)
The Breaker (Book 2)
The Chain (Book 3)
The Keep (Book 4)
The Test (Book 5)
The Spell (Book 6)

THE GIRL WHO DARED TO THINK (New!)
The Girl Who Dared to Think (Book 1)
The Girl Who Dared to Stand (Book 2)

THE GENDER GAME (Completed series)
The Gender Game (Book 1)
The Gender Secret (Book 2)
The Gender Lie (Book 3)
The Gender War (Book 4)
The Gender Fall (Book 5)
The Gender Plan (Book 6)
The Gender End (Book 7)

A SHADE OF VAMPIRE SERIES

Series 3: The Shade continues with a new hero...

A Wind of Change (Book 17)

A Trail of Echoes (Book 18)

A Soldier of Shadows (Book 19)

A Hero of Realms (Book 20)

A Vial of Life (Book 21)

A Fork of Paths (Book 22)

A Flight of Souls (Book 23)

A Bridge of Stars (Book 24)

Series 4: A Clan of Novaks

A Clan of Novaks (Book 25)

A World of New (Book 26)

A Web of Lies (Book 27)

A Touch of Truth (Book 28)

An Hour of Need (Book 29)

A Game of Risk (Book 30)

A Twist of Fates (Book 31)

A Day of Glory (Book 32)

A SHADE OF DRAGON TRILOGY

A Shade of Dragon 1

A Shade of Dragon 2

A Shade of Dragon 3

A SHADE OF KIEV TRILOGY

A Shade of Kiev 1

A Shade of Kiev 2

A Shade of Kiev 3

DETECTIVE ERIN BOND (Adult thriller/mystery)

Lights, Camera, Gone

Write, Edit, Kill

BEAUTIFUL MONSTER DUOLOGY

Beautiful Monster 1

Beautiful Monster 2

For an updated list of Bella's books, please visit her website: www.bellaforrest.net

Join Bella's VIP email list and she'll personally send you an email reminder as soon as her next book is out: www.morebellaforrest.com

CPSIA information can be obtained
at www.ICGtesting.com
Printed in the USA
LVOW10s0959240917

549870LV00003B/578/P